PRAISE F

"Burch weaves the challenges of family and the hope life can bring into a book that will touch readers' hearts in the most enduring ways."

— *BOOKLIST* ON *IN THE LIGHT OF THE GARDEN*

"An emotional journey that explores the deep roots of love … [*Something like Family*] is an outstanding read!"

— PATRICIA SANDS, AUTHOR OF THE *LOVE IN PROVENCE* SERIES

"Burch's latest combines a sweet, nostalgic, poignant tale of a true love of the past with the discovery of true love in the present … Burch's lyrical, contemporary storytelling, down-to-earth characters, and intricate plot make this one story that will delight the heart."

— *RT BOOK REVIEWS* ON *ONE LAVENDER RIBBON*

"Heather Burch reaches into your very soul."

— Carolyn Brown, *NYT* and *USA Today* bestselling author of *The Ladies Room*

Jenny—

WISHING BEACH

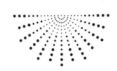

HEATHER BURCH

Enjoy this virtual vacation! :")

Heather Burch

DEDICATION

THIS BOOK REPRESENTS A COLLABORATIVE EFFORT WITH DIANE BURCH. LONG AGO, I SET WISHING BEACH ASIDE. SHE ENCOURAGED ME TO PICK IT UP AGAIN. WHEN I FOUND MYSELF FLOUNDERING, SHE TOOK THE PROJECT IN HER CAREFUL HANDS AND NURTURED IT. WHEN THE STORY WAS HANDED BACK TO ME TO WORK ON, I KNEW SOMETHING MAGICAL WAS HAPPENING. AND I KNEW IT WAS THE KIND OF MAGIC MY READERS LOVE.

ISBN 9781734449808

PROLOGUE

Winter, 1987
Wishing Beach, Florida

Along the coastline of Florida, on a tiny stretch of beach, something magical happens. Wishes gather. They fill the shoreline and glisten like diamond dust on the water's surface.

Standing guard on the beach, where dunes meet seagrass, is an ancient banyan tree whose dozens of wide, woody trunks are in fact, an aerial root system. The tree itself resembles a lone forest, its roots rising from the ground and attaching to its many branches creating a glorious—if not slightly mystical—canopy.

The tree sees all. And now and then, the leaves of the mighty banyan shudder and cause the wishes on this unusual beach to be visible to the human eye. But they are only visible to those with eyes to see—usually children who still believed in mystical things like fairies and dreams. Where others see the sun's reflection, these children see wishes, each one unique. Some are wishes that have lingered for decades and simply refuse to die. Some are new. Hurting people are inexplicably drawn to this stretch of shoreline and so they come, and leave their heaviest burdens in the shifting sand of Wishing Beach.

It is said that a person who visits Wishing Beach will leave changed. The magic isn't questioned. It simply is.

People come with open hearts. They come and they sit beside the water beneath the mighty banyan tree and shed tears only they understand. And in those tears, their deepest desires drop like Florida rain. Alone, wishes can do nothing. They must wait for someone brave enough to reach out and take one from the water. Every so often someone does reach out.

Angela Reed, nearly five, stood with her chubby toes curled into the sand. "Look Mommy," she whispered with more reverence than one would think a five-year-old could muster. "They're so pretty."

But her mother was busy snapping photos with her new Nikon and trying to stay out of the direct sun.

A particular wish caught Angela's eye as it bobbed on the surface. A translucent casing held shimmering sparks that danced with each swell of the rhythmic waves. Angela ran into the edge of the sea to grab the glittery orb.

"Angela, be careful!" Her mother hadn't planned for the five-year-old to get wet.

The sandy haired child scooped the wish into her hand. Her mother met her at the water's edge, careful not to get her new sandals baptized in seafoam.

Slowly Angela opened her chubby fingers. She cupped the wish with both hands and held it up for her mother to see. "Look Mommy."

Claire Reed tossed her head to keep her hair off her face. She stared down into the empty hands of her child. Claire was a good mother and understood games of make believe. She treasured them, in fact. In this busy era of television and boom boxes, she encouraged anything that helped children to use their imaginations. "What is it, honey?"

A tiny smile played about her baby girl's cherub face when her blue green eyes held her mother's. "It's a very special wish, Mommy."

Claire tousled Angela's hair. "And what is my baby girl wishing for?"

Angela pursed her bow mouth and two tiny dimples appeared. "It's not *my* wish. It's a wish from someone else. A long time ago, she stood on the beach here, and she cried, and she wished. She wished because she was sad, Mommy. But once her wish was said, she was okay. Her name is Olivia. And she's pretty like you."

Claire's heart fluttered for a moment. Gooseflesh worked over her neck and shoulders. She cleared her throat and reached down to support her daughter's tiny hands by cupping them with her own. "It's very nice to meet you, Olivia."

A deep belly laugh bubbled out of Angela. "You're funny, Mommy. *She's* not here. This is her *wish*."

Well, of course. Claire didn't mind being corrected by the *oh so* precocious five-year-old. She'd be doomed as a mother when Angela hit the teen years, of this she was certain.

The wind kicked up, and the small girl hunched against it, protecting the wish. "Until I break it open, I won't know what's inside." With concentration furrowing her brow, Angela gently squeezed her hands tighter together then jostled them back and forth. Angela's determination amazed Claire. This must be a very serious game of make-believe.

Near her daughter's hands, Clair heard something crack

3

open. She looked to the left and the right, confused by the sound that seemed to come from everywhere.

Angela gasped. "It broke open. Oh, it's beautiful. It's a beautiful wish, Mommy. And now it's going to come true."

CHAPTER ONE

Early summer, Present Day
Wishing Beach, FL
Angela

No one expects their life to crumble like mushy baby cookies. But sometimes that's what happens. No one sits around thinking, *Hey, maybe I'll just throw out the last fifteen years and start over.* But sometimes you have to. We breathe. We live. We love. We die. We own our decisions. What is outside our power is the certainty that the life we planned and painstakingly created will remain. Is there life after? Or is it all just silly wishes?

Angela Reed-Baker tallied the things in her future. *Tropical breezes, palm trees, sunshine.* She stepped from her car and was immediately assaulted by the coastal wind. Digging her fingers into her hair, she let the breeze work on her, hoping it might brush off some of the internal dirt she carried. She was the emotional equivalent of Pigpen from the Peanuts comics, aimlessly wandering around in a cloud of sentiment.

The clatter of palm fronds reset her focus. *You're here. Life begins anew.* Salty air filled her lungs while her mantra continued like a song on repeat. *Jogging on the beach, sunrise coffee on the terra cotta patio. Midnight dips in the pool.* She swallowed the cotton in her throat.

Although she tried to stop the second mantra, it rushed forth unwanted, uninvited, and most definitely undeniable. Things that would be no longer in her future: cooking dinner for two, conversation with the man she loved, family meals, holidays with a house full of noisy people arguing about the stock market and politics.

And just like that, the ache was back, settling in the bottom of her heart so far down it would take a deep-sea rescue team to raise that sunken ship. Abandonment was a monster with teeth. And yet, this was a monster of her own design. After all, she was the one who left. The onset of fresh tears was all too familiar to deny.

The beautiful beach house she'd gotten in the divorce sat before her, a shimmering jewel on the edge of Wishing Beach. Yet her joy waned. Angela's mind had been a battlefield for the last several months. It was time to let it go. Let it all go. Brice, the marriage that was no more, the life she'd spent fifteen years building. At thirty-nine, surely life wasn't over. The thought niggled. Just as she drew a deep breath of warm Florida air, the front door of her beach house opened.

Jesse Malone stepped out, his deep Florida tan emphasized by the fresh white T-shirt, khaki shorts, and canvas topsiders. His face was creased with sixty years of age and the unrelenting sun. Dark wavy hair streaked with gray was pulled back in a short ponytail at the back of his neck. The scarring on the side of his face was barely noticeable, as were the fingers on his left hand that were frozen in a natural cupped position, injuries from some terrible incident in his youth. He made his way down the steps, his slight limp hardly visible as he approached. A smile overtook the concern on his face and the familiar sparkle lit his green eyes as he moved closer with outstretched arms. "Angie!" He scooped her into a strong hug.

He knows, Angela realized.

"Uncle Jesse." The warmth in her heart overflowed in the comfort and security of his embrace. She breathed deeply of his clean aroma that mixed with the magnolia scented air.

And then the tears came.

Jesse wasn't really her uncle, but he had been caretaker for the Baker family beach house for as long as she could remember. She and Brice, along with Brice's two boys Braxton and Bryan, spent every summer on Wishing Beach, fifteen summers in a row. And Jesse was always there for whatever was needed. He spent a lot of time with the boys since Brice was never around for them.

Early on, the boys began calling him Uncle Jesse instead of Mr. Malone. She couldn't remember at whose suggestion, it just was. Somewhere along the way she became Angie to him which always made her smile. Only a few close friends had ever called her that. She considered Jesse a friend.

Released from his tight hug, Angie pressed both hands on her cheeks and looked up at the mansion of a beach house that would be her permanent home. She'd never be able to handle the place alone. The fact that Jesse was there to fill some of the gaps made this whole thing possible. He'd never missed an opportunity to help with her many projects.

Jesse kept an arm around her shoulders as they made their way up the steps.

She sniffed and rubbed the remnants of tears from her cheeks.

"Come on inside." He nudged her toward the door. "I've

got a pitcher of that hibiscus tea you like in the fridge."

She watched him from the corner of her eye. "I'm surprised you made that. I thought you hated it."

"Well, I did, but you forced it on me so many times I just kinda took to it."

And as he always could do, he made her laugh.

Over a glass of iced tea, seated at the round table in the alcove of the spacious kitchen, Angela and Jesse looked out the bay windows while Jesse told her of the recent repairs he'd made—all small, but important. Beyond the glass, overlooking the screened lanai and pool, the sprawling backyard ended at the ocean. Waves rushed up silently and retreated as their conversation turned to normal things. Bougainvilleas, fire ants, the new roadwork just completed in the neighborhood.

Some of the tension left her as they chatted on and on. Life *was* going to be good for her here at Wishing Beach. Bit by painstaking bit, she started to feel more normal. Something she hadn't felt in a very long time.

Finally, she got around to the subject that hung heavy in the air. "Did Brice tell you about the divorce?"

Jesse nodded. "Yes, he did." He raised his eyebrows which told Angela that it had been, in all probability an unpleasant discourse.

Angela sighed, that was such a Brice thing to do. Until the divorce was final, Brice had worked overtime to strip her of everything in her world that ever mattered.

Jesse cleared his throat. "I tried to call you. Your phone had been disconnected."

Disconnected? No. Thrown against the wall and busted to pieces by Brice? Yes. She'd had to go to the store and purchase a new phone, new line, *no* family plan, thank you. "Why did he call? What did he want?" she asked.

Jesse leaned back in his chair and crossed his arms, giving

her a long look. "He fired me. He told me to be gone before you got here." A half smile played at the corner of his mouth.

Stunned, speechless, seething, a myriad of emotions washed through Angela. Just when she thought Brice couldn't stoop any lower, he managed to prove her wrong. And proving her wrong was one of his favorite things to do. She dropped her forehead into her hand. "I'm so glad you stayed."

"I don't respond well when something rubs me the wrong way." Jesse leaned forward, his elbow on the table. "You coming to a big empty house without a friendly face to greet you … that rubs me the wrong way."

Angela reached over and lightly touched his arm. "Thank you for staying."

"I'll stay as long as you need me," Jesse said.

"I want you to stay for good, everything the same as always. I have enough money to manage that." Angela thought for a moment. "He probably led you to believe that I don't. I know Brice. I'm sure he's hoping you've moved on, and with such short notice after so many years, that you would be angry enough to not have anything to do with a Baker, including me."

"I'd never judge you by his actions."

Appreciation caused her to smile. But it faded quickly. "He'll do whatever he can to make life harder for me. Whatever it takes to hurt me."

"Well, then." Jesse pushed away from the table and stood up. "I guess we're back in business." There was a twinkle in his eye. He held out his hand. "Give me your keys and I'll get your bags from the car."

Jesse had insisted she rest while he unload her car, but Angela wasn't ready to stay inside. She stepped out, crossed the wide front patio, and dropped into one of the cushioned white rocking chairs that were anchored by giant terra cotta pots of tropical flowers. The seat was a welcome reprieve from the long drive in the cramped sports car Brice had picked out for her.

Her gaze followed the expansive lawn to the property lines on both sides. This was a big place, too much for one person to manage. The sprawling grounds of the massive home backed up to the Atlantic and anchored the corner of Wishing Beach. It offered plenty of work to keep her busy. Busyness would be a welcome distraction. Angela massaged her forehead.

She could afford to pay Jesse, contrary to what Brice might have told him. The cottage where Jesse lived made up a portion of his compensation, so her monthly outgo would be less than having to hire a gardener, a pool service, a general maintenance person and the occasional—or perhaps frequent—need for a repairman. Jesse was a bargain, no doubt. Since he lived in the cottage on the property, she would feel safe and not so alone.

Her parents owned a vacation home only three houses around the cove, but her folks no longer came to the island. Growing up, she and her family had spent summers and every school holiday on Millionaire's Cove. That was the name locals had given to the cove. Five mansions and acres of private beachfront decorated the crowning jewel of the island. The Perrys—almost American royalty, with their generations of senators and philanthropists—had built the first, but other mansions quickly followed. This is where she'd met Brice whose family vacationed in the house that she would now call home. Permanently. A house he'd lost because, in the last possible moments of their divorce proceedings, he announced that he'd decided not to give her their Connecticut home. He'd thrown a curveball. But she'd thought quickly and said, "Fine. Keep the house. I'll take the Baker Beach House." She could throw curveballs too.

He'd balked, of course, until his attorney reminded him that he hadn't included the beach house in his list of assets. And that, my friends, is what you call unethical.

They'd dated while she was in high school, then lost touch, then reconnected years later—her, fresh from college and him, fresh from a failed marriage.

After spending fifteen years of being beaten down by Brice and his self-impressed family, Angela felt like a shadow of the person she so desperately desired to be. The divorce was final now. Her circle of friends back home in Connecticut was practically nonexistent. Maybe she'd look for a start-up to invest in. The thought brought a spark of interest. She'd made several investments on her own over the years. To her husband's oftentimes loud objections. *"What do you think you're doing? Leave it to the smarter, the qualified ..."* such as himself.

"Oh God," she breathed. She had broken away from the destructive world of Brice but at least it was a world she *knew*. Tentacles of fear wound around her heart. *Could she do this?* The suffocating thoughts were coming far too often.

In the back of her mind, the mantra began again.

After Jesse finished unloading her car, he patted her shoulder, told her to get some rest, and headed toward his place—the small home that stood as a sentinel to the estate. At the end of the long driveway, he cut across the grass. Suddenly, he turned back around and came towards where she was sitting. When he was close enough, he cupped his hands around his mouth and shouted to her. "Your friend Jenny has called on the house phone several times. I forgot to tell you earlier."

She waved her acknowledgement. Was Jenny in town? Angela had shut her phone off for the entire trip to Florida. Angela had friends on Wishing Beach, but they mostly only saw each other over vacations and not typically this early in the summer. She hurried into the house to find her cell phone. Having some real friends to ground her would make this whole thing more bearable.

It *should* be bearable by now. After all, she and Brice had been separated for months. Plus, *she'd* been the one to leave. Brice had crossed a line. A very clear doormat line. It was only a short time after the doormat incident that she'd served the divorce papers.

The doormat that ended a marriage.

But the finality of the divorce had created a whole new awareness of loss. She supposed it would be honest to admit she no longer loved Brice. She finally saw him for what he really was and not the man she'd thought she'd married. Still she continued to grieve for the sense of home and of family and especially for the close relationship she had with her stepsons. She'd raised them for the fifteen years of her marriage to Brice. The hollow place in her heart was real.

ANGELA OPENED the door and screamed. Jenny, on the other side, screamed too. It had been so long, too long, and Angela couldn't wait to catch up. They'd hugged, screamed again, hugged again. "I'm so glad you're here," Angela said as she led Jenny farther into the house. "I love your hair." The cute brunette had always worn a blunt bob but now it had dozens of shades of blonde added.

Jenny shook her head, letting the strands dance. "It makes me look ten years younger," she exclaimed. "At least that's what my stylist said as I was fishing a cash tip out of my wallet."

Angela chuckled. "I bet the amount of that tip doubled."

"Tripled!" Jenny considered her. "Hmm. I like your hair, too. Not so polished. Not so perfect."

Angela nodded. "Well, Brice always preferred it straight and sleek. He no longer gets a vote."

Jesse was just coming out of the kitchen and greeted the two women.

"Nice to see you, Jenny," he said, on his way to the front door. Jenny smiled and gave him a wave.

"Join us in the kitchen, Jesse." Angela motioned for him.

Jenny cast her a confused glance.

Jesse scratched his head, looking like he'd rather chew hot lava than suffer through "girl talk."

"Y'all go ahead. I've got work to do. Those fire ants are trying to set up a fortress in your front yard. Never gonna happen."

"Well, will you be around for dinner? I thought I'd toss something on the grill later."

Jenny bumped her friend's shoulder. "Aww. A party? For me? I'm honored."

Angie laughed and gave Jenny a squeeze. "I don't think I'd call it a party. And I'm sure Jesse's sick of watching me mope around here. It has been two days after all."

"Two whole days? I don't know how he's managed." They both laughed.

Jesse rolled his eyes. "As a matter of fact, I won't be around later. Mama Grace called. I was told to be at her house for a fish fry. Ladies, you're on your own."

"You don't know what you're missing." Jenny rested a hand on her hip.

"I don't know how I would've managed the last two days without Jesse. He's kept me sane," Angela said.

"You sane? Not likely." Jenny tossed an appreciative look toward Jesse.

When Angela and Jenny fell back into conversation, Jesse said, "I'll be in the yard if you need me. Glad you came by, Jenny. I know Angie's been looking forward to it."

CHAPTER TWO

Present Day

ANGELA AND JENNY sat in the lawn chairs at the table on the wide lanai. Beyond the swimming pool, the sea stretched forever, and the brilliant sun shone above the water casting long shadows beneath the banyan tree on Wishing Beach. She and Jenny wore sunglasses to guard against the glare. Angela was glad for the bit of cover they offered. Jenny would be relentless in her questions, and any armor was good armor. Even if it came in the form of Chanel sunglasses.

"Have you talked to the boys?" Jenny sipped the iced tea Angela had made for them.

"No. I've tried to call, but I'm fairly sure Brice had their phone numbers changed. Brice told me they were furious at me."

"At you? For leaving their abusive father?"

"Abuse is such a strong word."

"He was abusive, end of story." Jenny pointed her index finger at her, punctuating her remark.

"He's still their father," Angela said. "I'm not sure how much they actually know about how Brice treated me. I was pretty careful all along so they wouldn't feel insecure. I think Brice was somewhat careful too, he does love them, and wouldn't want them to see that side of him."

Jenny leaned forward. "And you're the mother they've known since they were, what, four and six? I don't know how you can stand not talking to them."

She'd been over and over this in her mind. "And what, Jen? Expect them to take sides against their father? At least they were both away at college most of the year. I could have never left if they were still at home."

"True." Jen snapped her fingers. "Remind me. Where are they boys right now?"

"Backpacking through Europe with a bunch of their college friends. Brice said to give them some time. That's really all I can do." Angela shrugged.

Jen shook her head, light brown strands dusting her shoulders.

Where the boys were concerned, Angela had made up her mind. She would take it slow, no matter what it cost her. "I believe him that the boys are angry right now."

"So they know that the divorce is final?"

"Brice said he told them. He said they need some space to wrap their heads around the divorce. Even though we've been separated for a year, divorce is absolute. It's so final. With the boys being away at school, I don't think they realized their father and I were leading separate lives."

"What about holidays? Christmas? Surely the boys came home and noticed you weren't there."

"No. I moved back into the house, and we pretended everything was fine. Well, fine as it ever was. Brice told me not to worry, the boys will come around eventually. He's probably right on this. Anyway, I don't have a lot of options." Angela placed her drink on the coffee table with a little too much force. Frustration drove her out of her chair. She stopped at the edge of patio. Before her, the Atlantic glistened. "It's killing me not being able to talk to them, to explain. Sometimes there's just no right answer. So, I'm going with the best wrong answer."

Jenny walked over and slipped an arm around her friend's shoulder. "I know you Angie, you'll do the right thing." She gave her a squeeze. "Or at the very least, you'll do the best wrong thing." They both laughed.

"I left my new cell number for both of them, for Braxton with Alicia, his ex-girlfriend. And for Bryan, I left the number with Mike, his best friend. They'll call when they're ready."

"There's always social media."

"That's just it. I can't be the one to reach out. I have to wait for them to make the first move, and it has to be after Brice has cooled down. If I want a relationship with the boys, I've got to do it his way. As usual, Brice holds all the cards."

"I should let you know I invited Ginger and Kari to meet us later, they're both on the island right now for family vacations. I think Kari said they would be staying for only a couple of weeks this year. Have you thought about talking to Kari?"

"I want to talk to all my besties," Angela said.

"I don't mean best friend Kari, I mean Clinical Psychologist Professor Kari."

"Oh. Talk to her in a professional capacity?" Angela rolled her eyes. "She's here to get away from work."

"Angie, she loves you, we all do." Jen took a breath. "So, where was I? Oh yes, Mimi, Missy, and Kara are vacationing as well, but you know how busy those three always are.

They've got a lot on their plates. I would have invited Donna and Gayla to drive out, but Gayla is at a landscaping conference and Donna is on vacation in Maui with her new foster daughter. Still, they only live a few hours away, so when you need them, you can reach out and they'll be here for you."

Jenny was the take charge one of the group. Angela was grateful, she could never have spearheaded even a casual get-together right now. Listening to Jen, it sounded like her friends wouldn't have much time for her. Well, what did she expect? "But you'll be back in a few weeks from your mom's right?"

"Actually, no. My company is sending me to Korea. I'll leave from Mom's."

"Oh." Angela felt a tinge of panic, she had thought that being nearby would mean she and her Wishing Beach vacation friends could meet for lunch or come over and hang out. But, of course, that was entirely unrealistic. People were busy. They had lives. Unlike her. A new heaviness settled in the pit of her stomach.

"We'll be here tonight," Jenny said, as if she could hear Angela's thoughts. "At least, most of us." Jen pointed at her. "You need a night with the girls. I've already texted them, so it's too late to back out. Speaking of texting, do you remember the text you sent us all when you left Brice? It was something about a doormat. Care to explain?"

The text had simply read,

HE THREW AWAY MY DOORMAT. I'M LEAVING HIM.

Recalling those fateful words brought a sudden flood of memories.

"Earth to Angie. I need to hear about this doormat." Jen snapped her fingers. She took another drink of her tea and made a face. "This sun is melting my drink. I'll bring out extra ice."

Jenny helped herself in the kitchen while Angela let the early sun work its magic. Shards of light slipped through the cracks around her shades, piercing her eyes and reminding her she wasn't in proverbial Kansas anymore.

Jen sat back down by the pool and took a few moments to freshen both drinks. Water ran in streams over the waterfall at the edge of the raised hot tub and into the glistening blue pool. "Now, the doormat story. We were all so shocked, and relieved that you were walking out that no one took the time to ask about that little detail. We all wanted to make sure you were okay."

The first was followed by more texts back and forth with her friends.

YES, I'M OKAY. NO, HE DIDN'T GET PHYSICAL. YES, IT IS HIGH TIME.

Right after those texts, Brice had shut off her cell, and then thrown it against the antique China hutch that had been in his family for generations. Both the phone and the beveled glass door had been casualties of his wrath.

Angela was tired of reliving that moment. She'd always known he'd been capable of violence. The incidences had been spiraling but that day he'd lost control. She'd feared what he might do next. "The doormat was important to me because it had been the last gift from my grandmother before she died.

"My gram always said the door of a place sets the tone for the entire home. A doormat is a foundation that either welcomes or pushes away. A doormat has value beyond the credit it's given. A doormat is the first place where you pause and sigh and know you're home. It's the first step into your sanctuary. It's the gatekeeper."

Jen's eyes narrowed. "So when she gave you this particular doormat, it was special for a lot of reasons?"

Angela giggled. "Yes. I know it sounds philosophical and

maybe even hokey, but I loved that doormat. It was the last gift I ever received from my grandmother."

"And Brice threw it away?"

She nodded. "Yes. He knew it was important to me. But his feet were muddy from the golf course. He'd gotten drenched on the ninth hole and came home and rubbed his feet all over it, forgot, stepped outside in his socks a half an hour later and got mud all over those. He proceeded to take the doormat to the trashcan by the road, and the garbage service picked it up before I knew what had happened."

"It was the very last straw, wasn't it?"

Angela nodded. "I grieved over a doormat. How crazy is that? And I knew it was over for Brice and me. I tried and tried to be the best wife and mother I knew how, but the more I did the more he took advantage. Finally, in his mind, I was nothing more than a—"

"Doormat," Jen finished for her.

"Mm hmm. And not the kind of doormat my gran talked about. To Brice, I was just a place to wipe his muddy feet."

"He's such a jerk." Jen scowled. "You did the right thing, Angie. You're not second guessing yourself, are you?"

"Only for the boys' sake."

Jen nodded. "Let's run to the store and grab some steaks. This isn't a wake. It's a celebration."

Angela sighed inwardly. Was there any way out of this party? No. She knew better. She wanted to see her friends, catch up, and maybe even laugh for a little while. Just not yet. At this point, it didn't really matter. Jen had spoken.

ANGELA and her friends had steaks and prawns on the grill for dinner. Not surprisingly, Jen had been right. She'd needed a night with the girls.

Ginger made drinks in the kitchen while the others watched her. "Has anyone talked to Mimi?"

Jen scrounged around in her purse and produced her cell. "I'm calling her and telling her to meet us here."

Angela sighed. "Is there no end to your energy, Jen? At some point we have to sleep."

Jen stood. "We can sleep when we're dead. How often do we get the chance to all hang out together?"

Ginger handed a drink to Jen. "About that. How long are you in town?" Jen had a townhouse on the southeast corner of the island. But traveling with work kept her away most of the time. Couple that with caring for her aging mother in New Orleans, and Jen was rarely on the island.

Jen was already punching in Mimi's number. Instead of answering, she waved a hand in Ginger's face. "Mims, I'm at Angie's. Did your dinner party go okay? You know what, I don't really care, all I want to know is, are you free, and can you bring some bagels, coffee cake, and OJ, and meet us here? Bring your swimsuit. I fancy a midnight dip in the pool. FYI, I don't have a suit, so I'll be bathing *au naturel.*"

When Ginger started to protest, Jen held up a flat hand in front of her face. "Don't judge. What, Mimi? Yes, of course it's a sleepover."

Was it? That was news to Angela. But she was glad her friends would be there for the night. Everywhere she looked inside her house, all she saw was Brice. She was desperate to make the beach house her own. Making new memories with her best friends would help. And if that meant she had to sacrifice sleep, so be it. Plus, she'd been thinking about getting rid of Brice's stamp on her life. For so many years, she'd been his sidekick. It was time to begin forging her own way. As she stared out the kitchen's French doors that led to the lanai, she began to get an inkling of one thing she could do. It was crazy. And she'd need her friends to help her. They made her strong. She needed some strength in her life right now. What she didn't need was that horrible hammock Brice had insisted on putting on the lanai a few years back. In fact, she had a whole beach house full of Brice crap she no longer had use for.

"Let's swim for a while, ladies. Then, we've got work to do." Angela grinned and dove headfirst into the pool.

$$\sim$$

ANGELA'S FRIENDS dotted the front yard when she knocked on Jesse's cottage door. She wouldn't have bothered him at such an hour, but she noticed his lights were on. He'd been gone for the evening—apparently to his Mama Grace's house for a fish fry, but his Jeep was in the drive.

Jesse opened the door and pulled a set of readers off his nose. "Angie? Is everything all right? Are you feeling okay?" Concern creased his finely lined features, more so when he cast a glance behind her and saw the collection of furniture on her front lawn and the parade of her friends carrying various pieces.

"I'm feeling great Uncle Jesse." She made a display of raising her hands and spinning in a circle. "I'm feeling free."

He scratched his chin. "I realized earlier you were having an all-night shindig with your friends, but I never imagined you ladies arranging the yard to look like a living room."

She hooked a thumb over her shoulder. "What, this? I'm done living my life by Brice's rules."

"Is that a fact?" The smallest of smiles grew on his face. He approved. That much was evident.

Angela's cheeks were flushed, she could feel the warmth even in the cool night wind. "I'm sorry for bothering you." She looked around him deeper into the cottage—he hadn't invited her in. Of course, he still looked mystified by what she and her besties were doing.

There was an awkward silence as he watched Jenny and Mimi carry out another end table.

Angela pointed into his house to a reading nook where a thick law book sat with a yellow legal pad bookmarking the center. "A little light reading?" she asked.

Jesse nodded, but didn't look where she had pointed. "I'll admit it. I'm a diehard reader through and through. I could be entertained by a phonebook or the dictionary."

"Oooooh, the dictionary," she said with wide innocent eyes. "Wait until you get to the M's. It's all mystery, murder, and mayhem."

Now it was Jesse's turn to point. "Is that—are they carrying your couch?"

"Uh," Angela uttered and turned just in time to watch Ginger, Jenny, and Mimi drop the couch in the yard. "They sure are."

"Has the furniture done something to offend you? I'm sure we could talk this through."

"That's just it, Jesse. The furniture offends me."

He nodded. Cleared his throat. Looked a bit like someone talking down a person in the midst of a nervous breakdown. "I heard a few screams and hollers followed by splashes when I got home from Mama Grace's house earlier. Figured you all were spending the entire evening in the pool. I also figured your friends for hot tub sitters, not pool swimmers with their fancy hairdos and all. One ought not make assumptions," he said.

"Very true, Uncle Jesse. Now, as to the reason for my late-night visit. I need the keys to the tool shed."

"Good gracious, girl. You're not after the chain saw, are you? I draw the line at mutilating perfectly good furniture."

Angela laughed. "No. Nothing like that. I just have to take

that horrible eyesore of a hammock apart to get it through the lanai screen door."

"So, you really are tossing out all your furniture?" He slowly stepped onto his porch. In front of the couch, a trail of pieces decorated the lawn leading all the way to the road where they'd propped open the wrought-iron gate.

"I really am. I'll be shopping for new pieces. Hey, you could come with me if you want." She didn't know why she said that, but there it was.

"You don't need anything in the tool shed for that hammock. I'll come over and help you maneuver it through the door."

"Oh, I don't want to impose." She placed a hand to her heart. Of course he would offer to help. She should have known that and left the hammock for tomorrow. But it felt so good, so empowering to haul that furniture right out her front door. Once they'd started, she didn't want to stop.

"It's no imposition at all. If you're erasing bad memories here and creating new good ones, well, I'd love to be part of it. Let me slip on some shoes and I'll be right over." He started to turn but stopped. "But are you sure you need to throw away the furniture?"

"I'm sure. In the morning I'm calling the island thrift store to pick it up."

He nodded, slowly.

"I promise I'm not crazy. Jesse, everything at this beach house was chosen by Brice … or his mother. How can I start fresh when everything I look at, use, or sit down on belonged to him, was hand chosen by him, and adored by him?"

Jesse pressed his lips together. "I reckon you can't. I'll tell you what. If you really want to get rid of all this stuff, I think I can get it out of your way tonight." He looked up at the star-studded sky. "We're going to get a shower later. That can't do these things any good. I know someone who will come pick them up and get them to the right people."

"Great!" Angela said.

Jesse held up a finger. "Now, you make sure you're not going to change your mind?" It sounded like a question.

"I won't be changing my mind." Angie shook her head, solid in her resolve. "All that's left to move is the hammock and Brice's heavy chair."

Jesse clapped his hands together. "I guess we're in business, then. I'll be right over."

ANGELA WAITED for Jesse to meet them at to the back of the house where wet beach towels and half empty drinks littered the lanai. Throwing out Brice's furniture was liberating beyond her wildest dreams. She felt alive. Reckless. Primal.

The hammock was easy enough to unfasten and cast aside, but when they went to lift the frame, it shifted causing Jesse to slip on the wet pool tile. The shift startled the girls lifting the other end, they pushed instead of pulled and Jesse tipped backward, arms flailing to regain his footing. In the end, gravity won dragging him into the pool.

He came up sputtering.

"Are you okay?" Angela reached a hand toward him.

He climbed out and first felt his front pockets for his cell phone. "Guess I left it at the house. Good." He reached to his back pocket and withdrew his wallet. Water ran out of the shiny leather corner.

"And your watch." Angela stood with her hand out. He handed her his wallet and unbuckled his watch. "Mims, hand me that towel," Angela ordered. She took the wallet from Jesse. "I'll dry these things out. Jen, will you see if you can get his watch dry before it's ruined? There's a hairdryer in my bathroom."

"Where are my helpers?" Jesse lifted his end of the hammock frame, the two girls hurried to pick up their end. Mimi and Angela spread the contents of Jesse's wallet onto the patio table. Ginger had grabbed a roll of paper towels and the three of them blotted at the cards and bits of paper.

"What's this?" Angela withdrew the small square photograph.

Mimi peered over her shoulder. "Pretty. Who is she?"

"I don't know. I've never seen her before." She gently dabbed the photo, careful not to ruin it. Angela flipped it over and examined the unmistakable curlicues that had once been words, but they had long since faded. Holding it in the light, she saw something near the top corner.

"That's a heart," Mimi said.

"Aw. Do you think they were in love?" Ginger's voice turned dreamy.

"Jesse has never mentioned her. I don't know." There was a lot she didn't know about Jesse. Like why a sixty-year-old man was reading law books for entertainment.

The girl in the photo had a perfect smile and long blonde hair cut into a late seventies or maybe early eighties style.

When Jesse and the girls returned, both Mimi and Ginger stepped back. He examined the contents of his wallet, splayed on the patio table. He reached for the photo.

"She's very pretty, Jesse."

He lifted the picture and lovingly ran a finger along the edge. "Yes, she is." There was a hint of a smile at the corners of his mouth.

A yacht glided across the water beyond them, its gentle hum breaking some of the thick tension in the air.

"What's her name?" Angela asked, her voice little more than a whisper.

"Her name is Olivia."

"Who is she?"

Uncle Jesse swallowed hard. "She was the one." Then he blinked, and the boundaries went up. He gathered his other belongings and piled them in one hand. He captured the photo of Olivia and disappeared through the side gate. "I'll be back to handle the big chair after I get dry."

The girls were quiet. Angela's mind began racing.

CHAPTER THREE

Beginning of summer,
Wishing Beach Island, 1981
Olivia

Olivia Murray stared at the open water.

"Come on out," her brother teased.

Olivia's lips twitched and her fingers dug into her upper arms. Brothers. Where had her fear come from? From them, of course. Two older brothers who delighted in torturing their *baby* sister—as they liked to refer to her. She wasn't a baby. She had just turned seventeen.

"Come on," Evan coaxed. "Baby!" He was treading water at the edge of the pier they'd sailed off after depositing their outer clothing on the worn wooden planks. "It won't be like last time."

When you held me under water until I nearly drowned? she asked, silently. Okay, maybe she hadn't nearly drowned, but her vision had dimmed and as she'd fought to right herself on the unforgiving sandy ocean floor, she *imagined* she was dying. Seventeen. Never been kissed. And about to expire.

The sad part was she *could* swim. She was an accomplished swimmer and diver. In a swimming pool. In fact, she'd spent countless hours in the Olympic size pool at the academy where she trained. She was on her school's swim team. Truth was she wasn't afraid of *water*. She was afraid of the *ocean*. The thought of getting in it was paralyzing.

Pathetic.

Still, she wouldn't give them the satisfaction of knowing how scared she really was. Chills ran up her spine even in the balmy summer air. She could practically feel the sting of salt-water in her mouth, her throat. Olivia shuffled away from the edge causing her brothers to laugh. She stomped off toward the row of beach houses sitting to the right of the pier. Ignoring their laughter, she concentrated on the bright colors of the beachside surf shop just before her. A wood plank structure and tin roof sported decorative exterior walls. Each wall of the surf shop was colored with bright swatches of paint in sea themed designs as if the building had been tagged by a gang of highly talented mermaid graffiti artists. Her favorite was the animated island and swooping palm trees where a table of dolphins sat sipping drinks. She tried to focus on the wall, but her emotions were high.

Stupid brothers. For as long as she could remember her brothers had filled her head with stories about sharks, riptides, and dangerous undercurrents. Even sea monsters when she was young enough to believe those tales. But sharks, riptides and undercurrents were real, and were dangerous.

She gritted her teeth and squeezed the oncoming tears back into her eyes. This had to stop.

Ten hours later, Olivia walked back to the same pier where her brothers had laughed at her. A darkened sky above held pinholes of light. Off to her right, a plane slid silently through the stars. Around her, all was quiet. Even the night fishermen were gone now. Of course, it was midnight and hightide. She'd checked because she didn't want to dive into shallow water. Beneath her cotton blouse and culottes, she wore her brand new Catalina bathing suit. Her first two piece with a halter top and bikini bottoms that rode low on her narrow hips and made her feel less like a thin gawky girl and more like a woman.

Slowly, she slipped out of her clothing and folded the items neatly. Over the past several hours, she'd imagined sailing off the edge of the pier into the water below. She'd done it so many times in her mind, she worked hard to convince herself that now was no different. But it was different. In all her imaginings, she'd never noticed the chill in the air biting her flesh or the intense quiet. Regardless, she was determined to swim.

Olivia placed the pants on top of her shoes and the blouse on top of the pants, all on the wooden strips of the pier. A single light shone down on the water while others lit the way to the pier's edge creating hazy halos of light against the ink black sky. It was strange how calm she was considering that only hours ago, the thought of getting in this water terrified her. Now, it beckoned. Olivia scooted to the end of the pier until her toes overhung the weathered boards.

NINETEEN-YEAR-OLD JESSE SAT in the quiet of the tiki hut awning at the surf shop. A row of lounge chairs stretched out beside him, all chained to the deck by Owen, the shop's owner. Owen knew Jesse loved the peace and quiet of the beach at night. He wouldn't mind him taking a break there before going home. Tonight after closing, Jesse stayed at the garage where he was employed so he could work on his own car. He did a bunch of system checks before he started tearing down the motor. Looked like it was going to be a complete rebuild. But he'd ask Wally, his boss, what he thought before he went any further.

Jesse was drinking a bottle of Coca-Cola when he first saw the girl. Like a beautiful ghost, she glided out to the end of the pier, her long blonde hair flying behind her. He sat a little straighter when she began undressing. Jesse's pulse picked up a beat.

At first, he'd figured she was just some tourist intrigued by the island and the water at night. But he caught the hint of something different about her, an intensity, a purpose. He didn't know if that was a good thing or a bad thing, but she certainly held his interest, especially now that she was stripped down to her bikini.

The swimwear showed off her long legs and a tiny waist. She took care situating her clothes, her body folding at the hips like a dancer to place the garments on her shoes. "Something's wrong about this," he muttered under his breath. She was all alone at midnight, getting ready to do what, exactly?

Jesse's heart pounded as he stood up. Determination—and a bit of apprehension—propelled him onto the beach, his mind trying to fill in the blanks and wondering how a pretty girl would feel about being approached at midnight by a stranger. Maybe she had plans to meet someone out there on the pier—a moonlit swim for two teen lovers. Then she leaped off the end of the pier into the water, her hair trailing her thin body like ribbons behind a kite. Jesse broke into a run. This wasn't swimming. No, not swimming. The splash echoed over the quiet beach. Jesse weighed his options. Swim out or run to the end of the pier and jump in. Swim. He raced out as far into the surf as he could go, then swam with all his might using the weathered posts as a guide.

He found her holding onto one of the pier's pilings as he rounded the end of the dock. Her eyes were wide with fright, and her hair floated around her like sheets on a clothesline on a windy day. She kicked her legs to the side, her features suffused with terror.

"I got you," he said, swimming closer.

She started to reach for him, but a rogue wave hit them full force. She gripped the rotting pier post tighter. A sound, something between a sob and a scream came from her mouth.

A thin ribbon of blood threaded its way into the lamp light.

Her eyes flashed to his, a silent question about how she'd managed to get cut floated to him.

"Barnacles are sharp as razors. The posts are covered in them."

Her gaze darted to the post, legs kicking behind her.

"How 'bout I help you get out of the water? Predators feed at night."

She glanced around her midsection as if sharks would materialize at his words.

Jesse reached a hand to her. "Best we get you to shore. I swear you're safe with me." A fifteen-foot hammerhead had been caught off that pier not more than a year before. He wouldn't mention that.

He kept his eyes on hers. They were beautiful eyes. He expected they'd be a different color in the daylight, brighter maybe. But the shape, the layers of lashes, the perfect placement on a delicate face, all of that would remain. In fact, she was the most stunning girl he'd ever seen even if she was drenched. His hand was still outstretched when he said, "I'm Jesse. I live over on Bayside. If you're new to the island, Bayside is the bay side of the island." He smiled trying to put her at ease, hoping to dilute her terror.

"I'm Olivia," she whispered and reached for him.

Blood ran down her arm. Still, she kept her grip on the pier with her other hand. He gave her a gentle tug and met resistance. "Olivia, I'm not a coward, but I'd rather not have to fend off hungry sharks. How about you let go, and I'll lead us back to shore?" He kept his voice calm.

With a tiny nod, Olivia slipped away from the pier, her small hand in his strong one. Together, they made their way out of the dark water and onto the beach.

He guided her to the surf shop. Once he had her settled, he ran back and retrieved her clothing. She was shivering by the time he made it back to her, looking small there on the beach chair, her legs drawn to her chest.

She took her things from him, but she wouldn't meet his eyes. His T-shirt and shorts were soaked, and the chill of the night forced itself on him.

"You're cold," Olivia whispered, glancing up. "I'm sorry you had to come in after me."

"I'm fine." He lowered himself onto the chair beside her. "Why were you out there?"

She turned away as she pulled her blouse over her delicate shoulders. "I don't want to talk about it."

"Okay." Then he remembered the stash of beach towels Owen rented to unprepared tourists. The narrow box was supposed to have a lock on it, but Owen usually forgot. "Good news," Jesse said as he opened the top and reached inside. "Warm towels."

She looked back at him. "How are they warm?"

"Oh," he said. "I just mean they're dry and warmer than the night air." He draped the towel around her, and a tiny smile appeared and lit her features.

She continued to shiver, so Jesse started at her ankles and tucked another towel around her legs, stopping mid-thigh careful not to get too close to her hips. "Better?"

"My brothers made me do it." Olivia's gaze turned to him.

Anger welled up in Jesse. "Your brothers told you to come out here tonight?"

She shook her head. The wind had plastered much of her hair to her face, but she didn't seem to notice or care. "No. They'd kill me if they knew I was out here. They just always torture me about being scared of the ocean. I read where the best way to overcome fear was to face it head on. Run to the roar. I thought I had a good plan, hightide and no people to see me if I made a fool of myself, which I did."

Jesse sank onto the chair beside her again. "I gotta tell ya." He shook his head. "A girl who goes swimming at night in shark infested waters is fearless."

Her eyes widened. "Shark infested? You sound like my brothers."

"Oops, sorry." He grinned. "Changing the subject ... how's your arm?"

She slid it out from under the towel and turned it over. "Okay. No worse than cat scratches. It stings like cat scratches."

He reached over and examined the long cut. "It's not deep, but barnacles are germy. You'll want to clean it out as soon as you get home. And speaking of that, it's late. I can walk you home. Where are you staying?"

"Where am I staying? How do you know I don't live here?"

Jesse raised his brows. "No one as pretty as you lives on the island. I'd have noticed."

She angled to look at him. "How do you know you haven't seen me and just forgot?"

His eyes met hers and held. "I'd remember you, Olivia."

A crimson stain appeared across Olivia's cheeks. "I admit I do spend most of my time at home and on the beach near the house where my family is staying. But I ride my bike into town to the library pretty often." She shrugged. "Yeah," she sighed. "I'm pretty boring."

"Boring?" Jesse gestured wide. "This is the most interesting, not to mention unusual, blind date I've ever been on." They both laughed.

Jesse draped the towel around his shoulders, shawl like, to ward off the chill. "Shall we go?" he said.

"Okay," I have to get my bike at the pier."

It was easy for Olivia to decide she liked Jesse. On the long walk as he accompanied her home, they never ran out of things to talk about, like they had known each other forever. By the time they had reached Millionaire's Cove and the McGovern house where her family was staying, they agreed Jessie would gradually introduce her to the ocean in such a way that she could overcome her fear.

Olivia cast a glance to the handsome young man beside her. Yes. She definitely liked him. She liked his laugh and the way he made her feel safe and protected. Olivia took in his profile as they walked along, her swinging her arms, him pushing her bike. His wet hair had dried in clumps that landed on his shoulders. Back at the Tiki Hut, she'd watched with newfound interest as he rubbed his bare chest with a large colorful beach towel. He was good-looking, about six foot tall, well built, strong jaw, great smile, straight white teeth, and in the low light he appeared to have green eyes. He'd be a great study. She wished she had her sketchbook. Olivia's passion was art. As they walked on, she continued to inspect him with her artist's eye. And Jesse didn't seem to mind. Tomorrow, she'd meet Jesse again. And one day, she'd draw him.

CHAPTER FOUR

Present Day
Angela

The doorbell rang, and Angela brushed the hair from her face. She'd been on her knees in the kitchen and her joints groaned as she rose. "Coming," she yelled, as if the visitor could hear her from the distance. It had been a week since she and her friends had hauled out her furniture. A week of cleaning, scrubbing, and repair work in The Reclamation, as she had begun to refer to it. She was reclaiming her home. And in doing so, she was reclaiming her life. Each morning was a little easier. The first day after her girls had left, Angela walked down the stairs to the living room she'd emptied, and she cried. Day #2 of The Reclamation, she'd only offered a pensive glance to the cavernous and lonely rooms on her way to the coffeepot. But Day #3, well, it was Day #3 she'd listened to each echo of her footfalls as she'd descended the stairs. At the bottom, she'd given her house a long, meaningful look. And then, she'd laughed. She laughed like a crazy woman and before the day was over, Angela had scrubbed every wall and corner of the sprawling entryway and living room.

"I'm coming," she repeated to the persistent knocker at her front door. Before she could get there, Angela stopped dead in her tracks. Was the cavernous room playing tricks on her ears? She swore she heard a key turning in her front door lock.

Her keys were hanging on the wall, and Jesse had left for the evening to go visit his mother. Was someone breaking in? The place was empty, a lot of good it would do them. The sound vanished and she decided she must have imagined it.

After the cleaning, she had called in a painter to freshen the downstairs. Honey butter for the walls in the main living spaces, and warm and inviting mocha for the library where dark woods welcomed visitors. The rest of the house had bright white trim and crown moldings. She'd decided to spring for a fresh coat on the trim work too. It looked fantastic. Like an altogether different place. *Her* place. She'd also chosen new light fixtures. Jesse, along with two boys from Bayside, had installed a contemporary chandelier in the entry where an ugly, ornate antique beast had presided over the foyer for years. She'd also added other fixtures supporting the whimsical design sense Angela had never known she possessed. Several times over the last few days of cleaning and painting, she'd tried to ask Jesse about the photo she'd found in his wallet. The photo of Olivia. But before she could get the words out, she always lost her nerve. Who was the mysterious young girl in the picture, a girlfriend? Had they been in love? If he wanted to talk about it, he would. Boundaries, his boundaries, she'd have to respect that.

She had just turned to leave the room when the jingle of

keys in the door lock returned. Angela grabbed a fireplace poker from beside the mantle and held it like a weapon. Whoever was coming in would be sorry.

She heard a woman mumbling on the other side of the door as the intruder struggled with the latch that always seemed to stick. Angela herself knew the trick to opening the door, but her evil side had never allowed her to share it with Brice. It was like the house was letting him know it never really wanted him there. Brice couldn't be on the other side of the door, could he? If so, his voice had morphed into a woman's.

Then, the door flew open to reveal Lorene Baker as she stumbled over the threshold. Brice's mother wore a pale green designer suit, and an alligator skin bag dangled from her forearm. Her frown poisoned any attractiveness she once possessed, and right now she directed all that venom at Angela.

Until, of course, she realized the house was empty. The sound emanating from her ex-mother-in-law was first a gasp and then a screech. A mind-numbing screech sending icy nails down Angela's back.

"What have you *done* to our beach house?" The sound became a voice ... with actual words. The shrill tone sliced straight through Angela. No doubt her ears would hemorrhage. Angela's first instinct was to explain.

Lorene took an accusatory step toward her. "And what do you plan to do with that poker?"

Angela glanced down at it. "I thought you were an intruder."

Lorene scoffed. "Intruders don't use keys, Angela." She'd always said her name with such contempt.

A thought occurred to her. She didn't have to put up with Lorene's condescension. She was, after all, no longer any relation to the horrible woman. Angela had always liked

Brice's father. How Cogburn Baker survived in the family of elite snobs, she had no idea. But he'd always been kind to her. She glanced past Lorene. "Is Cog with you?" Hopeful. Too hopeful.

"No, Cogburn is *not* with me." She planted her hands on her hips. "I'm glad. He'd be crushed to see what you're doing with our home. Our wonderful winter home," she whined.

"My home," Angela said, but it was only a whisper and too low for Lorene to hear. It was Brice who'd decided at the last possible moment that he wasn't willing to give up their home in Connecticut. It was Brice who agreed to give Angela the beach house in the divorce. He'd never cared about it—even if it had been in his family for decades. But what he did care about was uprooting Angela from her home in New Haven. He'd been shocked—she'd seen it in his eyes—when she agreed to give him the Connecticut home in exchange for the beach house.

"I arrived just in time." Lorene disappeared from the front door and before Angela could breathe a sigh of relief, she reappeared with a suitcase.

There were moments in everyone's life when they knew they were certain to die. Moments when all of life flashes through the mind, numbing the senses and creating a sort of haze of acceptance. For Angela, this was not one of those moments. It was, in fact, just the opposite. Instead of accepting her fate, a new sensation sprung forth, one that fought, one that wasn't above having a knock-down-drag-out with her ex-mother-in-law. "You're not staying here." The words burst unchecked from Angela's mouth. But if she had checked them, she would have stamped USDA Prime on them and still let them fly.

Lorene waved a hand in the air. "Of course, I am." One tattooed brow arched.

"Lorene." Angela placed the poker carefully on its stand,

removing the temptation to use the tool as a weapon. "This is not your house anymore."

Lorene placed her suitcase at Angela's feet and blew past her. "Is there tea? I have a dreadful headache."

Angela looked longingly at the poker. "No. Lorene. There's no tea." She followed her into the kitchen where Lorene began rifling through shelves and rearranging contents.

"Lorene! What are you doing here?"

She spun from the cabinet. "I spoke with Brice, of course. You've upset him. He may not be able to admit it, but you've hurt him." She pressed a hand to the side of her perfectly coiffed hair. The heavily teased strands stood out from her pink scalp, thinner than Angela remembered. The blonde shade chosen to best cover the gray.

"Brice sent you?"

"Good heaven's no. He's far too proud to admit that you've gotten to him."

Why were they discussing this as if they were talking about a lovers' spat? Angela leaned toward the older woman. "We are divorced." She said the words slowly. Meticulously. Enunciating every syllable.

"Nonsense. You're having a midlife crisis. I know the signs. I had one myself years ago." When she waved her hand, the giant stone on her finger caught the light. "You two simply need to kiss and make-up."

"Ah. Kiss and make-up." Was this really happening? No one in their right mind would suggest such stupidity. No one. Not even designer clad Lorene Baker. For an instant Angela hoped she was dreaming, and any minute she'd wake up and find herself once again alone in her house laughing hysterically about the nightmare she'd had. But Lorene's patronizing look was all too real. Angela had been the butt of numerous ill-timed and cruel jokes during her marriage to

Brice. Every flaw had been documented and presented to anyone and everyone willing to look down their noses at her. Even Angela's fear of flying over the ocean had been laughed about and used as entertainment for vast numbers of dinner guests.

She'd been the scapegoat whenever anything went wrong. Ran out of wine, Angela hadn't ordered enough. The poor quality of steaks? Angela knew nothing about choosing fine cuts of meat. Clothes. Shoes. Hair. Nothing was ever right. Nothing was ever good enough. If a blouse wasn't the right shade for a skirt, one would think she'd worn a bathrobe to the dinner party.

Throw her out. A voice in her head urged. *Throw the mean-spirited piece of work out right now.* Angela envisioned doing so. She could imagine it in glorious Technicolor. Grabbing her ex-mother-in-law and physically removing her from the premises. Just as she was getting ready to give Lorene a final verbal ultimatum, Angela remembered something.

She remembered her Gran. She remembered how Gran would tell her people like Lorene were a dime a dozen. They judged their own worth by how worthless they could make others feel. *They* were the small ones, the little bits of nothing making others as miserable as they felt. The strong, the shimmering stars of the world stood tall in the face of such attacks. Those who were strong enough not to retaliate were the real diamonds. *You're a diamond, Angela. Don't stoop to dirt's level.*

Angela turned from Lorene. "You can stay one night. It's late and I don't want to send you back out. But in the morning, I'm afraid you'll have to find somewhere else to stay or just go on home. You won't see me the rest of the evening. I'll be in my room."

Lorene raised a hand. "Actually, I sleep best in the master

suite. I just never took it from Brice because of his back trouble."

Angela bit her tongue. *But you'll gladly take it from me.* Ha. Back trouble. The affliction only arose when Brice was presented with a task he didn't want to perform. Angela grabbed the door frame for support. "You will manage fine in the magnolia room. The linens are fresh. Good night, Lorene. By morning, I hope you'll accept that Brice and I have irreconcilable differences. Our marriage is over."

DREAMS WERE STRANGE LITTLE CREATURES. Having just enough reality in them to cause one to question everything they'd done. When Angela woke to a stiff neck and a headache, she blamed the dreams, and the ex-mother-in-law in the nearby room. She'd stayed in bed an hour longer than usual, hoping beyond hope that Lorene had come to her senses and left.

Rather than trek downstairs to face the monster, Angela slipped into her jogging clothes, a sports bra, and her running shoes. She dragged her mass of hair into a ponytail. That didn't help with the headache.

Silently she crept down the back stairs after pausing on the landing to see if she heard commotion in the kitchen. She didn't, so Angela tiptoed down the remaining steps and slinked through the back door. The irony of sneaking around one's house when one lived alone? Not lost on her.

She grumbled as she stretched, even though a glorious beachline beckoned. The sky was a golden shade of morning and it refused to allow her to remain in a foul mood. Good. She detested being grumpy. Braxton and Bryan had always called her SpongeBob. Wake up happy and just get happier as the day goes on. Guilty as charged, she supposed. Why be grouchy in the mornings when happy was ready and waiting for you?

Mornings were why she'd taken up jogging again. Brice was a terror in the mornings. Grumbling and complaining about everything. She'd tired of it to the point of leaving the house as soon as he'd stepped into the shower. Her morning runs became her sanctuary. They'd become her lifeblood.

She headed down Wishing Beach in a comfortable jog, casting a glance to the long ancient banyan tree that stood guard over the mystical shoreline. Was it really mystical? She didn't know. She'd made wishes at Wishing Beach since she was a little girl, but who knew if a person made their own luck or if magic places like this beach poured out fate. Not her.

The place was desolate save for the occasional ocean offering that had washed up with the tide. Coconuts, seashells, and a few plastic drink bottles littered the pristine beach. She had just left Millionaire's cove and was jogging along where the houses were still elaborate but much more modest than on her cove. Angela lifted her gaze to the gleaming white house—the fourth one down past her edge of the cove. Apprehension threaded its way up her spine, but she tamped it down. Sea spray hit her cheeks as if rising to give her a kiss. Angela tasted salt on her lips.

It's not that the white house was particularly distressing, it was simply that she'd come this way twice, noticed the man on the back patio, waved, and been stunned by the way he'd ignored her.

Okay, so some of the full-timers disliked sharing their precious beach with the tourists, but Angela *lived here*. A full-timer. Besides, his behavior was just rude, and she'd purposed in her heart not to let people treat her with rudeness—like she could really control that.

As she neared, she watched him step out onto his patio

and sit down. He wore dark pants, a red T-shirt, and he was barefoot. He held a cup of coffee in one hand. When Angela knew she was in his field of vision, she threw a smile and a big wave in his direction. She'd holler a greeting, but he'd never hear it from this distance over the surf. If she wanted to get his attention, she'd have to trek into his yard—something she'd never do even though they were likely the only two people staying on this stretch of beach right now. The people who owned houses on Millionaires Cove came and went frequently. Summers, winters, every single holiday. Even Senator Perry and his family. But beyond the cove where more modest houses rested, inhabitants were few except during the winter months.

Her smile faded when he didn't so much as acknowledge her. Angela huffed and continued, her steps quickening in time with her frustration. Some people were just plain anti-social. She fought the sadness pressing down on her shoulders. She was all alone here. In so many ways. And the neighbor looked about her age. She'd fancied they might become friends. How juvenile. Angela scolded herself for her adolescent thinking.

Even though she knew she was right to leave Brice, everything *else* about her life felt wrong.

Angela returned to her house and noticed Jesse's porch-light was still on. That was good. She'd hate for Jesse to have to deal with the insufferable Lorene and her continual condescension. If Angela could rescue him from Lorene, she'd redeem a bit of this awkward morning. She angled toward his cottage and knocked on the front door. No answer. She knocked again and waited. Nothing. Then she realized his Jeep was gone.

Angela entered her house through the backdoor, knocking the wet sand from her feet before she did. Lorene breezed into the kitchen. "I assume you've gotten rid of all of our furniture?" She looked hurt, but Angela knew for a fact that Lorene hadn't been fond of Brice's choices while decorating the beach house. Angela remembered her reaction vividly, because it was the only time Lorene had found fault in her nearly perfect son.

"It's all gone. Some went to a family on Bayside who had a housefire, and the Salvation Army store downtown took the rest." Angela went to the coffee pot. "They were happy to get the donation."

"Well." Lorene had a silk scarf around her throat, hiding her chicken neck. "If you insist on redecorating, I suppose I could shop with you."

Uh. No. "Lorene," Angela tried to sound civil. "I thought I made it clear last night that this house is no longer your concern." Seriously, did she have to show her the divorce papers which clearly stated that the beach house was hers since Brice kept their family home?

"And allow *me* to make *myself* clear. You're going to come to your senses, young lady. My being here will save you from a lot of humiliation later. Trust me on this."

Angela was being haunted. She was being haunted by the soul of her living ex-mother-in-law. There was no justice in the woman's intrusion. And no. She'd never allow Lorene to go shopping with her. She was finally beginning to put her footprint on the house. Honey butter walls and mocha in the library. The last thing she wanted was the Baker Stamp blotting out all her shine.

Where was Jesse? Earlier she'd wanted to rescue him, now she was the one in need of liberation. She tossed a longing look toward the backdoor, willing him to appear.

"Are you expecting someone?" Lorene said over a teacup. She'd dragged the dainty china down from the high cabinet instead of getting a coffee mug like a normal human being. Pieces of china dotted the counter.

Angela threw a glance at the wall clock. "Jesse was supposed to be here by now." She failed to add that was because she'd in fact invited *him* to furniture shop with her.

Lorene waved a hand through the air. "Oh, I let him go."

Angela stopped in mid-drink. Surely, she couldn't mean literally. "What did you say?"

Lorene lifted her brows. "I'm staying for a few months and since *you're* planning to stay indefinitely, there's hardly need for a caretaker." She shrugged. "Besides, a woman alone shouldn't have a single man living on the property. Even though he's twenty years your senior, how would it look?"

Fire shot down Angela's spine. Her hands were trembling when she placed her coffee cup on the table. It teetered before coming to a full halt. "You—you *fired* him?" She could barely get the words out.

Lorene only pursed her mouth in answer.

Angela fisted her hands. "Tell me you didn't."

Lorene took another sip.

Angela's anger burned. Her teeth were clenched together so hard she thought the back ones might break.

"Angela, you're insisting on making a fool of yourself. It seems there's little I can do to stop that, but after all of this blows over, Brice has to be able to come here and hold his head high. I let Jesse go because of his insolence."

Angela face was engine hot. "His what?" *Insolence* and *Jesse* did not belong in the same sentence.

Lorene—still cool as a cat—placed her teacup on the delicate saucer. "Brice had given him direct orders not to get the house ready and to leave. He let him go. Jesse completely ignored those orders. He admitted as much to me this morning."

Angela's stomach churned. Once, she'd watched the boys play a video game that had a weapon that rolled then exploded. She took a single step toward Lorene. She must have looked a sight because Lorene's eyes widened with fear.

"Lorene, you had no right," she hissed. *Roll, then boom!* That's what the weapon on the video game had done. Angela was a weapon and right now, she was rolling toward Lorene.

Lorene stayed planted in her spot, statue straight. "When I spoke to Brice last night—"

"Get. Out." Angela took one more step.

When the woman didn't move, only gave her a pitying look, Angela pointed in the direction of the front door and yelled, "Get out."

Dimples appeared on the wrinkles of Lorene's face. "Really, a tantrum?"

Angela was trembling. "Leave, or I'm calling the police."

Lorene threw her head back and laughed. "And what? Tell them I'm loitering in my own beach house?"

That was it. Angela broke. "In all my life I've never met anyone as delusional as you, Lorene. You walk around like the world owes you, but you know what the world sees? A pitiful waste. You offer no joy to humanity and you spend your time sucking up other people's happiness in an attempt to make them as loathsome as yourself." She ended it with, "Your only saving grace is Cog. I don't know how he has put up with you all these years. As far as your son, Brice, he's as far from perfect as a human can get ... and still be considered human."

Lorene's face paled as Angela completed her rant. Surely, the woman would leave now. But true to her form, Lorene pulled a deep breath and said, "Are you finished with your little tantrum, because it's time to stop acting like a child."

Unbelievable. Angela pressed her mouth closed. Without a word, she turned from Lorene and headed straight to the phone on the wall. She hit three numbers and said, "Can you

46

give me the number for the Wishing Beach Island police department, please?"

Lorene scoffed. She obviously thought this was a bluff.

Her chin tilted when Angela began to dial. "Yes, hello. There is a trespasser in my house who refuses to leave. My name is Angela Baker. Yes, I live on the cove—" A hand appeared from nowhere and snatched the phone.

Lorene's eyes were ablaze. "You ungrateful—"

"Lorene, I spent my married life trying to make you happy. But I realized it's impossible. You're a miserable woman who tries desperately to control everyone around you. If you'd just give people a chance, you'd see that you don't have to be in charge to be happy. I want you out of my house. You have fifteen minutes to get your things and leave. If I ever see you here again, I will get a restraining order."

Lorene's mouth twisted into a grimace. She spun and marched out of the kitchen. Within minutes, Angela heard Lorene's engine as she sped away.

Angela walked to the front door and stared out. Shouldn't she feel better? Shouldn't she feel vindicated? Instead, she felt more alone than ever. Just as she was turning to go inside, a car pulled in. Oh Lord, she wasn't ready for round two. But it wasn't Lorene. A white SUV with WBIPD on the side, stopped in her circular drive.

A man in black dress pants and a gray shirt stepped out. "We received a call from this address."

Angela marveled at the speed in which he'd arrived. In Connecticut when they'd had a would-be intruder, it had taken forty minutes for the police to get there. "I didn't even give the house number."

The man smiled, lines around his eyes crinkling. "Small island."

His comfortable demeanor hinted at experience although he was probably younger than Angela. His hands slid into his

47

pockets as he spoke. "The dispatcher said you were cut off. Is everything okay?"

She looked back at the front door still standing wide open. "Yes. I'm fine. The uh-uninvited person left on her own. Thank you so much for coming." At least the Wishing Beach Island PD had her back.

He leveled his gaze. "Would you like to file a report?"

She realized he was studying her a little too closely. Her hands still trembled, so she placed them behind her back, her face heating under his perusal. "Um. No. I mean, it would sound very silly."

He took a few steps closer. He was likely a handful of years younger, yet he carried himself with a somewhat ageless wisdom. He tipped his chin toward the front door. "Do you mind if I go inside and take a look around?"

"What?" She really needed her brain to kick in and catch up with the conversation.

His sharp eyes missed nothing. "You seem visibly shaken."

"Well, yes." She'd just unleashed twenty years of pent up anger upon her arch enemy. "I wasn't in any danger." Angela shook her head and her ponytail bounced from shoulder to shoulder. "I'm not making a lot of sense, am I? And I'm being rude. I'm sorry. Please come in."

"I'm Officer North. Most folks around here call me Chris." He followed her into the house.

"Can I get you a cup of coffee?" Actually, she wanted him to do his quick inspection and go. She needed to find Jesse and make things right.

"Love one."

Well, that surprised her. She went to the coffeepot and poured him a cup. He sat on the barstool, his hand closing around the mug after she slid it to him. He rested his forearms on the kitchen island. "This granite?" Officer North asked, running a ruddy hand over the gray toned surface of the counter.

"It's quartz. We did it a few years back. I chose the color. My husband had a different one picked out, but the piece he wanted was sold to someone else. He lost all interest in making any decision after that." Pouting is what she called it. Pouting like a jilted teenager.

He gave it an approving nod. "I like it. Thinking about redoing my kitchen."

Why were they having this conversation? She needed to find Jesse.

"You planning to be on the island long? Not much is happening here now, but in a few weeks, Senator Perry will be here for a fundraising event," he said, hand still stroking the cool granite.

"Oh, I've met Senator Perry. Travis Perry, not Roy."

"Roy Perry passed a few months back. His wife still comes to the island to visit. Travis Perry hosts the Wishing Beach Ball at the end of the summer. Travis seems to be making an even bigger political splash than his dad."

She liked Travis Perry's politics, but she wasn't looking to dive into that conversation. "I'm going to be living here full time."

"Ah. We don't have a lot of full-timers. You have one neighbor down the beach."

"The rude one," she muttered.

Officer North leaned closer. "I beg your pardon?"

"Nothing. I just … I jog in the mornings. I've waved to him, but he doesn't respond."

North's mouth quirked into a half grin. "Odd duck, that one. You ever talk to him?"

"No." What did *odd duck* mean? Was she living down the beach from a psycho-killer?

North took a drink, but she thought she saw him hiding a

full-on smile just before his mouth disappeared behind the mug. "You should call him on it."

"What? How?"

North shrugged. "If he continues to ignore you, you should march yourself up his back steps and let him know you don't appreciate his rudeness."

Oh. No, she'd never do something so bold.

And yet, she'd stood up to Lorene. A vision of confronting him skated through her mind. For so many years she'd allowed people to walk all over her. Part of the new and improved Angela Baker was calling people on their crap.

"Would you like to tell me what transpired this morning to cause you to call the department?"

Angela gave a short rundown of what had happened. "I just didn't know how to get rid of her. She has no right to be here, and she's certainly an unwelcome guest."

North drained his cup and stood. He stretched. "You were right to call. These things have a way of escalating. Before you know it, someone's lying on the floor in a pool of blood."

Angela placed a hand to her stomach. "I can't imagine that as an outcome."

"No one ever does."

The gravity of his words left an unsettled knot inside her as she remembered gripping the fireplace poker like a weapon. She *could* imagine it. Maybe not with Lorene, but more than once when she'd made Brice mad, she'd wondered if he'd strike her. She had a slender runner's frame. She'd be no match for his fury. Sometimes, she thought it was only a matter of time until the hands he fisted in anger would release their wrath on her flesh. Maybe she'd escaped just in time. Or maybe she was being overly dramatic, the imprint of Lorene's presence still fresh.

As soon as Officer North left, she raced to her phone and tried Jesse's cell. It rang and rang, but no answer.

Still in her jogging clothes and unconcerned with the fact that she likely smelled like sweat and desperation, Angela grabbed her purse and headed out.

CHAPTER FIVE

Bayside, Wishing Beach Island
Summer, 1981
Jesse

Jesse's palms were sweaty, not sure if it was the Florida heat or the fact that he was seeing Olivia. He rubbed them over the freshly washed jeans he'd snatched from the clothesline at home. Mama loved the scent of clothes on the line and though she had a clothes dryer, she often left jeans, towels, and sheets swinging in the breeze while she worked the garden. These were Jesse's Sunday jeans. No grease stains, no threadbare spots.

He sat beside Olivia in the '66 Mercury Comet while he fought the urge to stare at her long legs. It amazed him that their chance meeting had turned into a two-hour long conversation on the patio of the surf shop then an hour at the beach wading and holding hands. Since that weekend, she'd been all he could think about. There'd been almost two weeks of dates on his hour lunch break—most days turning into an hour and a half lunch break—while he helped Olivia get over her fear of the ocean. Somehow along the way, he'd agreed to teach her how to drive.

She sat in the driver's seat of the Comet with a death grip on the large steering wheel. Olivia looked as scared as she had the night he'd fished her out of the Atlantic.

"Are you sure we should be doing this?" She let go of the wheel like it had burned her and fisted her hands at her chest. "What if I wreck your car?"

He'd picked her up downtown and driven her to the bay side of the island to a less traveled strip of road. "The car belongs to my boss. Mine is still in the shop."

She gasped. "You're not making me feel better about this!"

Jesse laughed. "Olivia, it's fine. You said you don't want your brothers teaching you how to drive, so here I am. At your service. Now go on, take the wheel in your hands."

A long sigh had her unfurling her fingers and slowly gripping the wheel.

Jesse reached over and moved her hands to the right position. "You're ready."

She shook her head and long blonde hair flew around her. "No, I'm not."

Jesse grinned. "You are."

"What if I crash?" she pleaded.

"You won't."

"I'm sure I will."

"I'll sit next to you." Jesse slid over on the seat. "That way I can grab the wheel if anything goes wrong?"

"Okay." She nodded.

As soon as he was beside her, he smelled flowers. Her perfume or shampoo or some such girly thing. Mm, she smelled good. He lifted an arm around her and placed a foot alongside hers resting his leg against her thigh. She was

53

wearing shorts and, *whew*, those tanned legs. He wished he had on shorts too, but he'd dressed in his Sunday jeans to impress her. He wondered what her skin against his would feel like.

"Jesse, I asked if I should start the motor. Are you having second thoughts?"

"No. No, I'm not. If anything goes wrong, just get your right foot out of the way. I'll hit the brake and steer. Okay?"

She swallowed. "We're going to die."

THEY'D HAD three real dates and that didn't even count the noontime surf walks to quell Olivia's fear of the ocean. Jesse splashed the new aftershave on his freshly shaved face. His reflection in the small bathroom mirror caused an unwarranted chuckle. He had to admit, he'd bought the *All Man* scent hoping Olivia would like it. Usually, he smelled like engine oil and gasoline. Although, he had to question if they were *real* dates. To him, yes. But to her maybe he was teaching her how to drive and that's all.

He shook his head to clear it and headed toward the kitchen in search of food. He was always hungry.

In the living room he stopped and planted a kiss on the top of his mama's head. She was bent over the desk that stood in the corner of the living room doing the books for the *Henderson Fishing Company*. Mama was Grace Henderson before she married Jesse's father, Joseph Malone. The only girl amongst five brothers. It was a given that her part in the fourth-generation family business would be just that, taking care of business. Jesse himself had never been much for fishing. But he could make an engine purr. He'd never planned to follow in the family footsteps and that had been just fine with his mama. She loved the business but had always wanted something more for him. Something different. Something special.

"You smell like a gigolo. Where you off to?" she asked without looking up.

He laughed and went on into the kitchen. He'd barely lifted the towel covering the pan of rolls resting on the counter when Mama's voice stopped him.

"Those are for dinner," she called from the living room. "There are leftovers in the icebox."

He dropped the towel. *How does she do that?* Mama could see through walls.

He turned to go to the fridge when she appeared in the doorway. She was 5'4" to his 6' and fifty pounds lighter but his mother could stop him with a look.

She could also coerce a confession with little more than a raised brow and her fists on her slim hips. "What's that look for, Mama? I ain't done nothing wrong."

"You *haven't* done *anything* wrong," she corrected.

"That's what I just said." He gave her a crooked smile.

She hmphed. "In the past couple weeks, you *ain't* done a lot right."

He feigned hurt. "What's that supposed to mean?" Usually, Mama saved the scolding for Jesse's older brother, Joseph Junior. He found trouble everywhere while Jesse kept his nose clean.

"Jesse, I talked to Mr. Caruthers. He says you've been skipping work."

"I have, some." He sighed. "I've had stuff to take care of."

"Look, I know how it is when you're nineteen."

"Almost twenty," Jesse interjected.

"I want you to have fun." She took him by the arm. "Jesse, this is a real break Mr. Caruthers is giving you. He wants to turn the shop over to you one day. And I have to be honest, knowing your feet are on solid land and not out there dragging fish from the ocean ..." As she said that, she threw a hand to the window where the bay lay beyond their small manicured lawn. "I just want you to be happy."

"I'm happy, Mama."

"But you can't cut work. You've done so well up to now. One more year—"

He cut her off. "One more year, and Mr. Caruthers' garage is mine." The garage was a profitable, established business whose owner was looking to retire. Jesse was a natural at mechanics which was one reason Sam Caruthers was willing to make him such a great deal. That, and that he respected Jesse's father. More than once, Sam told Jesse he couldn't stand the thought of some stranger coming in and destroying what he'd spent his life building. And to sweeten the deal, Mr. Caruthers was going to carry the paper, finance Jesse. A dream come true. All he had to do was stay on track. "You're right, Mama. I'll do better."

Jesse's dad, Joe senior, hadn't started life as a fisherman like those in the family he'd married into. But he quickly became one until a freak accident onboard took his life. Jesse was ten when his father died.

Thankfully, his mother had her share of the fishing business as income although that carried with it its own set of problems. New regulations had caused the business to take a dive in the past couple of years. Money was tight. But Mama always made what they had stretch. Jesse tried to help. Grace Malone was the strongest woman Jesse knew.

"Don't worry, Mama, I'll pick it up." He leaned over and landed a quick peck on her cheek.

"You off to see that girl?"

"Her name is Olivia."

"I don't care if her name is Queen Elizabeth." Her voice softened. "Son, you shouldn't be spending so much time with just one girl, especially a girl that young ... and from the cove. You have to use wisdom."

"She's different. I can't explain it. I've never met anyone like her, Mom. I really like her."

She offered a pitiful smile. "I know, Jesse. I can see it in your eyes, hear it in your voice. That's what worries me," Grace Malone said to her youngest son as she touched a small hand to his shoulder.

"Why are you worried?"

"Because she's too young. And most importantly, because she's from the cove."

"Why should that matter? She doesn't *live* there. She's a guest at someone's home."

"Like to like, Jesse. They travel in their own circles, and they don't take kindly to strangers breaking their carefully placed walls. You're an outsider to them. And in my experience, they don't like outsiders."

"Had a lot of experience with the richies from the cove, have you?" He grinned to lighten the mood if for no other reason. Mama didn't reciprocate.

"Folks on the cover are a whole different breed. And I don't want to see my brilliant boy getting tied up in that mess. Someday, the right girl will come along, and it will be magic," Mama Grace reasoned.

"Is that what you and Dad had, magic?" Jesse asked quietly.

"Yeah," she whispered. Her eyes shimmered with the onset of tears. "We did."

It had been almost ten years since Jesse's dad had died but to his mother, he knew it still seemed like yesterday.

"We were young. Very young, but we weren't from worlds that were that different." She patted his cheek. "I just don't want to see you get hurt, honey."

"Broken hearted, you mean." Like her, wandering around the house with an empty cavern where her heart used to be.

Mama blinked away the moisture from her eyes. She rocked back on her heels. "If you're really thinking she's the one, I'd like to know what *her* parents say about your relationship with their daughter? Do they approve? How did they react when you met them?" Her look burrowed into him. Grace Malone was still an attractive woman at forty-three years of age, green eyes, and strawberry blonde hair pulled back in a loose ponytail. Raising the three children she and Joe had made together was her primary love and focus. And in that she was unrelenting.

He swallowed the cotton in his throat. "Well …" The fact was, he hadn't met Olivia's parents. "For now, we're just friends." But that didn't quite seem honest. To him, they were so much more. "*Good* friends, that's all."

She waved a hand through the air. "You don't go off stinking pretty for your other friends," she snorted.

He flashed a smile. "You think I stink pretty?" Jesse waggled his brows and pulled his mother into a tight hug.

She struggled to get free. "You're not going to charm your way out of this, Jesse Everett." He'd inherited his middle name from his grandfather, Everett Malone. He'd also inherited his grandfather's set of movie star teeth, good looks, and his gift for charm. At least, that's what Mama told him.

When Jesse released her. She cupped his face with her palm. Jesse saw the worry in her eyes. He placed his hand over hers. "Everything's going to be all right."

He left the house, but his mother's words left him unsettled. Driving across the island, Jesse became aware of the invisible border he was crossing. The bay side of the island might be a stone's throw away from the beach side, physically, but in terms of the world they lived in, it was another planet. Parents in Millionaires Cove were generally not happy to have their daughters falling for a guy from Bayside. But all he was doing was teaching her to drive. As he turned onto the main beach road, he buried his concerns.

Jesse found Olivia just where she said she'd be. His earlier apprehension melted as soon as he set his eyes on her. She was always early.

She spotted him from across the park. Her face lit, and she jumped up from under the tree where she'd been sitting. Come to think of it, he never picked her up at her place. Was she hiding him from her family?

No matter, as she jogged toward him, Jesse's mouth went dry. She was dressed in a white cotton sundress, giving him a glimpse of her bare shoulders. The top had a low round neckline and a gathered waist. A common dress for the local types and tourists, but on her it looked sexy as could be. She might be young, but she looked every inch a woman today.

The rest of the world faded away as he neared her. There was no park, no marina, no brilliantly colored flowers, or tall palm trees. She made everything else disappear. Maybe he'd start calling her Houdini. His heart stuttered when her jog became a full-out run toward him.

She'd tanned over the weeks she'd been on the island, her skin warm and shimmery as she neared. When Olivia stopped at his feet and went up on her tiptoes, Jesse ceased breathing. She dropped a kiss on his jawline. It was probably meant for his cheek, but with all the surprise, he'd forgotten to bend so she could reach. There he stood, a statue of surprise. "Wha, what was that for?" he finally croaked.

"For being so kind to me. I love driving. It's neat."

Her hands lingered on his forearms where she'd propped them for the kiss. "Neat," he chuckled. "You ready for lesson number four?"

"Nope." She gave a one shoulder shrug. "I feel like I know enough about driving now."

When she released her grip and spun away, he wondered if this was the beginning of goodbye. Jesse's hand went to his heart. A painful twinge settled there. He'd been out with lots of girls, pretty girls. So why did this strange, beautiful Olivia make him feel so different than all the others had?

When Olivia got to the tree where she'd been sitting, she reached down and scooped up a large notebook from the ground. Then, she turned and frowned. "Aren't you coming with?"

He forced his leaden legs to move. He'd had to duck a little to tuck under the giant bald cypress where she'd been sitting. The branches of the cypress were heavy with Spanish moss that swung in the salty breeze.

"Will you sit with me for a few minutes?" she asked, her fingers cradling the notebook like a shield. She was suddenly nervous. He could tell. Her full lips twitched, and she kept blinking.

"Sure," he said, hoping he hadn't done something to scare her. They'd had so much fun over the days that she'd been driving. Once, they even had to pull the car over because they were laughing so hard.

She sat down, and before the wind could expose her thighs, she tucked the edge of her skirt around her legs.

Jesse stood above her.

She reached up and grasped his hand. "It'll be easier to sit down if you bend." Then a slow, teasing smile spread across her face.

Olivia continued to clutch the notebook, her gaze moving out to the marina before them. His gaze followed hers. Yachts, cabin cruisers, fancy runabouts and sailboats were all moored at the beach club. It was very different from the dock where his family's boats were anchored. These vessels were white and shiny, all new and seemingly unused. Might be pretty, but to him they looked lonely.

She must have noticed his interest in the place. "Do you like the boats?"

Boat meant work and smelly fishing. "Not so much. I mean, they're all in ship-shape here, but a boat needs a captain who loves her."

"I never knew boats had feelings."

"Everything has feelings, Olivia." For a moment, there was only the two of them. Jesse and Olivia and the rest of the world was merely a backdrop.

"Jesse, I want to share something with you." Slowly, she peeled the notebook away from her chest and placed it flat on her lap.

It wasn't a notebook at all. When she went to open it, he noticed the black smudges on her fingertips. Without realizing what he'd done, Olivia's hand was suddenly in one of Jesse's. He cradled it and used the index finger of his free hand to trace the dark smears and smudges that colored her fingertips and the pad of her palm. When he rubbed his finger against the smudge, it started to disappear. She trembled. Or maybe those tiny electric jolts came from him. His eyes met hers over their clasped hands.

Olivia's crystal blue eyes filled with tears, and he thought he must have crossed a line. He released her and leaned back.

"Jesse. I've never shown this to anyone. And I realized, it's because I don't care what anyone else thinks." She pressed her hand to the sketch book. "This is for me. But now ..." Her tongue darted out to moisten her lips. "But now, I feel like it's for you, too."

He opened his mouth, but no words formed.

"Can I show you?"

He nodded, not trusting his voice.

She lifted the cover to reveal a full page of small sketches. An eye, a folded hand, a palm tree. "These are just practice. I have some in color." She rushed past the page to another. "Here."

The sketch of an artistic rendition of the marina sat on his lap, highlighting a massive sailboat gilded gold and orange by a setting sun.

"You're not saying anything." She sounded nervous.

"I'm speechless." He spared her a quick glance, then his attention returned to the drawing. "Olivia, it's gorgeous."

She breathed a long sigh of relief. "You really think so?"

"Are there more?" He started to thumb through, but she placed a hand over his, stopping him.

"The others aren't finished." Her voice hitched up. "Most don't even have color yet."

"I'd still like to look."

She chewed her bottom lip. "Okay, but don't judge, all right?"

He turned to another page where a small girl stood at the edge of the sea with a beach ball in her hands. This drawing was every bit as compelling as the first. He flipped another page and another. "They're good. Really good, Olivia. Why won't you show them off? These should be in frames on walls, not hiding in a sketchbook."

She laughed and tossed her hair. "Sure. Whatever you say."

"Listen to me!" He hadn't meant to sound so stern. He angled to face her, and his free hand moved up to caress her cheek. He needed to hold her attention. "I'm not kidding. They're great, and people should see them."

She placed her hand over his, just like he'd placed his over his mother's earlier that day. "Jesse, I don't want any more driving lessons because ..." Her lips pressed together. "Because I just want to spend time with you. I ... I like you."

She liked him. Something fresh and delicious unfurled in his stomach. He hadn't meant to kiss her. But those words were precious, and it seemed the only way to capture them was to tilt his head toward hers. Warmth bloomed between them. Her thigh pressed against his. The scent of her hair and her skin enveloped him until he was drunk in the exciting new sensation. Her lips were moist and inviting when his mouth gently parted against hers.

She tasted like cherries and a hint of spearmint gum. Jesse inched closer, his hand sliding over her exposed shoulder and down to the bend in her arm. She melted into him, responding to every movement. Her mouth was supple, teasing a silent groan from the deepest part of his belly. His mind begged for more and his body was sure to follow. There was a tiny spark when they finally broke the kiss.

Her eyes drifted open. Olivia smiled as she glanced left and right to see if they'd had an audience. All around them, the world was abandoned. They were alone.

Olivia giggled. She reached over and placed a gentle kiss on his jawline in the same spot where she had earlier. But it wasn't the same because everything was different now. Olivia was the most unusual, delightful, the most captivating girl he had ever met. Excitement welled in him, he wanted to know more of her, more of everything about her.

She took his hand and didn't let go even after she stood. "Let's go get some ice cream."

Fingers interlocked, Jesse and Olivia walked past the marina toward the ice cream shop.

CHAPTER SIX

Present Day
Angela

Angela knew Jesse's family lived on the bay side of the island. Actually, now that she thought about it, Jesse had taken the boys, Bryan and Braxton, on a fishing day trip there years ago. They had loved it and couldn't stop talking about it. Maybe they loved it too much. Brice wouldn't let them go again. That's about as much as she knew about the bay side of the island. After she found Jesse and set this whole thing right, she'd have time to explore.

She'd need a distraction anyway or she'd spend the entire day brooding about Lorene and the horrible confrontation they'd had.

She forced her thoughts from Lorene and concentrated on the idea of discovering all the island's secrets. A fresh wave of expectation gurgled within her. But first, Jesse. She had all the time in the world to explore. This was her home now. Her forever home. Not just a stop off in the winter or a few weeks in the summer. The only pressing issue was finding Jesse.

Angela drove along as the streets narrowed and lost their center lines. Sidewalks also disappeared and the palm trees that were usually kept neat and trim were littered with dead palm fronds. Giant oaks with overhanging Spanish moss canopied the narrow road. This was old Florida. And it was breathtaking. She'd literally driven out of the pristine island atmosphere into a fairytale land where wind and ancient banyan trees with their upside-down roots swayed to their own music. She could hear crickets and night creatures even though it was early afternoon.

Seagrass and palmettos lined the street, vines twisting and twining them into one long living organism. Up ahead, a narrow bridge spanned an inlet. A smattering of old pick-up trucks had been haphazardly parked along the sides of the narrow lane. Even from a distance, she could see men fishing from the bridge, their poles dangling out over the water. If she wasn't in such a rush to find Jesse, she'd stop and admire the scene. There was something soothing and honest about the sight. Men and nature. Quiet water, a simple stick, string, and the possibility of a catch. She'd never been fishing herself. But she could see the draw.

Slowly, Angela rolled closer. By the time she reached the bridge, five sets of eyes were cast her way. They were all older men, retired, most likely, although two looked to be dressed in clothes suitable for a construction site. One had teardrops of white—paint, she decided—dotting the thighs of his faded jeans. When she stopped on the bridge and rolled down her window, the man nearest to her bent at the waist to look down into her car. "Look like you might be lost, ma'am."

He had a smooth deeply tanned face, and his hair was

thick and brilliantly white. He was a striking older man. "I'm actually looking for someone, Jesse Malone?"

He rubbed a hand over his cheek. "Nice ride you got there."

She waved a hand. "It's a ridiculous thing. My ex-husband bought it because of the horsepower. As if a tiny car like this needs, oh, I don't remember, something like four-hundred horses powering it."

He grinned and displayed a set of even teeth, only adding to his looks. "Why didn't he buy a red one?"

The joke was evident. It was a true, pure racing red. No blue, no orange in the paint base. Red. There could only be red for a car like hers. "After all," she chided. "He didn't want to draw attention."

He chuckled, shifted his weight and gave her an approving nod. "Why you after Jesse?"

A friend of his. Good. Angela opened her mouth to speak but was cut off.

He crossed his arms over his chest. "Whatever it is you think Jesse did, he's guilty." Their exchange had drawn the attention of the other fishermen.

She pressed a hand to her chest. "Jesse works for me, and I'm afraid there was a misunderstanding with my mother-in-law—my *ex*-mother-in-law—and I, well, I need him to know …"

The white-haired man's gaze was sharp on her. For the second time today, she was an open book being read by unfamiliar eyes. But they were sympathetic eyes. Both this man's and Officer North's had been. Like maybe on some deep and cosmic level they knew she needed looking out for. And they were willing to rise to the challenge. The feeling was most unusual. No one had ever really looked out for Angela. Even though she'd grown up with siblings, they'd always been busy with their noses stuck in textbooks. Too busy to take the time to read any pain in their sister's eyes. Certainly too busy to be a buffer for that pain. In fact, other than a long phone call with each of her siblings, she'd barely spoken to them since the separation. Not their fault. Their highly successful careers demanded their time. Even her sisters, Tess and Violet had expressed their love, offered a place to stay for a while but nothing more. She'd not wanted a *place*; she'd wanted a listening ear. Angela didn't harbor any indignation. They poured their heart and souls into work like she poured hers into home and family. Hmm. Maybe they'd had it right all along and she had it wrong, desperately wrong.

She forced the thought from her head. "I just need Jesse to know he still has a job," she finally said. That and so much more. Jesse had a home and a place of his own on the corner of her property. He'd chosen to stay there instead of living here at Bayside where the Spanish moss hung in glorious masses and gave an ethereal frame to the world below. She could settle here and feel—perhaps not at home—but at least feel at peace with her surroundings. Where life was less automated and rushed. Unlike her world where the signs of age and decay were swiftly hidden by fresh paint and power washers. It felt as though here one could age gracefully and that aging wouldn't be a tragedy, instead it would be a badge of honor.

That other world, *her* world had no resemblance. A person, a house, a car only had value if it was new and unblemished. Here, hidden beneath the banyan trees, anyone and anything could have worth. How Angela knew this, she couldn't quite say. Maybe it was a general attitude that wafted on the sea wind. Whatever the cause, she couldn't fathom why Jesse chose to live in her little cottage rather than the vast free-ness of the bay side of the island.

The older man smiled. "I'd say Jesse is a pretty lucky fella. You seem a nice enough employer. His mama lives over on Cypress Way. I expect you'll find him thereabouts. He's got all kinds of kin scattered over that neighborhood. But if you don't see him right off, Mama will surely know where he's gone off to."

"Thank you so much." She reached out of the car to shake his hand. "I'm Angela Baker. I live on the other side of the island."

He wiped his palm on the front of his fishing shirt. "Been cleanin' fish, you sure you want to shake hands?"

"I'm positive." They did so, and Angela nodded toward his bucket. "Good catch?"

"Enough for a meal. My name's Joseph Malone, by the way."

"You're—"

He grinned. "Jesse's big brother."

"What do you know? I guess it was fortuitous I stopped here."

A man behind Joseph leaned over his shoulder and said to her. "I don't know about that, but it was lucky."

Both Joseph and Angela chuckled. Joseph motioned with his thumb to the man behind him. "This is Hue." He turned to him. "*Fortuitous* and *lucky* mean the same thing."

Hue's wrinkled mouth became an o shape. "Well, isn't it *for-tu-it-ous* that I learned that today."

It was impossible not to like this crew. "What kind of fish are you catching?" Even in her hurry to find Jesse, she wanted to stay right here just a bit longer.

"Bass. Good eatin'." He pointed across the bridge. "This kind are usually a freshwater fish, but they can live in brackish. This is brackish water here."

The only thing Angela knew about bass was that she'd

had it at a wedding reception, once. Seabass. It had a delicate flavor and a garlic butter sauce. Her stomach growled.

She said goodbye and wound her way through the streets of Bayside. Colorful little houses with vibrant walls and white trim slipped past. The rows of homes put her in mind of the bright seaside huts in the Caribbean, the front porches decorated with hammocks and rockers. No potted plants, though. The foliage of the island and its ever-encroaching nature made the perfect frame for the porches. No need to add decorations.

She passed three teens, and one gave a cat call after she drove by. Angela laughed, surprised by the deep belly sound that rose from the basement of her stomach and gurgled out of her mouth. Instead of feeling embarrassed, she gave a cat call right back to them. She watched the confusion flicker across their faces in her rearview mirror. Then their laughter caught up to her and she laughed too, right along with them. This time, it was easier, as if the well to her joy had been busted open and now the stuff could flow easily, effortlessly. Angela used to laugh a lot. Growing up, she'd been the one who would laugh so loud and long, she'd have the whole family infected before she'd finished. She missed that girl. Then again, maybe she still *was* that girl. Underneath the fresh paint and the power washing. Maybe young Angela lurked inside her skin waiting ever so patiently to be the debutante of a new age.

How could a drive through old Florida be so liberating? Maybe because she'd stood up to her ex-mother in-law. Whatever it was, Angela didn't want this feeling to leave.

When she turned onto Cypress Way, a trio of small children followed her to the third house on the right where Jesse's black Jeep sat in the shell driveway. She lowered her window just as the kids caught up to her. Two of the three were tall and lanky. The last, short and round-faced. All girls. "Hi. I'm looking for Jesse Malone. I see his car."

None of them spoke, but the two taller ones turned and dashed into the house.

A slim elderly woman materialized in the doorway with a pot in her hands and a kitchen towel slung over her shoulder.

Angela got out of her car. The third little girl fell into step beside her. Angela smiled.

"Help you?" The woman at the door asked.

"Yes." She cleared her throat. "I'm looking for Jesse."

Jesse appeared from inside the house and placed a hand on the woman's shoulder. "Angie! What brings you way out here?"

"Jesse, I'm so sorry about this morning. Lorene was out of line." The words tumbled from her though a trio of young girls moved ever closer to hear the conversation. Angela didn't care who was eavesdropping. She'd found Jesse and that was what mattered. The girls moved in until they were a tight circle around Angela. The elderly woman's eyebrow notched up slowly. "So, this is *Angie*," she said, sing-songy as if she'd said her name many times before.

"Angela Baker, meet my mother, Grace Malone."

Grace adjusted her hold on the stockpot, and Angela could see green beans peeking out from the top. "This the woman who fired you?" They looked to be fresh beans like the organic ones she used to purchase at the farmer's market in New Port.

"Her mother-in-law fired me," Jesse corrected.

"Mmm-hmm." There was a long pause while Jesse's mother slowly looked her up and down.

Deeper in the house, a radio was on and the voice of an angel sang about lost love. But the sound bounced around, then emanated from the doorway and stopped just as an attractive woman filled the space over Grace's other shoulder. She was the grown spitting image of the two tall girls, with her green eyes and strawberry blonde hair. Hers was salon streaked with a variety of blonde and deep sunset shades, adding drama to an already striking woman. The trio of youngsters had lost interest in the conversation and were now standing nearby swinging their arms and inspecting the fancy car.

Then the woman behind Grace spoke and Angela realized her voice was the same as the one she'd heard singing. "Hi," she said and flashed Angela a smile. "Here, Mama. I'll do those." The tall, stately woman stepped gracefully onto the porch, sat down in a wooden rocker, and started snapping the ends off the beans. She hummed and kept one eye on the unfolding scene.

Angela pointed to her. "That sound. That song was you? I thought it was a radio."

The woman who owned the glorious voice smiled. "I'm Willow, Jesse's sister. Sometimes I tend to forget how far these pipes carry."

She said it like an apology. But Angela was fascinated by what she'd heard. She loved music, and Willow's voice was unearthly good.

Finally, Grace stepped out, commanding the attention.

Jesse followed her. "So, why did you come, Angie?" He looked a bit perturbed. The angle of his head and the almost frown on his face.

"Lorene. This was a huge misunderstanding. She had no right to …" She placed a hand on her heart. "Good Lord, I can barely say it. She had no right to fire you. Jesse, why would you listen to her?"

"Why would you let her into your house?" Jesse stated, flatly.

All the air left Angela's lungs. "You're right. This is on me.

One hundred percent. I should never have allowed her to stay. Please, can you forgive me?"

"I really didn't pay any attention to her." He shrugged. "But I decided to get out of her way and not complicate the situation." He offered a smile to lighten the mood.

Relief flooded Angela. "Thank you, Uncle Jesse." She narrowed her eyes on him. "You could have let me know and saved me all the trauma and drama."

Grace Malone took a step closer. "Trauma and drama. Good Lord." Her voice had a mocking tone. "It really must have been horrible for you. Thinking you'd lost Jesse over some—what did you call it—misunderstanding?"

Angela was being baited. Oh, she knew the signs well. She'd been baited by Brice's family for the last fifteen years. She knew what she was supposed to do. She was supposed to make light of the situation, admit she was overreacting, laugh it off and chalk it up to her own silliness. In essence, make her own emotions into a joke. Instead, she moved closer to Grace and looked her dead in the eye. "It was horrible." Angela planted her feet at the base of the steps. "It was awful because I've come to depend on Uncle Jesse since my divorce. He's been a true friend, and I could never replace him."

Grace's brows hitched up, but she remained silent.

Angela continued, feeling a rush of adrenalin as she defended herself. "And the thought that someone could enter my home and make that decision for me, it—"

Grace cut her off. "It what?"

Angela's fingers began to cramp. She realized she'd fisted them at her sides. "It made me realize that you don't *allow* people to walk all over you because if you do, they'll hurt the people you care most about." And quite suddenly, Angela experienced an epiphany. She repeated, "You don't let people into your circle if they have the capacity to hurt the ones you care about."

"You said that twice," Grace offered, but there was the tiniest hint of a smile on her face.

Angela's mind raced. "I may say it again. I'm learning a valuable lesson here." When she gave Grace her full attention, she saw the knowing smile on Grace's face. It mirrored the one on Jesse's. Even Willow glanced up from her pot of garden beans to offer Angela a wink. "It's important to protect the ones we love, isn't it, Uncle Jesse?"

He grunted in agreement.

"Well," Jesse's mother said. "If you're calling him *Uncle* Jesse, then I guess you can call me *Mama* Grace. Everyone else does."

"Thank you."

Mama moved to Willow and plucked a bean from the pot. She held it out to Angela.

Angela moved onto the porch and took the offering.

Silence stretched, and Angela felt a trickle of sweat down her back just beneath her Victoria's Secret sports bra. She held the bean to her nose and sniffed. "Fresh. These aren't from the grocer, are they?"

Mama's eyes narrowed, and her chin rose.

Angela snapped the bean in two. "Really fresh. Just off the vine. Organic, right?" She wasn't sure what Mama Grace was waiting for, but to pass the time, Angela could certainly sing the praises of organic farming and eating. She was a true believer. After visual inspection, Angela popped half of the green bean into her mouth. *Crunch, crunch, crunch.* She closed her eyes. "Oh, wow. Flavor. Mmm."

Mama Grace's chin dropped, and she smoothed some of the stray strands of white hair that had all but taken over the original strawberry blonde. "Sweet as apple pie."

Angela agreed and ate the other half. "It'd be a shame to cook them."

Mama stuck out her chest a bit. "Mmm-hmm. It certainly would be a shame to cook them." Then, she turned an eagle eye on Jesse.

He shrugged. "Mama, you said if I fixed that leaky faucet, I could have anything I want out of the garden. Slow cooked green beans with bacon. That's heaven on earth. I'm not changing my mind."

She swatted him with the towel from her shoulder.

Angela took a step forward. "You grew these? Amazing. What variety? Why are they so perfect? No dark spots at all." To tell the truth, she'd tried her hand at gardening and found it to be a skillset unattainable for her. A person simply had a green-thumb, or they did not. She most unequivocally did not. Though now she realized why Jesse knew so much about it and had been her saving grace when she'd planted a garden years back.

Mama kept her sour expression on Jesse. "Why can't you be more like your brother and be happy with swamp cabbage instead of insisting on ruining perfectly good *fresh* beans?"

Angela reached for another green bean, pausing only long enough for Willow to nod and lift the pot closer to her. "Swamp cabbage. Is that the same as hearts of palm? I've never tried it, but I read in my travel journal that it's delicious."

Mama Grace shifted her weight. "You'll have to try it sometime."

One of Angela's shoulders tipped up. "I don't know anyone who cooks it. I mean, the local restaurants don't."

"I do once in a while. I'll send some over for you with Jesse."

"Thank you." Angela said, warmed by how welcome she felt. She guessed Jesse had told them about the divorce and the boys, and that may have conjured up a little sympathy, but Mama Grace had challenged Angela and apparently, Angela had passed the test.

"You seem to be interested in the growing of fine vegetables." Willow grinned. "Maybe you would like to see Mama's fantastic garden. It really is something to behold. I've got to do some cultivating and also pick some leaf lettuce and other salad fixins for dinner." Willow looked up from the beans she was snapping. "We'd love to have you stay for dinner ... that is, if you're not busy."

The invitation surprised Angela coming from someone she had just met. She and Jesse were planning to furniture shop but that had lost its appeal at the moment. She looked at Jesse. He gave her a *why not* shrug. "I'd love to."

Willow cocked her head studying her. "You remind me of someone ..." she snapped her fingers. "A movie star. Can't recall her name."

Willow was being sweet. If she looked anything like she felt, she resembled a middle-aged sweats and scrunchie wearing housewife. Decidedly un-movie star-esque. Although she had to admit it made her feel good to hear it. She stood a little taller.

The three little girls who had been silently watching must have decided things were back to normal and moved in around Willow each securing a fresh green bean from the pot.

"Willow? Are these your girls?" Angela asked. "They look just like you."

Everyone laughed, and Angela suddenly felt like the butt of a joke.

"These two are my grandbabies, Bella and Jules. My daughter Katelyn is their mama. Corinne here, is our little neighbor."

Angela's mouth flew open. Willow didn't look old enough

75

to be a grandmother. "I need to know your skin regimen. If we could bottle it, we could make a fortune."

 ～

ANGELA ATE DINNER at a long picnic table outside Jesse's mother's house. She'd spent the afternoon learning about Grace's gardening techniques from Willow—who also seemed to know enough about the island's flora and fauna to write a book.

Throughout the day and into the evening, Angela had caught Mama Grace's long looks at her, sympathetic but questioning, as if she wanted to get to the core of who Angela was and discover what she was made of.

Jell-O. That's what Angela was made of and anyone bothering to sift through her soul to get to the root would find themselves bitterly disappointed if they'd suspected there might be more. Living was scary. But not living was worse. So, fear or no, she was going to live. *Somehow.*

Angela finished dessert—freshly baked peach cobbler— delicious because the fruit had been brought to the island by a neighbor who'd transported the goods from Georgia yesterday. The long picnic table that anchored the banyan covered backyard of Grace's house was filled with Jesse's family and neighbors. Angela couldn't stop the joy that gurgled up as she watched this—a most humble of gatherings —rival any she'd ever presented. Spanish moss hung above them, swaying to the melodic breeze off the bay. Decorating the table were sets of old milk jars half filled with water and offering brilliantly colored blooms from various local plants.

"You're staring," Willow leaned over and whispered in her ear.

Angela had taken an instant like to Willow. Spending the

day with her had only added to her admiration. "The flower arrangements are beautiful."

Willow shrugged. "Eh. It's just to draw attention to the backdrop."

Well, the backdrop was also gorgeous. The setting sun glinted off the bay causing millions of diamonds to dance across the water. "The bay is kind of amazing. The beach is barren other than the Wishing Beach banyan tree and the seagrass." Angela turned to face Willow.

Willow gave her a quizzical look.

"The beach. It's stark. A solid line of sky and water and sand. Don't get me wrong, I'm a beach lover through and through. But this is so …" She couldn't really find the words.

"Warm? Inviting?"

Ah. Willow understood. "Yes. I feel cocooned here." Angela shook her head. "Did I really just say that?"

Willow tilted her head back and closed her eyes as if she were beckoning those last few sunrays to come. The sun would certainly comply. Finally, Willow spoke. "I guess it's why we work so hard to stay right here."

Angela leaned onto an elbow. "What do you mean?"

"Well, there are other opportunities, more lucrative opportunities off the island. And for generations, we've gone. And then we always return. Some go off to college, some find jobs, careers, spouses. But sooner or later, the island calls us back. Maybe everyone feels like that about their hometown."

"No. I can almost assure you everyone doesn't. It's an incredible gift, Willow. To have a place you love so much. Did you leave?"

Willow hesitated, staring off into the distance. "No. I wanted to. But it wasn't in the cards for me." She looked at Angela and quickly answered the question in her eyes. "Circumstances." She could tell that wasn't going to be a good enough answer, "I'm glad I didn't leave. I would have never married the love of my life." She smiled.

"Oh. Is your husband going to be here for dinner? I'd love to meet him."

Willow shook her head. "Bo's out on the water, he's a fisherman. He'll be back in tomorrow morning."

Grace, sitting at the head of the table cleared her throat. "After we clean up, Willow will sing."

Willow rolled her eyes. "I don't want to sing tonight, Mama." She flashed a quick look to Angela. "Sorry."

Was she saying that because Angela was there? She thought she'd seen a crimson stain over Willow's cheeks.

Mama Grace pointed at her daughter. "God gave you a gift. And I want to hear that gift. Just like he gave you a gift for doing flowers, decorating tables." She gave a sweep of her hand.

"You did the flowers?" It was no surprise, the round, wide blooms had been expertly placed, sophistication offset by a touch of whimsy.

Willow nodded. "I own the flower shop downtown. My daughter runs it now most of the time. I'm there just enough to keep her on track."

"A flower shop, that sounds like a wonderful job to have."

"I love it. That being said, it's a lot of work, and I was ready to slow down. Katelyn was eager to go to the next level. I had a choice. Stay in charge myself and lose my daughter to someone who could see how much talent and drive she had or put her in charge." Willow's eyes twinkled in the firelight cast from the nearby tiki torches. "Hey, if you'd like we can meet at the shop sometime and I'll show you around. Katelyn's only a few years younger than you. I bet you two would hit it off."

"I would love that." Angela nodded.

"It's a date then," Willow said.

Angela stood and started clearing plates.

"You're a guest, Angela. Let us do that." Willow took the plate from her hands.

"I'd rather help if you don't mind."

Willow shrugged. "There's plenty to go around."

Angela was surprised at the way everyone at the table started stacking the plates, gathering the silverware and drink glasses, and generally making the whole mess disappear. Several people had placed their plates on top of hers while others whisked away the pans and serving bowls. "Huh," she mumbled. The table was clear.

She followed Willow into Grace's kitchen where they began the task of filling the dishwasher. "I could live here," Angela said, surprising herself.

One of Willow's brows arched. "Yeah, I bet you're just jumping at the chance to trade your mansion on Millionaire's Cove for a cottage in Bayside."

"A house is just a house without people. Family." She choked on the word and instantly wished she hadn't said it.

Willow, hands soapy, released the pan and sponge she'd held. She faced Angela. "Family can be made, you know? All family isn't always blood, Angela. Half the folks here tonight aren't relatives."

It was a beautiful sentiment—one Angela would like to believe.

Willow directed her attention to the dishes and began to hum. The sound was full and rich, and Angela wanted to hear more. "I used to sing," Angela divulged.

"You did?" Willow flashed a smile.

"All through high school—honors choir—and in college. I dated a guitar player slash songwriter with his own indie band. I'd write songs and sing backup for him. He was 6'4" and weighed about 130 pounds. I'm not sure how that factors into the story, but there it is."

"Wow, you sang on a stage."

"Such as it was. We mostly sang to half empty coffee houses. Free coffee though, so that was a perk."

Willow eyed her suspiciously. "Was that a pun?"

"It was." They both laughed. "Anyhow, I sang harmony. Actually, I learned most of what I know about harmony at Choir Camp."

"Choir Camp?" Willow looked at her wide-eyed with her mouth ajar. "I've never heard of such a thing. Choir Camp?"

"Yes, there is such a thing." Angela nodded. "My parents are big believers in education even during summer vacation. One of my brothers went to Science Camp, one to Space Camp, my sisters went to Computer Camp and believe it or not, Business Camp. And I went to Choir Camp."

"Wow." Willow gave a shake of her head, strawberry blonde hair floating around her. "Choir Camp. I thought summer camp was for fun."

"That's just it. That's what we each thought was fun. I think mine was the most fun, though," Angela admitted. "The following year I went to Art Camp. I'm an art lover, through and through. But I love music too."

"Well, everything I know about music came from being a Malone," said Willow. "My dad and brothers play instruments, and everyone sang. I don't remember it being any other way so I guess you might say it's in my blood."

"Really? So, Jesse plays an instrument?"

Willow's face sobered. "He used to, before …" she hesitated.

"Before the accident?" Angela finished her sentence. She was thinking about the fingers on his hand that were practically useless.

Willow looked down at the dishes in the sink, "Yes ... the accident."

The atmosphere in the room took a turn from laughter to

something Angela couldn't name. She didn't want to leave this alone, so she forged ahead. "What was his instrument of choice, guitar?"

"No, he liked the piano or keyboard. He was really good. He even wrote a few songs." Willow brightened. "Joseph, my other brother, plays the guitar. He'll probably play along tonight."

"Oh, great!" Music wasn't usually a part of the Baker family gatherings. Their leisure time was filled with talk of politics and business. She had another subject she wanted to bring up, but delicacy was vital. "Did—uh, did Jesse tell you about falling into the pool?"

She stopped with a sudsy frying pan in her hand. "He did? How'd that happen?"

She shrugged, trying to be nonchalant but already her heart was kicking up. "Long story. But his wallet got wet. When we took out the contents, there was a photo."

Willow went back to scrubbing the pot. She'd missed a spot. "A photo? I've never known him to carry pictures in his wallet."

"It was a photo of Olivia."

The pan slipped from Willow's hand and landed in the sink, dousing the fronts of their shirts with bubbly dishwater.

Angela used a kitchen towel to dab at her top. "We salvaged the photo, luckily. But you know, I was just wondering about Olivia."

Willow didn't take the towel Angela offered. Instead, she pivoted and looked Angela in the eye. "Wondering what?"

Was someone holding a spotlight on her? Sure felt like it. Her throat was tight. She rubbed at it to alleviate the muscles that had gone fibrous under Willow's inquisition. "Could you tell me anything about her?"

Willow's eyes narrowed. "Like what?"

Angela shrugged. "Like—I don't know, like anything."

Willow's full pink lips softened from the hard line they'd been. "Have you asked Jesse?"

Angela tilted a shoulder. "I tried. I wanted to. Jesse is such a private person."

"Yes, he is."

Angela huffed. "You know what? Forget I asked. I'm too nosy sometimes. He's helped me so much since I've been here. He's been a listening ear and a true friend. I'd like to return the favor."

"Good," Willow said. "Be a friend. Drop it."

Well then. They finished the pans and by the time they were done, they'd slid back into the easy conversation they'd had before she'd opened her big mouth about Olivia. Lesson learned.

When they stepped outside, it was fully dark with the sun hidden behind the watery horizon leaving only an orangey glow as its echo.

There were seven children in all, and it looked as though the smaller ones were chasing the preteen girls with a frog. The string of Tiki torches flickered, and the scent of citronella hung softly on the cool evening air.

Most folks were still gathered at the table, but some had drifted to the various lawn chairs scattered in small groupings in the yard. Angela sat on the edge of the picnic bench and Willow faced Grace. "What do you want to hear tonight, Mama?"

"Amazing Grace," Mama said without hesitation.

Willow reached down and took Angela's hand and tugged.

Angela stood, reluctantly.

"Only if Angela sings with me."

Angela withdrew her hand with force, heat rising to her face. "Willow, no. I haven't sung in years."

82

Willow flashed a frown. "Well it's not like your voice ran away. If you can speak, you can sing."

Jesse, sitting by his mother clapped his hands. "Come on Angie, sing for us."

A few others joined him, and Angela may as well have been standing there completely nude for as naked as she felt.

Willow put a hand on her shoulder. "Calm down," she said in a soft quiet voice. "You look like you're about to have a heart attack. It's just singing, Angela. There's no judgement here."

No judgment. She swallowed the cotton in her throat and glanced around the yard. Eyes flickered in the firelight on friendly, encouraging faces, the sound of children running in and out of the yard, the taste of citronella on her tongue, but no judgment. There was *definitely* no judgment. "O—kay," she whispered.

"I'll start, and you can join or pick up harmony." Without another pause, Willow began to sing. Each word was a symphony, each breath created a desire for more. In all of Angela's life she couldn't remember ever hearing a clearer, more perfect tone. Willow made it look effortless, but Angela knew that getting deep, rich sounds like that was anything but. For the first verse, Angela could only listen, awed by the sound and practically lost in it. The world around them hushed, the children gathered at the adults' feet, some of them curling up on laps, some sitting on the ground and drawing their knees to their chests, listening as intently as the grownups.

Willow nudged Angela as she started the second verse. Angela found her harmony and added her voice to Willow's. She had to admit, together, they sounded good. Really good. The truth was evident on the faces surrounding them. Angela's voice offered a second dimension to Willow's as they flowed together seamlessly. On the chorus, Joseph chimed in on the guitar then someone on a harmonica. By the second time through most everyone joined in singing including Jesse and Mama Grace.

Peace decorated each face. As they ended the song, Angela looked around the crowd who'd begun to clap, her eyes landed on Jesse who gave her a nod and a wink.

Angela smiled, it felt good to be an appreciated part of something instead of the odd man out, always trying to measure up.

CHAPTER SEVEN

Summer, 1981
Olivia and Jesse

As the days wore on, Olivia and Jesse continued with the daily swim sessions. He had convinced her to swim out a good distance into the ocean, but she would only do it clinging to his back or shoulder. Her fear was dwindling but it wasn't gone.

"I gotta head back to work," Jesse said. On the shore, Jesse playfully pulled Olivia around and into his arms. He looked into the crystal blue pools of her eyes then tasted the salt on her waiting lips.

It had been like that almost from the beginning. They played hard, they laughed long, they did everything to its fullest, only to conclude their time together with an unfulfilled connection that went beyond the physical, a connection he knew they both felt but neither could explain. They called it *The Magic*. Perhaps it was theirs because of destiny, or maybe it *was* magic, maybe it was because they were on *Wishing Beach*. Whatever it was, Jesse was falling hard for the enigmatic Olivia, who would dance at a shooting star and cry at the beauty of a sunset. She possessed a depth of understanding he had never seen in any of the girls he had known. And it was important he didn't screw it up.

So, he'd taken Mama's words about work to heart. He became more conscientious about his work habits. Getting back from lunch on time was a good start, along with spending evenings working on his own car because he'd taken up the garage bay long enough. Mr. Caruthers hadn't said anything, but Jesse knew an open bay meant they could take in extra work. Building for a future suddenly became huge for Jesse. Because he could imagine the future—one with Olivia at the center—and he was determined to give her everything she could ever want.

WHEN SHE COULD, Olivia spent her evenings at the garage with him. She brought along her sketch pad and curled up in the worn leather chair by the snack machine quietly sketching what she saw. Jesse leaning under the hood, Jesse wiping the sweat from his brow, Jesse rubbing the grease from his hands on a shop towel, Jesse frowning in concentration, Jesse laughing, Jesse handing her a soft drink, Jesse reaching for her. She watched and studied him intently. The more she studied him, the more she fell in love with him, every inch of him. It was one fine evening with the light of his overhead lamp casting a haloed glow over his features that she simply asked, "Did I ever tell you that I love you?'

Jesse bolted upright hitting his head on the raised car hood. Her words had stolen his. He'd imagined telling her he loved her. But he hadn't been sure ... not really sure if she felt the same. And here she was, spilling the admission as if it were the most natural thing in the world. Jesse dropped the wrench from his hand and took three long steps to where she sat. He smashed her sketchbook between them when he drew her into a deep, delicious kiss.

They were in love, sweet and perfect. "Let's get out of here," Jesse whispered. They left the garage and walked out on the pier where they had first met. It was their place. Plain and simple, and every step they took together seemed to lead them back here where the moon cast diamonds over the night water and the fish moved in slow motion beneath them in the single pool of light on the pilings of the pier. Jesse pulled Olivia into his arms and there—with the stars as their audience, they danced. There was no need for music. They were music. After Jesse kissed her again, this time deeply, hungrily, Olivia asked him to sing to her. Jesse sometimes hummed, but tonight he twined his hands into the strands of her long hair, then pulled her to his chest. Quietly, Jesse began to sing.

One week later, they found themselves on the same pier with the same moon watching over them. It was an unusually hot island night with only the cool ocean breeze as relief. The wind gently ruffled their hair, coiling Olivia's around Jesse's neck and shoulders. Her thin skirt wrapped around her long, tanned legs. They clung to each other and swayed to no music while a kind of desperation settled in. Summer would soon be over. Olivia would be leaving the island with her family. Her grip tightened on his shirt as she pressed into him, strain in her voice. "Jesse, I don't want to go."

"I know," Jesse whispered into her hair. "I know."

"Let's just leave ... together." Panic filled her words. "Please."

Jesse groaned, holding her tighter. He would like nothing better, but he knew it wouldn't work. "Livi, we have to stick to the plan. Just one more year and you will be free to do what you want."

"You're what I want, Jesse."

Jesse set her back and looked into her eyes. "You're *all* I want." He lightly kissed her lips. "But it's the best way, you know that."

"I know." She put her arms around his neck and pulled him to her, kissing him hard, tears damping her cheeks.

But Jesse didn't know. Not really. What he knew was that he had a chance to marry the only girl that had captivated his heart, his very soul, and he wasn't taking it. It was the hardest thing he had ever done. Listen to me, Livi. You're barely seventeen. You deserve to live seventeen, to experience the last year of high school—complete with a diploma and a graduation with the kids you grew up with. And you need to go to college because your art is incredible, and people need to give you the respect you deserve. College will do that for you."

"I don't care about that. I don't care about anything but you."

"Maybe not now. But one day you will. You'll have regrets. And I refuse to be a regret for you. I won't do it. Never gonna happen." Jesse was nearly twenty, and he'd had his chance to live seventeen. And eighteen, and nineteen. "Those years only come your way once, baby." Of course he loved Olivia. Loved her enough to give her that, even though he knew it was a huge risk. He remembered what his great grandfather used to say. "Living is risky. But risk keeps you alive."

Olivia came from wealth and opportunities, the kind he really knew nothing about.

"Who needs college when you have love?" she whispered.

Jesse's father flashed in his mind. The accident that took his life. The depression his mother had slid into. How her work at the family fishing business kept her occupied though sometimes she didn't shower for days. Joe Junior worked on the fishing boats that summer. Willow spoon fed their mother who drank coffee, but rarely ate. Where would his mom have been if she hadn't had her job as the Henderson Fishing Fleet's bookkeeper? She'd have been alone, with three children all under the age of thirteen, and destitute.

It wasn't like the garage business was a particularly dangerous one. Still, accidents happened. He knew of a man on the mainland who'd been pinned under a car in a nearby garage. No. Jesse wouldn't take any chances with his future. "You're going to college. That's final."

"How do I know you'll wait for me?"

"You see this pier? This is ours. We may not own the deed, but we belong here. Right here hand in hand. As long as this pier stands, I'll wait for you. If it takes years, I'll wait. If you fall out of love, I'll wait. Olivia. You're my heart. A man can't live without a heart, can he?"

"And I'm just supposed to go along through my senior year and then college without you?"

He pulled her snug against him. "I didn't say that. There are colleges in Florida. We can spend every weekend together. Wherever you are, I'll drive to see you."

She huffed. "Why are you so adamant about college?" Her mouth tipped into a pout. He'd like to kiss it, but he didn't.

"I wanted to go to college. Maybe law school. But Mr. Caruthers started talking about me taking over the garage. I mean, it's a right fit. And an incredible opportunity. What twenty-year-old has his own successful business?"

"Jesse," she whispered. "Do *you* have regrets?"

"No," he lied. "But I will if you don't finish school."

~

OLIVIA TOYED with the sculpting clay her Aunt Sylvia had sent her. After Jesse's approval of her art, Olivia sent a few of her drawings to her aunt who lived a glamorous life in Paris —of all cities—the city of love. One day, Olivia would take Jesse there. They'd stroll along the Seine holding hands and when the romance of the city overtook them, they'd stop right there and kiss. That was a common sight on the streets of Paris, couples locked in intimate embraces. At least that's what was portrayed in the many novels she had read. She loved to read but not as much as she loved to draw and paint. She often got so lost in her art, her parents would find it necessary to encourage her to go out and spend time with her friends.

Olivia's feelings for Jesse had deepened to the point of taking over every part of her. At first, he'd been a sweet friend to her in her moment of need. Ever since the day at the marina when they'd first kissed, she noticed not only his gorgeous smile, but the breadth of his strong shoulders, the indentation at his narrow waist. How his jeans fit so well over his frame. How the muscles of his upper arms bunched when he worked on his car.

All the world seemed right when she was with Jesse. He made her fearless. He made her believe in herself. And to her mind, there was no greater gift on the planet.

She sculpted the clay sent by her aunt Sylvie into two distinct human shapes, then she intertwined those shapes. Two becoming one. An entirely new and glorious thing. It was her and Jesse. It wasn't a bad attempt for her first try.

Olivia had been careful not to get bits of clay on the Persian rug in the room where she stayed. This wasn't their house, after all. Her father had brought the family here because he had some big business deal in the works with Mr. McGovern and Roy Perry. Mr. Perry was a senator with lots of influence and Olivia's father planned to use that influence to push his project through—a project that was going to add to their finances.

Aunt Sylvie had married into French money and lived in an apartment building she owned right in the middle of Paris. Although Olivia's father was good at business, they didn't own two houses or an airplane, and they certainly didn't own an apartment building in France. Ever since Aunt Sylvie found a happy life and good fortune, Olivia's father seemed desperate to outdo her. Olivia's parents were well off, quite well off, but they weren't rich like the McGoverns. And they weren't rich like Aunt Sylvie.

When Olivia was finally finished tinkering with the rough edges of her sculpture, she set it on the windowsill to dry and went downstairs to join her family and the McGovern clan. She wasn't seeing Jesse tonight. Her parents asked that she be there with them for dinner and family time. Sometimes she wondered if they thought she and Jesse were getting too close. If they only knew. Even though she'd seen Jesse a few hours ago, she missed him. And she blamed her mom for that, but it wasn't her mom's fault. Tonight, Jesse was helping his uncle fix something on one of the family's boats.

Olivia glided down the marble steps and into the living room where her brothers, along with their new best friend, Ricky McGovern, were taking apart a skateboard while the moms watched television. Mother wasn't much for television usually, but since she'd once met Marlin Perkins and had found him to be both delightful and intelligent, she never missed an episode of Wild Kingdom.

Olivia was just getting ready to ask where her father was when he burst through the front door with Mr. McGovern on his heels. Roy Perry entered last.

Her father looked pale when he stepped inside, his mouth drawn into a tight line. Mr. McGovern motioned toward the boys. "Get your jackets, boys. We're taking the boat out."

Olivia cast a questioning glance to her mother who addressed Olivia's dad. "Benjamin, what's going on?"

His attention went to his sons, Olivia's brothers. "You two. We'll need all eyes on deck." He pointed a finger in their direction, then motioned for them to go upstairs. "Sweatshirts and jeans. It's chilly on the water tonight. Grab flashlights."

It was strange to Olivia how men could enter a room visibly upset and bark orders while not bothering to explain their urgency. Later, she was certain they'd complain about their *nagging women*. When in reality, the women weren't nagging, they were just asking *what in the world was going on.* Olivia stood. "Father?"

He exhaled a long breath. "The fishing boats were headed in this evening when an unusually thick fog emerged. One of the boats collided with the ferry."

"Oh no," Mrs. McGovern said. "Was anyone injured? Sometimes there are dozens of people on that ferry."

Olivia's mother stood and put a hand over her mouth. "Those poor people."

"One fishing boat made it back, The Portly Miss. The others are still out there ... they're saying one went down. Maybe two."

"How many boats are involved? You said one boat hit the ferry," Mrs. McGovern said.

"Yes, but a second vessel hit the debris, maybe even the wreck. It's going to be a mess out there."

Jesse's family owned The Portly Miss. "What other boats?" Olivia said, her fear growing and her voice rising. "Father, what boats sank?"

"Andy's Luck ... I think, and ... I'm not sure."

Olivia drew a quick breath. Jesse's family. Maybe even Jesse. Oh, which boat did he say he'd be working on? Had they finished the repairs and taken the boat out on the water to check it? Her mind was racing to remember details. Olivia slipped her feet into her Mary Janes and went to the coat rack to grab her sweater. "I'm coming with."

Alton McGovern laughed out loud. Olivia's father frowned. "And do what?"

McGovern gave her a hard pat on the back. Maybe his intention had been to assure her they had things well in hand, but she wondered if the motion was to demonstrate her weakness. She pitched forward with each snap of his hand. "Let the men handle this, honey. You'd just get in the way."

His dismissal riled her, but she persisted. She wanted to go out on the water. "My night vision is excellent."

"Are you sure you want to see what's out there tonight, little girl? Can you haul a body into the boat?"

"Alton, really!" His wife scolded him.

Olivia bit down on the rejection that sounded to her like insults. Even as early as the beginning of summer she would have spun and stomped off. Instead she stayed in complete control calculating what she would do next. She surprised herself. She knew the maturity she was exhibiting could have only come from one place, Jesse. "Father, I'd like to accompany you. My night vision is incredible. Are you willing to risk a life by not taking me?"

She watched as his carefully constructed armor began to crack. She spoke the truth and he knew it. Wow. She'd stood up for herself as an adult, and her dad was about to commiserate.

Her mother, always one for decorum, leaned forward. "Over my dead body," she said with enough venom and certainty that Olivia's father shrank back. She then turned her scrutiny on her daughter. "Go to bed, Olivia. I'm sure everything will be okay by morning."

Olivia's nostrils flared, but that was the only visible reaction to this injustice. She wanted to scream. Instead, she counted to three and said, "You're probably right, Mom. Boat crashes. Ewww. Besides, my friend Sasha is supposed to call me about watching a movie together at her house."

Placated, Olivia's mother focused her attention on readying the boys for their rescue mission. Olivia turned and ran upstairs to her room pulling off her blouse as she went. She closed her bedroom door and quickly stepped out of her skirt while kicking off her shoes. She pulled on long shorts and a T-shirt and pushed her feet into a pair of sneakers. Grabbing her purse, she bounded down the stairs. "Mom," she called on the way down. "I'm going to Sasha's house since family night is off."

Her mother was giving orders to Olivia's brothers about being careful. "Wha—Okay, Olivia. Don't be late. Do you want Dad and Mr. McGovern to drop you off on their way to the marina?"

Right. Because that made sense. "No. I'll be fine." Olivia called as she turned down the hall, her mother's response fading as Olivia ran into the kitchen. There on the counter sat her Mom's purse, car keys nestled in a side pocket. She grabbed the keys and headed to the door that led into the garage then waited for Mr. McGovern's big truck to leave with the men of the house. The car was backed in—which made her a little less nervous. She ran around to the driver's door and as she did, she spotted the stack of packing quilts in the corner. She ran back and opened the trunk and loaded the half dozen or so quilts. Purely an instinctual move. With the headlights remaining off, she carefully pulled down the long driveway and onto the street. The fog wasn't terrible, but as a new driver it was a first for Olivia. On the plus side, there was virtually no traffic on the cove.

What if Jesse was on the boat that sank? What if he'd disappeared amidst the fog and the waves? He might be floating alone in an ink black sea right this minute. Or worse. What if he was dead?

She forced her mind away from that possibility.

When she finally arrived at the marina on the bayside, Olivia scanned the faces, searching for Jesse, but it was no use. Black smoke mingled with white fog shrouding everything in an impenetrable gray haze.

Rising from the dark water like a phoenix, fire licked the sky and dropped giant glowing teardrops onto the inky water. She sucked a breath, scarcely believing her eyes. Her stomach turned. She was watching people die.

Among the burning pieces of debris, a myriad of boats slowly trolled the water. The main wreckage wasn't far from shore. Along the shoreline beside the marina, a woman was being dragged from the water. Olivia's hand went to her heart. The woman was still, her body limp, limbs dangling. A head of dark hair plastered her face. As soon as the body hit the beach, a crowd huddled around her. A man shouted and waved them out of the way. Then he dropped to his knees and began mouth-to-mouth resuscitation. Olivia crowded her way into the press of people over the woman.

Stunned, Olivia could only stand there staring down at the lifeless figure. Then she remembered the blankets. She ran to the car and scooped up a quilt from the trunk, then ran toward the woman.

She elbowed her way through the crowd. "Here," she said, reaching out to the man who was giving the woman mouth-to-mouth.

He motioned for Olivia. "Tuck it around her."

Olivia sprang into action. She wrapped the blanket around the woman and tucked it under her cold, wet legs, not unlike the way Jesse had tucked the towel around her weeks back when they'd first met.

Screams nearby drew some of the onlookers' attention,

but Olivia stayed planted, staring down at the lifeless woman. With a great choking sound, the woman jerked. The man rolled her onto her side where she spewed water, coughed, and made a strange gurgling sound deep in her throat. The woman began to shake.

"She's in shock. Get another blanket." The man pointed at Olivia, and she hurried back to the car.

"You have others?" someone asked as she returned.

She nodded.

He threw a hand toward the marina. "Go. Help as many as you can."

Olivia took her charge and sprinted to the car. She searched left, then right to see where she could do the most good. Several people were standing out on the pier and even from her distance, she could see a few with the slimy sheen of fresh seawater. With her arms loaded, she made her way toward them.

A woman approached Olivia as she swung a packing quilt around the shoulders of a shivering man. Olivia opened her mouth to inquire if he'd been on one of the fishing boats. She was interrupted.

"Thank you!" The woman reached around her and pulled the quilt securely around the man. Her pale skin showed through her white cotton blouse where water spots stained her shoulder and arms. She must have helped drag people from the water. "We're gonna need more blankets."

"I have two more. I'll get them." Olivia went to the car again, her heart beating with the cadence of her footfalls. She was desperate to know if Jesse was okay, but immediate needs kept stealing her focus. She was helping save people's lives. She jogged toward the pier, her arms aching from the weight of the heavy packing blankets. A set of strong hands clamped around her arms causing her to stop cold. It was such a shock, Olivia nearly screamed.

Her captor spun her around so fast her hair whipped her face. Before she could focus, his hands tightened.

"Olivia?" It was part question and part command.

"Jesse." Her head stopped spinning, and she peered at him. His eyes reflected fear and questions.

Words rushed out of him in a flurry. "You weren't on the ferry, were you?" he asked, his voice hoarse. "You—you couldn't have been. You're mostly dry."

"No. I came to help."

He exhaled a long breath and dragged her into his arms, crushing the blankets between them. He was warm, his body pressed against hers. She pulled away, discarded the blankets, and immediately returned to the circle of his arms where she held him with every ounce of her strength. Adrenaline waned, leaving her limp and shaken.

He tucked her head beneath his chin. "Thank God you're okay."

"Me? What about you? I heard your family's boat might have been in the accident."

His arms tightened their grip and he made a sound, almost a sob. She felt the rock-hard abs of his stomach tighten against her. Olivia knew this nightmare had only begun. She drew in his scent, dragging strength from it, from him. But she would need to be the strong one tonight. Olivia gathered her moxie. She could do this. She wasn't a child.

Jesse smelled like a mixture of motor oil and the intoxicating aftershave he used. His thighs shifted, and Olivia moved a margin as if she were strong enough to shore him up. He held her, his fingers threading through her hair. Olivia didn't understand everything that was happening, but what she did know was that Jesse needed her and she wasn't about to let him down. "Your family?" Olivia tried to pry herself from him to look into his eyes.

Jesse only tightened his grip on her. "My uncle. They've taken him to the hospital. He's badly burned."

Olivia squeezed him hard, trying to hold him together, trying to shield him from the pain. "Oh, Jesse. Were you on the boat?" Tears welled in her eyes.

"No. We'd just finished working on the motor, and he decided to take it out for a test run before fishing tomorrow. He asked me to go along, but I was hoping I'd see you, and… I-I let him go alone. If I'd been there …"

"Stop. You couldn't have done anything. He's alive, Jesse. Let's just concentrate on that."

Nearby, someone yelled. They were on the far side of the marina, away from the bulk of the commotion. Jesse and Olivia stepped apart. Taking her by the hand, he said, "Come on. There are still people here who need us."

Together, they jogged to the edge of the water where a woman was standing. "There!" she screamed. Her skirt and blouse were soaking wet and plastered against her flesh. She pointed again and ran a couple steps back into the water.

Jesse grabbed her arm. "Whoa there."

Olivia trained her eyes on the water. Far from shore, something white floated on the waves. Jesse searched the woman's face. "What are we seeing?"

The woman jerked away and started to run into the water. "Ma'am, you're barely standing. What's out there?"

The woman's face froze with terror. Her soaking wet hair hung in haphazard clumps around her face. "My daughter!"

Jesse leaned forward, eyes scanning the sea. "I don't see anything."

Olivia stared out into the fog and smoke. A waft of wind curled the haze and there, on the other side of the driftwood, she made out a tiny face. She grabbed Jesse's arm. "Jesse, there."

He shook his head. "I can't see—"

Olivia grabbed him and dragged him a few feet into the water. "Come on, I'll lead you." The water rose around them, but Olivia kept her wits by keeping her eyes trained on the piece of wood the child gripped.

"I see her," Jesse cried. "You go on back to shore, Olivia. I'll get her." He pushed her back toward the beach. "Go. I don't want to worry about two of you."

Olivia stayed in place treading water while she watched Jesse swim like a champion toward the girl. When she realized he and the child weren't swimming back to shore, Olivia moved out farther. So far, she could barely touch the sandy ground beneath her. Her arms shifted front to back in a semicircle around her.

Jesse was at the massive piece of driftwood. She caught sight of him between the curls of smoke. He was with the girl, but he wasn't swimming back. Something was wrong. Olivia started pumping her arms, swimming deeper into the water where the two seemed to be frozen. A wave rushed over her face and her mouth filled with seawater. She coughed it out just as she reached the jagged piece of wood.

"Olivia!" Jesse gripped the child with one hand and reached for Olivia with the other. The motion caused his head to go under and Olivia grabbed for him.

"I'm okay." Her limbs ached. She anchored her chest against the large piece of debris.

The girl's tiny face was streaked with tears and black smoke. She was crying, silent sobs racking her little shoulders.

"We've got you," Jesse said, and coaxed her to let go of the wood.

She had a death grip and wouldn't release it. "Maybe we should swim the driftwood in?" Olivia's mouth flooded with water and she coughed it out.

"It's too big. I already tried to move it and it wouldn't budge. We gotta get her to let go."

Olivia tried to untwine her hands from the wood, but her little digits were slick. She'd found a crack in the wood where she'd dug in. Probably saved her life. "What's your name?" Olivia said. When the child only stared at her, she asked again, this time with more force. "What's your name?"

She opened her mouth, but nothing came out.

Olivia looked behind them at the shoreline dotted with pinholes of light from the marina and the rescuers' headlights. The shore looked to be getting farther and farther away. Olivia's legs were tiring. She couldn't keep this up much longer. In the opposite direction and much farther out, the rescue boats were circling. "We're going to take you to your mom. Do you want that?"

The child looked past them toward the shore.

"Young lady." Olivia sharpened her tone the way her mother always did when she was in trouble. "Let go of that right now."

Instinctively, the child released her grip. She slipped into Jesse's arms, clawing to get a good grasp on his neck. They pushed off the wood. Relieved, Olivia and Jesse swam toward the shore.

The little girl's mother sobbed hysterically as she ran out to take her daughter. Jesse and Olivia collapsed on the beach, breathless. Someone dropped a quilt over them in passing. Olivia lifted the edge and sniffed—must and boat fuel. Exhaustion and a kind of hysteria spread over them. She began to laugh.

Jessie dragged her closer, and soon, they were both laughing. Until the tears took over.

"WILLOW SAID you can wear something of hers," Jesse said to Olivia as they walked up the steps to a cute little yellow house with white shutters. A small front porch with two rocking chairs and a porch swing greeted them.

"You don't lock your front door?" Olivia asked as he pushed it open.

He gestured her in. "No, the neighbors look out for each other. Besides, nobody comes to this side of the island to rob a house."

He flipped on a lamp and she looked around. Cozy, lived in, like a family loved the house, the furniture, even the carpet. "Take anything you want from Willow's room. It's that one," he said, as he pointed down the hall.

"Do you have a clothes dryer? I could throw my things in. It won't take them long to dry."

"Yeah, sure. Bring them to me when you're ready." He swallowed hard. "I'm going to check on my uncle." Jessie picked up the phone's receiver while Olivia went to Willow's room.

She flipped on the light. Willow's room was a bright, cheery, sanctuary. Gossamer curtains billowed in an open window, and posters littered the walls. A record player and a stack of albums took up an entire corner. Olivia wandered over to take a closer look. A forty-five rested on the turntable, so she placed the needle and started the song. Leo Sayer singing *When I Need You* filled the room.

While it played, Olivia stripped out of her wet clothes and found a soft and fuzzy pink robe in Willow's closet. She wrapped it loosely, tying it at her waist. She hugged herself as she swayed to the music.

This was one of Olivia's favorite love songs, and it brought her a measure of comfort on this night that had been so horrible. She closed her eyes and got lost in the lyrics and the music. *Just a few moments.* She just needed a few fragments of normalcy. She too owned this very record. Home felt so far away. She was a different person now. Back at home in Boston, she was just a teenager who couldn't swim in the ocean or drive. Everyone believed she was scared of everything and knowing so ramped up her fear. She was someone else here on the island. She had swum in the ocean tonight helping to save a child's life. Jesse had taught her how to drive. She'd somehow reinvented herself in the weeks she'd been on Wishing Beach Island. Maybe the island really did make wishes come true. No one knew how desperately Olivia had wanted to leave that scared, meek version of herself behind. *You swam tonight.* The last bits of adrenalin drained out of her leaving her knees ready to buckle at the reality. *You could have drowned.*

It didn't matter. She'd been needed, and she'd helped people. She'd helped Jesse. What a horrible night this had been for him. His family must be devastated.

She left the record playing and picked up her wet clothes and went to look for Jesse. She found him sitting where she had left him with the phone still in his hand. He was staring straight ahead. "Jesse? Jesse, what is it?"

He hung up the phone. "He died." He looked at Olivia, disbelief in his eyes. "Uncle Louis died."

"I'm so sorry, Jesse." She reached out to touch his shoulder. He ignored it and stood up. He took the wet clothes from her hand and started walking to the other room. She heard the dryer open and close and then turn on.

He walked back into the living room stopping in front of her. "They've accounted for everyone else. I guess if there's a bright side to this, it's that more lives weren't lost." After he said it, he slowly turned away and headed down the short hall.

Olivia watched him go, her heart breaking all over again. This was supposed to be Wishing Beach, Florida. How could a place known for wishes coming true be a place for disasters? The unfairness of it all sent icy fingers down her spine causing a new batch of shivers on her already clammy flesh.

Jesse paused in the hall and ran his fingertips over a framed photo on the wall. Then, he disappeared into the darkness through the door at the end of the hall.

Olivia didn't know what to do, so she went back into Willow's room because the song had ended, and the silence of the house screamed too loudly to ignore. Olivia wandered over and placed the needle starting the song again. Leo Sayer singing *When I Need You* filled the room once more. Only this time, it wasn't soothing her, there was no soothing her right now. Tears filled her eyes.

It all seemed so inconceivable. That on a night like any other, three boats had crashed. With the fog, the fishing vessels never saw the ferry—which had apparently stalled in the water. And just like that, Jesse's uncle lost his life. For a long time, she sat on Willow's bed. She'd left only once and walked to the end of the hall, but the room Jesse had slipped into was dark. Too dark even for her night vision. She paused at the spot where he'd stroked a photo on the wall. She stifled a sob when she realized it was a picture of Jesse with a huge open-mouthed smile and an arm slung over who she assumed was his uncle Louis.

Silently, Olivia had made her way back to Willow's room and sank onto the bed where she sat with her hands clasped in her lap. Jesse would need her. Eventually. And she'd wait for as long as it took.

Finally, Jesse padded into his sister Willow's room. He wore only a pair of jeans and a white buttoned shirt, no shoes. His eyes carried the look of a man haunted by too many ghosts. Olivia stood, reached out, and drew him against her side. She rested her head on his chest. A long sigh escaped from him as he circled his arm around her waist.

Caught in the moment, they swayed to Leo Sayer's song about love and need. Each time the record stopped, Olivia started it again.

This time when the ballad ended, it was Jesse who restarted the song. She caught his arm and raised it toward her face, dropping a kiss on the inner curve of his elbow.

Her action elicited a groan from deep in his chest. The primal sound fueled her. Olivia angled her head and placed another kiss against his shoulder blade, then one more at the V of his buttoned shirt. Jesse remained still except for his shuddering breaths.

Olivia studied his face. She grazed her fingertips along his lips. She wanted his mouth on hers, wanted his kiss more than anything. She rose onto her tiptoes, her fingertips falling away, making room to kiss him.

Jesse raised his hands between them. "Olivia …"

She cradled his face with her palms. "Jesse. Don't stop me."

He pressed his forehead to hers and closed his eyes. "I don't want you to do something you'll regret."

She stiffened. "Will you regret this? Regret me?"

He drew back. The wound appeared in his eyes and seemed to work its way through his entire body. "Never. All I ever do is dream about you."

She smiled up at him. "Then stop dreaming." Olivia slipped her fingers inside his shirt and began unbuttoning.

Jesse moaned at her touch. His muscles were warm and hard beneath her hand, and she was in no hurry as she peeled away the shirt and explored the curves and valleys of his chest and stomach. She'd done this many times with her eyes. Her artist's eye removing the clothing from his body to reveal the perfect form beneath. But never with her hands.

He was beautiful. His tanned skin glorious against the

paleness of her fingers. And she was brazen. She was fearless. Only with Jesse could she truly be herself.

When his hands finally began to explore her beneath the fuzzy pink robe, her boldness melted into a languid state of euphoria. Jesse was everything, and she wondered how she'd ever lived and breathed and survived before she'd met him.

Olivia drank in the dreamy world, its dizzying mix surrounding her. Jesse's personal scent, pine from the open window, and the saltwater that had long dried but still clung to their skin heightened every sense. When she finally drew his mouth down on hers, she was lost. Gloriously, utterly lost. As their mouths fused, a new consciousness arose. A feverish desire to get closer, mingle souls, become one overwhelmed her.

With his hands firmly planted against her shoulders, Jesse pushed her away.

Before the humiliation could register, he drew her back to him, pressed his mouth to hers again, then pushed her away a second time.

She was confused, the intensified sensations causing panic. "Jesse, what are you—"

"I love you, Olivia. I don't want to mess this up." The words came out in a rush, the anguish evident.

"I love you, too." She placed her hands on each side of his face and looked intently into his eyes. "I want you Jesse, all of you. I can't bear to leave the island without having all of you to take with me."

Jesse lifted her hand, laying soft kisses on her palm. "I want all of you, too. In my heart and in my soul forever." He gently kissed her lips. Threading his fingers through hers and with only the breeze standing guard, he slowly led Olivia into his room.

CHAPTER EIGHT

Present Day
Wishing Beach
Angela

Angela placed a headband on her forehead and stretched first her left leg, then her right. She used the base of the stairs to balance as she evaluated the previous evening's visit to Mama Grace's house. Even though everyone and everything was new to her, she couldn't remember when she had felt so relaxed. Or maybe a better evaluation … perhaps never had there been a time in recent memory when she felt so free to just be herself.

To actually just be.

Jesse's family had given her that. Even Mama Grace had commented on how beautifully she'd sang with Willow. Even though Willow was twenty years her senior, Angela felt as though she had a new best friend. She'd only really screwed up when she'd asked Willow about Olivia.

But the evening was also bittersweet. She missed her own family, Brice and the boys, dysfunctional as it was. She didn't miss Brice's abusive ways, but she missed the family unit. When she finally left Brice, she lost all of that. Living without that family dynamic, she could sort of understand why some women stayed in spite of the abuse. There was such a great price to pay.

Second guessing again? No, that was dangerous territory. Bit by bit, she was letting go of the dream that could never be as long as Brice was who he was. Angela locked her fingers over her head and stretched, reaching for the sky.

Wishing Beach waited at the edge of her property. Its ancient Banyan ruffling lightly in the breeze. "Maybe you can tell me how to move on," Angela said to the Banyan as she ran toward the long stretch of Wishing Beach.

A great shuddering sigh seemed to pass over its leaves, giving Angela pause. She shook it off. "Translation please. I don't speak tree." But the tree had nothing more to say on the matter, so Angela turned her attention to the gorgeous landscape before her. Sand, water, an orange glowing ball above that gilded the early morning. Not a single vessel corrupted the rolling surface of the sea. It had been a red sky last night, and the old rhyme about a red sky at night being a sailors' delight was certainly proved this morning. Angela pulled a lungful of sea air into her being and jogged up the beach. Just past Wishing Beach sat the house with the dismissive neighbor. Angela no longer felt the need to get to know him, but she found herself slowing as she neared his place.

He appeared at his back door and though she didn't want to look over at him, she did. Since she looked, she felt compelled to wave. Blasted good manners. There had been numerous times when she'd ran past, waved, and then made excuses for the fact that he'd snubbed her. Excuses like, "He just didn't see you." "Maybe his mind is somewhere else."

Today she was wearing a bright pink jogging suit—no, she hadn't chosen it because of him—and since she was dressed like a flipping neon sign, there would be no way to excuse his rude behavior and she could once and for all chalk it up to pretentiousness. She threw a giant—okay, yes, maybe a little over the top—wave in his direction.

Nothing.

Forget it. Move on and never wave at him again.

But that wasn't what she did. Fueled by years of mistreatment from her in-laws, Angela angled and headed straight for his back patio. Her feet stomped out her resolve. Something stirred deep in her belly. She wasn't going to defend *herself.* She was suddenly carrying the futile frustration of a thousand other people who'd suffered at the hands of ill-mannered snobs.

As she neared, she could see into his house. Nice, not as fancy as Millionaire's Cove, but an attractive beach house with comfy looking furniture. Cool beach colors and breezy window treatments. Lovely. She also noticed the strong features of her neighbor. Sunglasses hid his eyes, but he had a chiseled jawline and long, lean body. That would also be lovely … if one could ignore his elitist ways. She could not. He was very tan.

If it wasn't for his stark impoliteness, she'd want to get to know him. Wow, her libido kicked in and there she'd been thinking it was all but dead. Well, nice to know there was still some coal in the engine, though she'd not be chugging her way down this particular track.

Instead of speaking as she neared, she just smiled … giving him enough rope to hang himself as it were. She'd met men like him before. Stuck-up types. But she'd always had the decorum to ignore their impoliteness. Not today. Not any longer.

She stopped at the base of his stairs. He rose to his feet

and took a step closer to the edge of the patio, but still didn't speak. Good Lord.

He did have a bit of a frown on his face. A confused looking frown that she could barely see around his shades.

"Hello," she said, a little too loudly.

"Oh, hello."

She huffed. "You know, I didn't want to come up here, but I've passed your house multiple times and waved, and you've never waved back. Not once. I know some of the full-timers don't like the tourists, but I *live* here. And we're *neighbors*. And it wouldn't kill you to wave." The intensity of her voice surprised her.

He ran a hand through his hair. "I'm really sorry. I—I didn't see you."

She let out a sound somewhere between a laugh and a cough. "You didn't see me? Really?" Under her breath she muttered, "Jerk." Angela shook her head, turned around and started jogging again.

"I'm Ryan," he said. "I didn't get your name."

She stopped, planted her hands on her hips, and turned to stare at him.

A smile was on his face as he stood barefoot on his deck.

She returned to her post at the bottom of his steps. "So, now you want to be friends?"

He shrugged. "I don't know. I don't know you. All I do know is that you sound like a lovely person except for the bite in your tone."

The word psycho killer slipped back into her mind. "That doesn't even make sense. You know what, never mind. I shouldn't have stopped here. I wouldn't have but Officer North suggested it." There, any serial killer would back off if they thought she was connected to the local police department. Find another victim.

The man chuckled. "Officer North said that, huh?"

She wasn't in on the inside joke, but she could tell there was one. "Yes. I asked about you and said you'd never waved back." Her sense of honesty kicked in and she added quietly, "I might have called you rude."

"Officer North is a jerk. Total jerk." The guy tilted his face to the sun. "He's also my baby brother."

Flame worked its way to Angela's cheeks. "Oh."

"He say anything else about me?" The man asked, tilting his head of dark hair.

"Uh, no."

"Didn't mention any details about me?"

"Like?"

"Like the fact that I'm blind."

Her eyes narrowed. "That's not funny."

Ryan didn't smile. Only stood arrow straight at the top of his steps, facing just a little bit akimbo to her.

Oh. Oh dear. "You really are blind?"

He nodded. "Eighty percent. So, when a lovely neighbor is jogging past, I can't see her. I do see some close up."

"Ryan, I am so sorry. I mean, really. I'd been waving, and you never acknowledged me, and I had no idea. I'm—" She huffed again. "You know, you can stop me anytime."

"Stop you," he said, with a wicked smile. "This is the most fun I've had in ages. A beautiful woman shows up at my back door and wants to chat. Then, I explain about my sight, and she's putty in my hands. Why would I want this to end?" He scooted to the edge of his steps and Angela fought the urge to help him navigate the steps.

She was torn between frustration and embarrassment. Ryan navigated the stairs *easily* without any help at all. He stopped close to her. "There you are," he said.

She let a long breath escape her mouth. Blind. She knew she shouldn't feel sorry for him, but she did. She felt guilty for being so mean, and now she felt bad for him—which was even worse. Typically, the last thing a person with any kind of disability wanted was pity. But she wasn't good with people with disabilities. In her desire to help, she always felt like she somehow made things worse. "Yes, here I am. Am I close enough?"

"Depends. Are you going to hit me?" His mouth was tilted in a half smile that made his row of perfect white teeth gleam.

"What?" She was taken aback.

"You know, for ignoring you."

"No. Of course not."

"Why not? Is it because I'm blind?" he questioned, but there was a distinct playfulness to his tone.

"Are you messing with me?" she finally uttered.

"Maybe. Are you interested in being messed with?"

Something seductive about those words coming from this man caused Angela to swallow hard while white-hot fire shot into the depths of her stomach. "Uh," she said in a breathy voice. Do you want to be messed with? That's what he'd asked her and yet the words felt too intimate to ignore. How long had it been since she'd been *messed with*? Over a year.

When she failed to string more words together, Ryan let her off the hook. "Other than telling me off, you seem like a nice person, and I don't get a ton of visitors."

Angela chewed her lip. "You think I'm a nice person? I believe earlier you used the term beautiful woman."

"Ah, yes. But how would I know?"

"My question exactly." A tiny part of Angela wanted to move away. He was close. So close, standing at her feet.

He grinned. "I know your eyes are narrowed on me. Head tilted just a bit to one side. There's a half grin on your face, and a dimple on that side."

Angela swallowed.

111

"Now, you're frowning. Head still tilted though."

Angela found it impossible to move, though all the parts of her wanted to. Nose to nose with Ryan, she remained still. "You're not really blind?" she whispered.

"Not totally blind. I have an eighty percent vision loss. I can see shadows. But my observation just now was more about human nature. I study it, you might say. And I'm making an assumption about your stance based on the conversation. I'm also making an assumption about your looks based on your scent and your voice."

"My scent?" She'd been jogging but not quite long enough to work up a good sweat.

"Laundry soap, shampoo or body wash that's citrusy, and something chemical. Not sure what that is."

She stepped back. "The spray I use on my running shoes."

"Ah." He nodded. "It's working."

How could she feel so exposed to someone who could only see her in shadow? She held out a hand between them. "My name is Angela Baker and I live on the cove. I'm recently divorced—yay, me—and I have no job. Also, I'm holding out my hand for you to shake."

He looked down between them, took her hand and shook it, and slowly let go. "It's nice to meet you, unemployed Angela Baker. I'm between projects, Ryan North."

"Hmm. I feel as though we've met. I mean, I don't think we have, but maybe I knew someone with your name. Ryan, why would your brother set me up like that? I mean, he said I should call you on your crap and not allow my neighbor to be rude and not wave back."

"Eh, brothers. Chris and I have always been this way. We're thick as thieves actually, but I told him I didn't want to be treated any differently since the accident and so the pranks have continued."

"Seems heartless."

Ryan shrugged. "I can't leave him alone in the house. He rearranges all the furniture then laughs when I trip over things."

"What is wrong with him?" Her brothers had never been like that.

"I get even."

"Well, it's really immature." Her stepsons had enjoyed a bit of good-natured pranking, but Angela had never allowed it to go too far. She'd drawn the line at rubber snakes enclosed in the bath towels.

"Yeah," he said, rubbing a hand over his freshly shaved chin. "It is immature."

She cast a long glance down the beach, the sun was bright and yellow, casting off sparks across the ocean while seagulls searched for breakfast. "I guess I should get back to my jog before the sun turns up the temperature."

"Hey, maybe I'll smell you jog by."

She chuckled. "It was nice meeting you, Ryan."

"It was nice meeting you too, Angela. Please keep waving, but next time give me a shout too. I swear I'll wave back."

"It's a deal." Angela turned and jogged toward town with a smile on her face.

FIVE DAYS of jogging and true to his word, Ryan had waved each and every time she'd hollered good morning to him. She liked that. She could admit she looked forward to seeing him and with each passing day, the anticipation grew. Today though, she had other things vying for her attention. She'd had a conversation with Jesse that had left her with more questions than answers. Olivia Murray. That was the young girl's name. Angela had asked Jesse what had happened to her, and he'd said she left the island at the end of the summer without so much as a goodbye. He'd changed the subject before Angela could ask more. But this wasn't the end of it. Not by a long shot.

Angela turned her thoughts to today. After yesterday, she'd decided that her little infatuation with Ryan the neighbor had truly and completely gotten out of hand. Why? Because she'd found herself buying new perfume for her jogs. No one in their right mind buys perfume for jogging. Oh, she'd crossed some invisible line, for sure. She'd argued that point with herself in the mirror this morning as she spent extra time pulling her hair into a ponytail and applying makeup. Yes, of course she knew that a man who only saw in shadows couldn't see her hair or makeup but having them in good shape helped her feel confident. The makeup was for her. Not him.

Angela neared his house, and the familiar fluttery sensation began in her stomach. As she got closer, she searched his back porch. Strange. Ryan was nowhere to be found. At the edge of his property, she paused at a palm tree and stared up at the sunny white house.

His patio door was open. But no Ryan. Angela chewed her cheek. She glanced down at her running shoes. She bent at the knees and re-tied each one while casting glances up to his place. When she'd stalled as long as she felt appropriate, she fell into a jog, watching the house for any sign of movement as she went past. She set her sights on her new target, the giant sea green and dark green sign at the end of the beach. It read, *1954, Fresh Caught Seafood.* In smaller letters, it touted, *Best in the Business Since 1954.* It was her favorite restaurant on the island. The establishment's colorful history only added to its charm.

After the two-mile run up the beach and back, she neared Ryan's house again, this time from the opposite direction. She sped up when she saw a red swatch of material and figured it was a T-shirt. Close enough to make out a shape, her heart lightened. Instead of jogging past, she angled and jogged right up to his steps. "Morning, Ryan," she said, and yes, even she could hear the excitement in her voice.

A wide smile spread across his face. "I was afraid I'd missed you this morning."

She'd been afraid of that too. "Am I to assume you didn't want to miss me?"

He took a few steps toward the back of his patio. "I look forward to seeing you. You want to come in and check out the house?"

She opened her mouth, but nothing came out. Honestly, Angela hadn't expected an invitation. She ignored the fact that he'd said, "I look forward to seeing you," and instead, concentrated on the idea of going inside. Should she? No. Definitely not. She didn't really know Ryan. Coffee on the patio, maybe, but inside?

Ryan brushed a hand across the top of his railing. The motion drew her attention. Was he nervous? "I'm sorry, Angela. That sounded kind of cheesy, didn't it? I'm not used to uh—I don't know, flirting? I mean, is this flirting? One thing eyesight helps with is knowing where you stand with someone of the opposite sex."

Angela didn't know how to answer. Fact was, she *had* been flirting with Ryan. Whether he knew it or not. She'd assumed he hadn't, but he'd known all along. "I—well, I—"

He leaned back a little. "Oh, wow. You don't have to explain. My mistake. I thought the signs were there, you mentioned being divorced."

"I was flirting," she blurted, a little on the loud side.

The embarrassment that had been on Ryan disappeared, replaced by a long, slow smile. "You were?"

She tipped one shoulder in a shrug. "Don't make a big deal out of it."

"At least let me enjoy the moment. It's been a while since anyone flirted with me."

She took the stairs and landed at his feet, a half grin on her face. "How would you know? You never wave back until you're told." Where was this coming from? Angela didn't have a sassy bone in her body and yet ... she couldn't seem to stop herself from bantering with Ryan.

Instead of moving away, Ryan slid closer, his voice dropping. "How do you know this isn't how I get women to come to me?"

She threw her head back and laughed. "Ha. If that's the case, you need more practice."

"And yet, here you are. Beautiful woman standing at my feet."

"Let's change the subject, shall we?" Over the last few short visits, she'd confided in him about Jesse. Even about the photo she'd found in Jesse's wallet. "Remember the photo I mentioned to you?"

"How could I forget? Your voice went all dreamy with intrigue."

"Okay, okay, slow your melodramatic roll."

He laughed. "You should talk."

"Her name is Olivia Murray. Jesse admitted that they were in love—or so he thought—and that she left at the end of summer without so much as a goodbye." She didn't know why she had confided in Ryan, but bits and pieces of the story kept falling out of her. "On another subject, I was talking to Jesse this morning and he told me an interesting secret about *you*."

"Is that right? And here, I thought I wasn't interesting at all anymore."

She grinned. "Quite the contrary. He said you're a writer. A novelist, in fact. He's familiar with your work. Me on the other hand, I'd never heard of you." There she went again with the sassiness.

"Well, I'm not surprised. I write complicated thrillers." He half grinned. "You seem like more of a trashy romance kinda girl."

She sucked a breath. "Is that so?"

"Just an assumption."

"Well, Mr. Literati, why don't you loan me one of your modern classics, and I'll tell you how it stacks up to my romances." Truth be told, she was out of her romance phase and now she liked book club fiction. But arguing with him was the most fun she'd had in ages, and she didn't want it to end.

"They're violent. You sure you're up to the task?"

"I'll manage."

"Scary too, sometimes. You'll be double checking your doors at night. I'm just warning you."

She placed a hand to her breastbone. "That is if your work suspends my disbelief. Thank you for the warning, but I don't scare easily."

He stepped closer to her, and though his eyes were hidden behind his aviators, she felt the change in the conversation. There was a long pause before he spoke. "I'm counting on that, Angela."

She could only stand still and try to force some air into her lungs. Counting on what, exactly? That she didn't scare easily? The possibilities were endless. "You had invited me in to see your house. Does the offer still stand?"

"It does." He turned, and she followed him inside, grateful for the distance between them.

His house smelled like he looked. Fresh, masculine, a scent that was decidedly Ryan. She liked it. It was unassuming. Unlike the expensive cologne Brice slathered on which never quite hide the stench of his self-importance.

"Jesse is a fan of yours. We've had a lot of conversations about classics, but he also loves a good modern-day thriller."

Ryan walked to the cappuccino machine built into the wall beside his refrigerator. "Cappuccino?" he asked.

He moved with ease and so gracefully around his home, one would never think his vision was impaired. "No thanks, but a glass of water would be great."

He got a glass from his cupboard. "Crushed or cubed?"

"Crushed."

"Would Jesse want a signed copy? I just got a box of my next release."

"He'd love it. Thank you."

They took their drinks as he showed her around the downstairs of his house. It was cool and breezy, interior matching the beach house exterior. The welcoming soft colors that splashed across paintings and furniture screamed Tommy Bahama designs from the furniture store on the island.

After the tour, they settled on his lanai where she could watch the morning's armada of various boats head out to the open water.

Ryan took a sip of his coffee. "Has Jesse told you anything else about his first love, Olivia?"

"She's apparently not dead which is what I'd begun to wonder the way everyone was so hush hush about her."

"Interesting." He looked thoughtful. "So, where is she?"

Where? Angela had no idea. In fact, it hadn't occurred to her to ask where Olivia might be. She was more interested in what had happened between the two to break them up. "I don't know."

"Haven't you looked?"

What? Why would she do that? Angela couldn't stop herself from leaning a bit closer to him. "What do you mean?"

Ryan shrugged. "You're interested in what happened, yes?"

"Very."

"Well, I'd do an internet search for her. If you discover where she is, that might give you some clue as to what happened." He must have sensed her uncertainty. "It's like a puzzle, Angela. You can't put the pieces together until you have said pieces."

"You don't think it's an—" she searched for the right words— "invasion of privacy."

His jaw dropped. "I'm talking about searching the internet. That's public."

"Oh, right." She certainly wasn't getting any information from Jesse. What could it hurt? She could just peruse the net a bit. See what she found. "I wouldn't know where to start."

Ryan smiled. "Research happens to be my specialty. And as I told you when we met, I'm between projects."

"Yes, you didn't happen to mention you were a successful author."

"What of it? Right now, I'm your research assistant."

"Hm." She watched him from the corner of her eye. "I don't pay well. Unemployed, remember?"

"Eh," he said with a shrug. "I'll do it pro bono. If you're game."

She was. Maybe nothing would come of it. Maybe she'd learn a little about the woman who so fully and for so many decades still managed to hold Jesse's heart.

Angela had all but stopped believing in that kind of love. That earth-shattering, feel it to your toes kind of love. Maybe it did exist. Maybe she'd unlock some of those divine secrets in her quest. Maybe.

CHAPTER NINE

End of Summer, 1981
Olivia

It appeared that all the locals on the island had come for the funeral. Olivia stood beside Jesse and the other members of his family, next to the floral draped casket waiting to be lowered into the ground. The minister finished the service with the announcement *"a reception will take place in the fellowship hall."* The family slowly filed out, each one laying a single white rose on the casket as they passed by. Olivia did the same with the rose she'd been given by Jesse. She watched Jesse and the others as to what to do next. She had never been to a funeral conducted like this, so informal and inclusive.

Olivia wasn't sure she would feel comfortable or even welcome, but Jesse wanted her to be with him, so that was enough. She stood beside him at the front of the crowd holding hands and just as the minister requested a few moments of silence. She chanced a peek at Jesse's family members—but no one looked over at them, no one cast her even a fleeting glance. Just as well, she had met almost none from his family. She'd been in every room of Jesse's home, though. She knew the size of bed and what his linens smelled like. She knew if his pillows were soft or firm. Firm. But meet his family? No.

"You're squeezing my hand," Jesse whispered in her ear.

"Oh. Sorry." Olivia loosened her death-grip.

The summer wardrobe she'd brought with her from Boston contained nothing black or even dark. She ended up with a tan skirt and a silk ecru blouse, her long hair secured at the back of her head with a pearl clip. Jesse wore black pants, a black shirt, a black jacket, and a black tie. Wavy dark brown hair brushed his shoulders. He looked very handsome. He looked older.

The cemetery grounds adjoined the church property. A wide expanse of mowed area between the two was filled with a few hundred friends, relatives, and acquaintances paying their last respects to Jesse's Uncle Louis. Jesse tugged on Olivia's hand, and they made their way through the throng. There were so many people, and wearing such a wide array of clothing, she realized it wouldn't have mattered what she wore. It was clear that these people were just glad to be together.

The *Island Friendship Church* was a picturesque white building with stained glass windows and a tall steeple. An addition attached to the rear proved to house the fellowship hall. Inside the spacious hall, lined across one end, were tables laden with every kind of food imaginable. And so many people. Hugging, greeting, kissing, even laughing as they recounted stories of the deceased that only they could appreciate and enjoy. Jesse was inundated with hugs, kisses, and condolences, along with the rest of his family.

Eventually it settled down and people gravitated toward the kitchen area and the food tables. Just as Jesse started to steer Olivia in that direction, a pretty woman dressed in black put her hand on his arm. A young girl stood behind her, and Olivia recognized her from photos at Jesse's house.

"Oh, honey," the woman said, and kissed his cheek.

Jesse pulled her close and hugged her. "You okay, Mama?"

"I'm okay." Teary eyed, she patted him and let him go.

"Olivia, this is my mother. And this is my sister, Willow." He nodded in the younger girl's direction. Her face was delicate and her body long and thin. She was as tall as Olivia but with a set of sparkling eyes and a round, baby face. She was probably a few years younger than Olivia.

"Nice to meet you." With a soft smile Olivia nodded to them.

Jesse's mother studied Angela. "I'm Grace. I've heard about you. I understand you're the one who helped Jesse save that baby girl from drowning."

"She was hardly a baby girl, Mama," Jesse said. "Ten or eleven, at least."

"They're all babies 'til they're grown," Mama corrected him, but her piercing eyes never left Olivia's face. Clearly, she was waiting for Olivia to answer.

Swallowing hard, Olivia hoped her voice would comply when she opened her mouth. She curtsied. "Yes, ma'am. I have good night vision and could see the girl clearly."

"I guess it's a good thing your family brought you to the island, then. Otherwise, we'd be having a double funeral today. Nothing sadder than the death of a child." Grace slowly extended her hand to shake Olivia's. But her glance darted to Jesse locking with his for a split second. She smiled at Olivia and instead of following through with the handshake, she reached over and gave her a hug. Olivia appreciated the gesture of acceptance but felt a little awkward, it all felt so personal and her family just wasn't the huggy, kissy kind. Her gaze fell across Grace's shoulder to the young teen quietly watching. Willow, the owner of the pink fuzzy robe.

TWO WEEKS after the boat tragedy and the funeral for Jesse's uncle, Olivia dressed for the Wishing Ball. She'd purchased the gown, a tea length white dress with spaghetti straps and a fitted waist, on a shopping excursion with her mother. Standing in her full-length mirror, Olivia spun around and let the gauzy skirt tickle her exposed calves.

The original plan that her mother and Mrs. Perry had contrived was that Travis would escort Olivia to the ball at the Perry Estate. So when Olivia told her mother she planned to attend with Jesse instead, her mom had thrown a fit—the likes only a well-bred catty Boston woman could achieve—effectively cutting Olivia into tiny bits without so much as breaking a sweat. The admonishment had reduced Olivia to tears.

Olivia *did* understand. She had been told—most of her life —how one day after college, she and Travis Perry would marry. A status marriage, the closest thing to an *arranged* marriage she could think of. The families had lived next door to one another in Boston since Olivia was six years old when she and Travis had first met and become lifelong friends. The idea of marriage had built up in her parent's minds, especially her mother's, to the point it had become real.

Olivia did like Travis, he was ultra-popular and good looking, but the chemistry just never happened. His interest in politics bored her to tears, and her talk of all things artistic and creative caused him to yawn incessantly. He was a good friend, a very good friend, but that was all.

"Fine, Mom." She had conceded. "You're right, I said I

would go with Travis, and I will." That put everything back on track in her mother's mind, and all was well once again.

It was the final weekend before Olivia and her family would leave to return to Boston. School would resume shortly thereafter. It was the moment Olivia had been dreading, but for tonight those thoughts were pushed aside. Jesse had planned a surprise date for after the ball. He'd let it slip that they would be going to *1954*—for starters—the most extravagant and expensive restaurant on the Island. *For starters*, she spun again, wondering what that could mean. She had no idea what to expect. The promise of a magical night kept her heart a flutter in spite of the ugly scene she'd had with her mother just hours ago. Which reminded her, she needed to call Jesse and tell him of the change of plans.

She glanced at the clock. Jesse should be off work now. She picked up the receiver on the extension phone in her room and dialed his work number. It was short notice, but she knew Jesse would agree to whatever she wanted concerning the ball. He picked up on the second ring. "Jesse, I'm glad I caught you. There's been a change of plans. I have to go to the ball with Travis. Before you say anything, I want you to know, Travis and I are just friends."

There was a long pause. "Will I still get you after the ball, Cinderella?"

"After the ball and for the rest of our lives." That had been enough for him.

She had already reset the plan with Travis to pick her up and escort her, though she planned to leave a couple hours into the party to sneak away with Jesse. Travis had laughed but understood. He knew her mother. And her predicament. Travis had wholeheartedly agreed to do whatever was needed to help Olivia and Jesse pull off their special evening. She'd been his excuse a time or two during their growing up years. He was happy to return the favor.

It was seven on the dot when Travis arrived at her house. Punctuality, a learned and practiced trait that would serve him well as a statesman, which of course was his future. He was a Perry. When she first saw him at the front door, she did a double take, she couldn't help but notice he did the same to her, much to her mother's glee. He was good-looking, no doubt, even better than the last time she had seen him. He had been away to college, and then off with his friends most of the summer, so she'd seen him very little in the past year. He was tall, broad shouldered, with piercing blue eyes that set off a conventionally handsome face crowned by pitch black hair—but he carried a new maturity in his outward appearance. He had the Perry looks—beautiful and perhaps a bit dangerous. She pitied the girl who fell for him. She'd be a hopeless mess. Who could enter that Perry family world and not be swallowed up by it, by the egos, by the pretentiousness? Her thoughts sounded harsh toward the family, but she wasn't. Not at all. The Perrys were like the Kennedys. They swallowed souls. They couldn't help it.

The Wishing Ball was held at the Perry Mansion each year. It was the grandest of the five mansions on the cove and sat in the center of the cul-de-sac like a majestic king holding court. It was the kind of beach house her father had always wanted to own. Olivia's family was well-off but not generationally rich.

They entered the Perry house—a hive of activity. "Come on, the ball is out back." They hurried through the lavish beach house. Energy and expectation crackled in the air around them.

"I really miss hanging out with you," Travis said, giving her food for thought. He seemed different now that they were actually together. On the phone, when she was asking him for help, he seemed like the "brother" she knew and loved. Now that they were together again, she sensed something far different. A year ago, back home, they'd chatted on the phone about how fun it would be to spend the summer on the island—a place Travis knew so well and a place she'd never been. He'd told her he'd show her around, and she'd sworn not to be afraid of everything. But that was a year ago. Since then there has been college and friends for Travis. And Jesse, for her. Both their lives had taken different paths, perhaps if that had not happened, they would be on their way to a different future. But it had happened. They had both grown.

They passed waiters and caterers as they headed out to the back patio. The entire Perry yard, including every banyan tree and palm was decorated with tiny white lights. The space had an ethereal glow that ran from the giant marble patio to the shimmering Atlantic beyond. Off in the distance, she could barely make out Wishing Beach. She wished she'd stopped there and offered up a wish. Magic and summer nights. What could be more perfect?

Travis touched her shoulders until she turned. Her breath caught when she saw the bandstand. Perched in the naked branches of a giant banyan tree, a wooden platform held the orchestra. It was a marvel. Olivia couldn't stop staring at the spot where music rained down on the party goers below. "It's a work of art," she whispered, reverently.

"You should have seen the workers trying to maneuver the stage into the branches. They ended up having to dissect the stage and place it in sections."

"I've never seen anything like it." The banyan tree looked to be barely holding the band—almost as if they were floating there—on a cloud—trimmed with white lights. The orchestra, dressed in formal gowns and tuxedos, gently swayed with each soothing note as if they were oblivious to the fact that they hovered five feet above the rest of the world.

"My mom's idea," Travis said. "Her friend Patricia had seen a similar one in France. My mother had to recreate that magic."

"It is magical." Olivia was breathless.

For the next ninety minutes, she enjoyed the evening. There were people from Boston that had flown in for the occasion, adults and young people...several that Olivia knew. She enjoyed catching up. The young people hovered around the pool, a large gathering including a bunch of new guys, Travis's college buddies. Olivia tried to steer clear of them. Between the drinking and their remarks, they weren't the sort she enjoyed hanging out with.

The thing that really surprised her had nothing to do with college guys—and everything to do with Travis. She hadn't expected to have fun. She'd thought she'd spend the time staring at her gold watch wishing Jesse was there. And she *did* wish he was there. But she'd had fun without him. She was having fun. With Travis.

She and Jesse had decided it would be best to meet down the beach at the public access gate around nine o'clock. By that time, she would have made a solid appearance with Travis, her mother would be settled in with the adults, and she would no longer be noticed or missed.

"One more dance?" Travis snaked an arm around her waist and nudged her closer.

He smelled like Polo cologne—one of her favorites. It was surprising how well they fit together as they glided around the floor as one. A tiny voice niggled that time was slipping away. She didn't want to keep Jesse waiting. "I need to leave."

His disappointment was whisked away by his infectious smile. "Go find your island boy. I've got things under control here."

"But my parents think I'm with you. If they see you and not me—"

"I've got this, Liv. Don't worry. I'll get word to your mom through my mom that a bunch of us are leaving to go build a bonfire down the beach—which we are. Once you're gone, this party will be lame."

When she sank her teeth into her lower lip, Travis chuckled. "Don't look so concerned. We do it all the time. You can come with us and wait there for Jesse, that should take care of any questions. It's only eight-thirty. You've got a little time." His gaze caught hers, and he tightened his hold.

Before she knew what was happening Travis' lips touched the edge of her mouth. The soft pressure of his lips on her face caused a sudden intake of air. Heat rose to her cheeks.

When he slowly leaned away, that half smile was back. He'd done this with such expertise, he must have kissed a lot of girls. Still, she was embarrassed. What if someone saw? What if *Jesse* saw? Of course, she knew he wasn't there. The awkwardness trickled down her body and caused her to look around the dance floor. There, on the other side of the stage, her mother held a Cheshire grin. As soon as she realized Travis had also noticed Olivia's mother, she hooked her arm around his waist.

He bent and whispered in her ear. "Let's put on a good show. We've got her as a captive audience."

Olivia allowed herself to be glided around the dance floor. Travis was a good dancer. Of course. She let his arms linger around her. Then, before the song ended, he took her by the hand and slowly led her to the side of the house.

They tucked beneath a palm tree where there were no prying eyes.

"I can't thank you enough," she said.

He shrugged. "What are friends for?" But instead of

letting her hands go, he used his thumbs to make tiny circles on the tender flesh of her wrists. "Liv…"

"Yes?" Under the scrutiny of the guests, Travis's touch seemed natural, but alone with him, little teardrops of wariness descended on her shoulders.

He drew a breath and released it, slowly. "Liv, I … we've been friends for a long time, right?"

"Forever almost."

"Yeah. And we've always been honest with each other, haven't we?"

She nodded. "As far as I know."

"I had a really good time tonight. Even if it was only a couple of hours. I mean, I didn't expect to have so much fun. What I'm trying to say is, maybe our parents are right."

"You mean my mother," Olivia corrected.

He smiled. "Our mothers."

Olivia raised her eyebrows.

"Okay." Travis back tracked. "*Your* mother."

Having set the record straight, she focused in on a single word. "Right?" She frowned.

"Yes. About us. I never realized how beautiful you are until tonight. I always thought of you as a kid. Liv … I have to tell you … you're no child. You grew up while I was gone to college."

No. She grew up here on the island. Love, driving, boat crashes, saving lives, all of those things had grown her up.

He took hold of her arms. "You are an incredibly beautiful, smart, sexy woman." His charming blue eyes were piercing her soul. Another day, another time, a time pre-Jesse Malone, well, those words he'd spoken might have meant something. Words. She needed words. Instead, she swallowed the cotton in her throat.

"I know you told me you care about this Jesse guy. I'm not discounting that." He let go of her. "I've had some fantastic summer romances, practically every year we were on the island. They're great, Liv, really great." He ran a hand through his ink black hair. "But summer's over and you'll be back in Boston and real life. All I'm saying is, I'd like to see you when we're back in Boston. I think we'd be good togeth- er." He took her hand and brought it to his mouth kissing her fingers.

Olivia pulled her hand away. "Travis, it's more than that. I'm going to marry Jesse."

He chuckled. "You can't be serious."

"I'm dead serious." She looked away.

Travis sobered. "Look, I'm sorry. Summer romances burn hot and burn out fast. I know this is your first—"

"And my last. Jesse is my everything, Travis. That's not going to burn out."

He took a minimal step back so he could look at her fully. "You'll see."

"We're in love. Is that so hard to believe?"

"Nah." But Olivia could see him putting on his practiced smile. "I didn't realize it was like that. If you and Jesse do get married, I'll be the first to congratulate you, okay?" He put his hand on her chin gently turning her face toward him. "Okay?"

She finally looked at her old friend. "Okay." She gave him a little smile.

Travis took her hand and secured it in the crook of his arm. "Let's get the others and go have a bonfire. As they walked, he added, "If you decide not to marry Jesse, I meant every word I said, I would like a chance to date you. Deal?"

Olivia laughed. "Deal."

❧

It LOOKED like most of the young people had decided to leave the party to the older folks, of which there were plenty, and they all seemed to be having a good time. There was a double row of shoes on the ledge at the end of the veranda and barefoot girls and guys with rolled up pant legs were making their way down the beach. Olivia carried her sandal heels by the thin back straps. She swung them with the rhythm of their walk. She and Travis were back on their normal footing, laughing and talking like the friends they were. She loved that.

It was a pretty good trek to the bonfire site although if you kept walking you would end up at the pier right in the middle of the tourist district. The good part was that this was a public access area between houses and prying eyes. The college guys Travis had invited already had the fire burning, there were coolers full of beer and bottles of wine, snagged from the party's open bar. Someone had driven a dune buggy down the beach and turned up the radio to supply the music. There were blankets stacked on the seat for anyone to use and a few folded beach chairs strewn about the sand.

Two of the college guys were already loud and drunk. "Hey, Travis!" the big one yelled. "You bring that pretty little girl for me or are you saving her for yourself?" His words were slurred.

"No, Bull, she's leaving pretty soon. She has a boyfriend she likes better than us," Travis said, his well-honed good-natured spirit stopping the inquiry. Two of the boys laughed, some booed.

Olivia realized there weren't a lot of girls there. "Where are all the girls from the party?"

Travis looked around. "They'll be along. Some wanted to run home and change out of their dresses."

It was still a few minutes before she should leave to meet Jesse—and she didn't think waiting for him alone was a great idea, so she'd wait here. Even if she was feeling uncomfortable. She made her way to the dune buggy and claimed one of the chairs. She unfolded it and placed it where she had a view of the slope with the public access. That's where Jesse would be coming for her. As soon as she saw him, she'd leave. Drinking and parties and bonfires on the beach were not her scene and she couldn't get out of there fast enough.

Travis grabbed a drink and was mixing with the crowd as they continued the party. Such a charmer, he had a girl on each arm. It made Olivia smile.

The big drunk jerk named Bull walked over and leaned down right in her face. "That smile for me, Princess?"

She turned away from his alcohol breath. "No."

"Don't be like that," he persisted. "Come on, let's dance."

Ignoring him, she stood up. Pushing her way past him, she grabbed her shoes and went to the other side of the fire, closer to the access path and farther away from Bull. He called a few choice remarks after her, those being echoed by his buddy, another drunk jerk who had become interested in the exchange between her and Bull.

They staggered their way toward her bumping into the dancers as they moved along. Olivia looked back and forth between the road where Jesse would be any minute and the staggering jerks trying to get to her. She cast a long look to her watch. Nine o'clock. But no Jesse. Still, she wasn't going to stay here and be mistreated by these troublemakers. When they turned their attention to a pretty brunette who'd just arrived, Olivia seized the moment to disappear down the accessway.

She paused in the shadow of a lamppost, holding her sandals to her chest and calming her racing heart.

"Where ya goin' Princess?" Bull yelled for her. "I didn't get that dance yet."

Olivia half walked, half ran away from him.

Headlights were on the road. Bull was right behind her now. He reached his meaty hand out to grab her arm. She jerked away and hurried her pace.

"What's the matter? You too good for me?" Bull was still coming after her. He wasn't playing anymore. His voice was angry.

As she left the sand, Olivia started running up the moonlit slope toward the lights and the lot where Jesse would park his car before meeting her. She wasn't going to wait for him on the beach like they'd planned. At least in the parking lot there were ample lights and maybe even a few people.

She kept looking over her shoulder to be sure Bull or one of his buddies wasn't coming after her. Halfway to the road she ran into Jesse. Literally. He grabbed her shoulders to stop her. Olivia squealed.

"Hey ... what's your hurry?" Jesse chuckled.

She put her arms around him and hung on for just a second. She looked back once more. "Let's go." She couldn't see Bull, but she wasn't taking any chances. Nothing was going to spoil the rest of her and Jesse's last night together.

"What's going on?" Jesse said.

"Nothing. Let's just go." She hurried them the rest of the way to Jesse's car sitting under the bright light of the sign that read, Cove Road.

Jesse opened her door for her. She was shaking and her knees were weak when she got in.

When Jesse was in the driver's seat, he turned to her. "We're not leaving until you tell me what happened. Olivia, you're trembling."

"All right." She let out a big sigh.

He didn't start the car. He listened to her recount the episode with Bull. When she was through, he opened the car door and started to step out.

"What are you doing?" Olivia shrieked.

"I'm going to have a discussion with Bull." He moved to get out again.

"No, Jesse! Don't." She reached across the console and grabbed his shirt. "Please!"

That stopped him long enough to listen to her. But fury continued to burn in his eyes.

"Please," she pleaded. "Don't let him ruin our night." Olivia could easily see Jesse fighting for control.

Finally, he said, "You're right, baby, nothing is going to ruin our night." He leaned over and gave her a soft kiss.

DINNER WITH OLIVIA at *1954* had been everything Jesse had hoped. They'd sat on the restaurant's patio. He'd ordered a steak and lobster, and she'd ordered seared scallops. After dinner, they'd indulged in dessert, putting everything out of their minds for the moment. No Bull, no party, no school, and biggest no of all, no mention of her leaving. And now, they were locked arm-in-arm as they moseyed toward the pier. It was after ten p.m., so they practically had the town to themselves. Only a handful of couples—like them—were making the most of the gorgeous island night.

"Jesse, do you really want to marry me?" Olivia asked out of the blue.

Did he? More than anything. He held up a finger. "After you finish school, even college. You have hopes and dreams, Olivia, and I wouldn't be much of a man if I stood in the way of that."

She sighed. "I don't want to wait that long. It seems like you don't mind, like maybe you don't really want to."

Jesse stopped, his hands on her shoulders, he turned her to

face him. He looked deep into her crystal blue eyes. "Don't ever say that again ... or even think such a thing." He swallowed loudly. "It's all I can do to keep my head on straight and do the right thing. I want you more than anything on this earth. But I want you forever, not for just a little while. That's why I'm trying with all that is in me to do it the right way. And I can't do it unless you help me. I'm not that strong, Olivia. Do you understand?"

"But Jesse, what if we drift apart?"

He pulled her into an embrace. "Never gonna happen. They say God has the perfect woman for every man." He looked into her questioning eyes again. "Livi, you're my perfect woman."

He'd managed to quell her fears. "I love you, Jesse."

"And I love you, Olivia. We love each other!" He pressed his forehead to hers. "If that won't pass the test of time ... nothing will. We're talking about forever. At least I am."

"Yes ... forever." She hugged him.

He kissed her hair. "It'll all work out, trust me. We just have to get past this first year." Jesse let go of her. "I have an idea." He began working the snug ring off his finger. He brushed it on his shirt then held it out to her. "Here, take my class ring. When you bring it back next summer you can exchange it for an engagement ring."

"Oh... I love it!" Olivia squealed. "I love it, I love it!" She took the ring from his outstretched palm and put it on her thumb.

"I'm glad you like it." Jesse was laughing. "I don't think your mother would take too kindly to an engagement ring right now, anyway." He put his arm around her waist, and they continued their stroll to the pier.

A breeze from the sea trickled over their skin and the palms above clacked in answer. They were alone on the pier, a scene that may have been created solely for the purpose of this moment. The moon shone, glistening on the water. A single boat slipped silently over the horizon.

Jesse began to hum. He reached out his hand and she glided into his arms as she had done so many times out there on the pier, just her and Jesse. "So, did you dance with Perry tonight?"

She grinned up at him. "Yes, I danced with *Travis*."

"Did he try to steal you away from me?"

"Actually, he did." She related to him the conversation between her and Travis Perry.

"Tough decision, huh?" He raised his brows as he continued with the good-natured banter. But with the slightest undercurrent of needing affirmation.

"Very funny," she said, eyes flirty. "No contest."

He twirled her out and spun her around and back into his arms. Pulling her close, he kissed her hair and down the side of her face. She'd told him what he needed to know. He began humming a tune, and they slipped into soft, sensual swaying and gliding around the deserted pier. They didn't need music; they were the music. "I wrote this song for you, Livi," Jesse whispered. Olivia smiled and held him closer. He began to sing softly.

All of the moments we've shared together
Forever are sealed deep in my heart
Although we've come to the end of the summer,
Nothing will ever keep us apart.

Forever and ever like moonlight and shadows,
Forever together like sunshine and rain,
I lo-o-ve you
Yes, forever and ever
Forever together

I lo-o-ve yo-u!

Look up in the sky to the star shining brightest
That's where I'll watch each night over you
Until you're back in my arms once again
This song that I sing is forever for you

Forever and ever
Forever together
I lo-o-ve you.
I lo-o-ve you.

~

NOT WANTING the magical night to end, they walked hand in hand down the beach. Barefoot and with Jesse's pant legs rolled up like the party goers, they waded in the surf letting it play around their ankles. As town life and streetlights slipped away, they moved from the water to the sandy beach with only the moonlight to guide them. Their night was perfect, their world was perfect, their future was perfect. They did have it all.

They stopped and kissed.

An unease crept up the back of Jesse's neck. He broke the kiss and glanced around. Two forms materialized from behind a palm tree up ahead. He tried to shake the feeling, but it intensified as the figures moved closer. People shared the beach, he tried to reason, but his gut told him this was different.

"Come on, Olivia." He didn't need to urge. She had sensed the change in the atmosphere and was already moving in the direction of town, her hand firmly gripping his.

From behind them, they heard a craggy voice. "Hey

Princess. I remember you from the party. You're Travis' girl so what are you doing out here with this piece of trash?"

A second voice joined in. "Maybe she's being held against her will. Looks like she needs us to rescue her." They were getting closer.

Jesse turned and called back to them. "You're drunk. Just move on."

They laughed, moving up quickly. "You're the one going to move on, pal."

"Jesse," Olivia whispered. "That's Bull." Her fear was evident, and the urgency in her voice hurried their steps. Sand kicked up around them as Jesse searched for lights from town. The problem was, it was late. And they were alone.

"Slow down, Princess. We just want to talk."

"Travis isn't going to like this!" she yelled at him.

"You're right. He told me not to mess with you. He said you belonged to him. So, I'm just going to persuade your boyfriend here to get lost."

Olivia looked over her shoulder and shouted back at him, "I'm going to report this to the police if you don't leave us alone." She sounded brave but her hand was quaking in Jesse's.

Jesse was trying to keep cool hoping it would play out and be over by the time they got back to town. He knew he could hold his own in most cases, but Bull was a hulking figure, and he had a buddy. They'd been drinking, and that was always a bad combination.

"Call the cops, we don't care. Travis' dad owns the cops here." Bull kicked over a beach trashcan as he sailed past it. The sound made Olivia jump and she cast a hopeless look to Jesse.

"We'll be okay," he whispered. "We just need to get to town where there are people."

Before they could get farther, the two guys rushed them.

"Get lost," Bull goaded Jesse giving his shoulder a shove.

Jesse turned with his fists clenched.

The other guy rolled onto his toes, clearly a fighting posture.

"Hold her," Bull said. "We don't want anything bad to happen to her."

The guy grabbed Olivia's arms from behind and she yelped.

Jesse flew toward them but was stopped by Bull's meaty grip. He jerked him back and readied for the first blow.

The other guy laughed. "Don't worry. I'll take *real* good care of her." He pulled her tight against him, letting go with one hand and encircling her torso. Then, he let go with the other hand and brought his arm around her, pinning her arms against her sides.

"Let me go," she screamed and tried to kick free.

"Feisty. I like that in a woman." The guy said while Jesse watched helplessly. He was in Bull's grip and couldn't get free yet. He'd have to wait for the best moment—when he could throw them off their game and get Livi out of there safely.

Olivia's struggles only encouraged the guy holding her. He wrestled her around to face him then pressed his drunken mouth over hers.

Jesse exploded toward them, fists flying at the guy and ignoring Bull who'd been holding him. But as soon as he got close, he was propelled back. Bull was grunting and yelling at him, and Jesse felt something solid connect with his head, sending stars in an arc around him.

Livi fought and twisted trying to get free from the guy who'd ripped at her gown.

Jesse shook off the fog he felt, fists ready and jumped at the guy.

Bull hit him hard across the back bringing him down to

the ground. "You need to learn some manners," he said, tossing a large piece of driftwood aside. "We're only after a little fun."

Olivia was screaming, crying, and kicking her attacker.

Jesse struggled to his feet and landed a right hook to Bull's face. It surprised the huge man. He fell backwards onto the sand. Then Jesse turned his wrath on the guy holding Olivia. He lunged at him delivering a blow to his face which made the guy let go of her. Bull jumped on Jesse from behind throwing him to the ground. Jesse tasted blood, realized it spewed from his nose.

Bull wasn't laughing anymore. He was furious, his fists flew into Jesse wherever they could land, pummeling him. Bull grunted and screamed curses with each blow.

Jesse raised his head. "Run, Livi! Run!"

She shook her head. "I can't leave you."

"Go, go!" Jesse shouted.

The blows were relentless. A foot kicked him in the face filling his eyes with sand. He tried to blink past it. A blow landed against his ribs, and he felt several crack. Blood ran into his eyes blurring his vision, but he strained to find Olivia. The other guy was just standing there, watching the beating. That would mean Olivia got away. Jesse struggled to draw a breath, then he realized that Bull had stomped on his chest. He wheezed as another blow came, this one to his ribs. His hand was trampled, he couldn't move it. Another kick to the face. His mouth filled with blood. Something cracked against his knee, he felt the bones give way. He couldn't cry out in pain. Then ...

Nothing.

CHAPTER TEN

Wishing Beach
Present Day
Angela

The bells jingled when Angela opened the door to *Island Floral* and stepped inside the shoppe. Immediately, her senses were captured by the large beautiful space where light softly illuminated the room from the enormous window to her left. An intoxicating fragrance of fresh flowers wafted over her. And of course, there were lovely green potted plants. Everywhere.

"Ahh," she whispered, then inhaled a deep breath filled with the floral perfumes of earth, sunshine, and life. This was the kind of place she could stay forever.

"Be right with you," a voice she recognized as Willow's called from somewhere in the back of the store.

"It's just me … Angela. No hurry," she called back as she glanced around trying to take it all in. A functional credenza sat in the foyer area. A vase of assorted fresh flowers rested there, no doubt intensifying the pleasing fragrance in the air.

Next to that was an array of *'take one'* information brochures for *Island Floral,* as well as for the neighboring merchants. Over by the window sat a round glass table with four chairs, a small stack of floral arrangement catalogues waited on top. The service counter sat further back in the room, banked by the glass doored refrigeration unit that displayed the pre-made arrangements and bouquets.

That's where the *usual* ended.

Angela's gaze was drawn to a massive painting that hung on the right wall. It summoned. She walked across the dyed concrete floor of beige, rust, and sand that glowed with a satin sheen to the center of the room. Two fawn colored low back settees faced each other with a small coffee table between them. That space was anchored by a bright, multi-colored rug. From the settees, you could see both the table and chairs by the window as well as the massive painting on the opposite wall.

Angela stood, mesmerized by the work of art. There was something about it. Although there was a flamboyance to the brushstrokes, the painting itself was somehow soothing … wistful. She'd never seen a painting quite like it. Angela closed her mouth, she realized it was gaping as she tried to take it in, tried to sum up a response, an opinion. She could come up with neither. There were splashes of color amid the bold strokes, abstract yet … not abstract. In the midst of it all, was an impression—and an almost tangible motion—of a man and a woman. Angela had seen all manner of technique, but this … she couldn't define. Not that she was a qualified critic, of course, but she was an art lover.

She cocked her head trying to decide what was behind the two impressions … rising stairs? A jungle? As she peered, it seemed the two figures were moving away from each other. Yet when she stood directly in front of the painting, the man and woman appeared to be coming together. She frowned, squinted her eyes, and looked again, giving her head a slight shake.

"So, you see it, too."

Angela turned toward the voice behind the counter. "Oh, hello Willow." She laughed at her own preoccupation.

"Hi, Angela, I'm so glad you could come on such short notice. Sorry for the wait, I was on the computer with a client, making some final adjustments for wedding flowers. What can I get you, coffee, hot tea, a cold drink?"

"Tea sounds good."

"Make yourself comfortable." Willow made a sweep of her arm around the room.

Angela decided to sit at the table where she could have a good view of the painting. She sank into the comfortable chair and placed her purse on the one next to her. Her gaze panned the room again but homed in on the painting and stayed there. She leaned forward, squinting to read the signature.

Willow came out from behind the counter with two cups of steaming tea in her hands. "The artist is Marco ... Marco Del Sands." She sat the cups down in front of them. "I am so glad we're finally getting together."

"Me, too." Angela took the cup Willow offered.

"I know I told you I would show you our shop, but truth is, I don't come in very often anymore. The girl that works for us couldn't come in today, so in a little while Katelyn has to go and tend the plants in the homes and businesses. So, here I am!" She flipped her hands in the air.

"Oh, your daughter's here, I'd love to meet her."

"She's in the office finishing up some things. She knows you're here. She should be out in a minute."

Angela nodded. "The place is lovely. Truly, Willow. I'm so impressed." Her gaze surfed the room.

"Well, thank you. We've tried to make it inviting."

"Accomplished!" Angela took a sip of the hot tea while her eyes drifted over the rim of the cup and turned once again to the painting on the opposite wall.

"You like the painting?" Willow asked.

"Like? Uh ... I'm captivated by it. And befuddled at the same time."

Willow laughed. "You're not the only one that it strikes that way. Then, too, it doesn't strike some, at all."

"It is an enigma." Angela frowned. "I don't recognize the artist, but I—"

"I'm leaving, Mom." Katelyn burst into the room, ponytail swinging, a pretty woman a few years younger than Angela and full of energy. She had a strong resemblance to her mother.

Willow beckoned her daughter over to the table. "Katelyn, I want you to meet Angela."

"It's so nice to meet you." She shook Angela's hand. "I'm sorry I missed you at Grandmama Grace's a few weeks ago."

"Me, too." Angela leaned on her elbows on the table. "It was delightful."

"Mom said you fit right in," Katelyn said. "Even won Grandmama Grace over by singing."

"I could hardly call it singing. I just harmonized a little with your mother. Isn't that right, Willow?"

Willow shrugged. "You've got a good set of pipes."

"Nothing like yours. Do you sing, Katelyn?"

"Not really," Katelyn admitted.

Willow slashed a hand through the air. "She's being modest. Beautiful voice. She just doesn't exercise it enough. Moving on, Angela and I were just talking about Marco's painting." Willow gave Katelyn a knowing grin.

Katelyn cradled her cheeks in her hands. "Oh, dear."

Willow chuckled.

Katelyn turned to Angela. "Then, I guess that means you saw it?"

"I'm not sure what I saw." Angela frowned in thought. "I think I saw a man and a woman, some stairs or some kind of jungle. I don't know." She left out the part about seeing them moving. They'd think she was crazy.

"What were they doing?" Katelyn asked.

Angela hesitated. Tricky now, should she tell them? *What the heck.* "That's the strange part," she stated hesitantly. "Initially, I thought they were moving away from each other. But then, when I looked again, it looked like they were moving toward each other.

Willow and Katelyn shared a look.

Angela's eyes moved back and forth between the two women. "What? What?"

"It's just a little phenomenon that happens to *special* people." They raised their eyebrows in a woo woo expression.

Angela was puzzled, but she was also intrigued. "Did *you* see it?" She addressed the question to both of them.

"Yes," they said in unison.

"I saw them moving toward each other. And Katelyn saw them moving away."

"So, what is it supposed to mean?" Angela was enjoying their little game.

"Well," Willow spoke first. "It is said that if they move toward each other, you have a good relationship. And ... I do."

Katelyn chimed in, "And I didn't ... at the time."

"So, what does mine mean? I have both."

"It means you want someone out of your life, that's what you saw first. But you're not sure if you really want them gone," Willow explained.

A shiver went up Angela's spine. There were moments when she wanted her family back, so much so, she would entertain thoughts that maybe the verbal abuse wasn't all that bad, or worse, maybe it was worth it. She never stayed there but entertaining that thought at all frightened her. "This time the painting's wrong." She protested too quickly and too loud. "I mean it's creepy, like witchcraft or voodoo."

"Marco *is* from a small island in the Caribbean, but that's not what it is. He said he painted *Magia,* that's Spanish for magic, with a technique that Da Vinci used when painting the Mona Lisa. It's called *Sfumato* technique."

Recalling her college days, Angela sat straighter. "Oh, I remember this! Sfumato suggests things in the painting vanish—like smoke. That's why it feels like the Mona Lisa's eyes follow you or at the very least move with you."

"Exactly," Willow explained. "But Marco swears there is no power in the painting, it's in the people. People's minds are immensely potent. You see what you want to see ... or maybe what you need to see."

"It sure resonated with what I needed to see." Katelyn rolled her eyes. "Not that I made a life decision based on a painting. It did, however, confirm what I had already decided to do. I just wish I could have seen it earlier."

Willow placed a reassuring hand on her daughter's hand.

Whatever had happened to Katelyn, Willow must feel as though she still needs a bit of shoring up from it. Or at least a bit of reassurance. "*Magia* doesn't actually belong to me. It's on loan. I have several of Marco's paintings I can choose from, but I bring this one back on occasion because it's such a conversation piece."

"That it is," Angela agreed wholeheartedly.

"We provide plants for Marco's store, and he provides artwork for us. That's what living on the island is all about. Symbiotic relationships."

Would Angela ever feel so connected to the island that she'd be in symbiotic relationships with the other islanders?

She sensed that would be easier if she were a business owner. What kind of business would she own on the island? Was she cut out for business? Probably. But not like her siblings with their big business ventures. No. A small island shop where she greeted customers as they entered, and she closed the doors at lunch if she fancied a walk to a nearby restaurant. Art. She loved art. She could sell paintings and sculptures and even island photography. At nearly forty, she was deciding what she'd be when she grew up.

"I better get going," Katelyn said. "I've got plants to tend. I wish I had longer, but gotta stay on *schedule*." She made little air quotes when she said it. "But hey, if you want to do lunch sometime—"

"I would love to!" Had Angela said that too quickly? She liked Katelyn—who was about her age, give or take five years. And since all of Angela's friends were gone now or in their sixties, well. It seemed like a great idea to get to know Katelyn.

"Call me anytime." Katelyn headed toward the door. "I usually close the shop at four, so I'm always up for a late lunch or early dinner. 1954 has a fabulous happy hour."

"Kate, could you bring us over one of Marco's brochures before you leave? I want Angela to see what beautiful work he does." She winked at Angela. "This painting's fun, but maybe not a fair representation."

Angela took the brochure Katelyn offered, and she and Willow waved goodbye to Katelyn as the front door jingled, its merry sound so delicate it could be pixies tap dancing. Willow was right, the paintings in the brochure were beyond her expectations. Most were amazing island landscapes so realistic she could almost feel the mist off the waves on her face.

"Wow. He is really good. Oh, here's one of *Wishing Beach* and my banyan tree. Well, not really mine, but I love it." She looked at the front page again. "I see he does commission work. I'll have to give him a call. Jesse helped me get my furniture picked out, but I still have to decide on pictures, accessories, you know. All the details." She hadn't looked up the whole time she was talking, she was intently studying the half dozen or so paintings pictured in the brochure. Angela flipped the brochure over to see if there were others on the back. No more paintings, merely a picture of the artist, *Marco*. She felt her eyebrows lift, and she had to stop her jaw from dropping. "Oh. Oh my."

Marco was shirtless, barefoot, and poised at the helm of a boat holding a spear or some sort of weapon, like a Norseman, or a pirate, Angela thought. He was muscled and golden bronze, black hair swept from his face and trailing behind him. He wore nothing but a pair of fitted pants that stopped just below the knee and a leather belt draped from his shoulder across his chest. Marco's smile was dazzling white. The painting behind him was of the sea and a rising sun, all oranges and golds. He was real in the make-believe world.

"Mm hmm." Willow grinned. "Beautiful, isn't he?"

"Uh, yeah-h." Angela felt her face blush. "I mean … yes, I guess he is."

They both laughed.

Willow leaned closer so she could admire Marco as well. "Early forties, been here seven or eight years, and yes, he is single. However, only use him for fun, not for keeps. Every woman on the island knows that. The tourists have to find out for themselves."

Angela felt heat rise to her cheeks. Had sixty-year-old Willow just instructed her to *use the hot guy in the brochure for fun, not for keeps?*

"Any more questions?"

Angela hadn't asked any questions, at least not yet, but of course she wanted to know *now*. "How's his track record?"

"Looooong. He's a ladies' man, been married a couple of times, I think. Probably why he doesn't go back to the Caribbean where his mama lives."

Angela thought how strange it was for a person to be expected to live where their mama lived. Strange. And kind of wonderful.

Willow raised her index finger. "But, in Marco's favor, he is a really good guy. He doesn't play you. He's well known in the community not only for his paintings, but as a huge supporter of all the arts. He attends every event, and that includes fine dining events—which makes him the perfect date in my estimation. I know the way to my heart is through my stomach." Willow rubbed the hollow place where her stomach should be. "He loves having a beautiful woman on his arm. He'll be the first to tell you that. He treats women with respect. He's harmless unless ..."

Angela leaned forward. "Unless what?"

"Unless you don't want him to be." She grinned and gave her a playful look. "But, seriously, in all the years we've known Marco, he's always said art is his mistress. Believe it. Like I said, he's a fun date, but not a keeper. So, if you don't expect more than that, you won't be disappointed."

"Well, I ... um ... don't ..." Angela sputtered. She could feel her face blushing again.

"On that note, I think I'd better show you around." Willow stood and pushed her chair back into place.

Angela tucked the brochure into her purse and followed her into the working area beyond the counter. A large pale green sign with ornate calligraphy hung behind the customer service counter. In bold black letters it read, *Earth Laughs in Flowers.* That was one of her favorite phrases from the Ralph Waldo Emerson poem. The back room was a substantial space with a sink, two long counter height tables, coolers, a door leading to a bathroom, and another to an office that held a small but inviting lounge area with a couch, coffee pot, and microwave.

Willow explained the functions of her business as they wandered through. She was an interesting and detailed tour guide. "I started *Island Floral* about thirty years ago, only it wasn't called that then. I was fresh out of high school and always worked a summer job at the ice cream parlor. But I wanted a *bigger* job once I was *grown-up*. My mother had taught me about flowers from the time I was a little girl. You saw the flowers at her house."

Mama Grace's garden was a marvel. Angela had been thoroughly impressed.

"There were always too many blooms. So I started cutting fresh flowers from her massive flower garden. I set up a stand near the pier, across the street from here actually, with a black and white sign that simply read, *FRESH CUT FLOWERS.*"

"That's inspiring, Willow. I have a friend named Melinda who always says that if the job you want doesn't exist, invent it," Angela said.

"I guess that's what I did. I was there every day during tourist season, and every day that the weather was nice in the off season. It wasn't always easy ... or prosperous. Fresh cut flowers have to be 'fresh cut'." Willow laughed. "So I had to try to judge how many I should cut for the day. You can imagine. Some days I had enough left over to fill every vase in Mama's house!"

"But you loved it, right?" Angela said. "I mean you must have, you're still here."

"I did love it, and I did okay especially with no formal training. I just loved flowers and being around them." Willow's look went distant. "I think they were also cathartic for me. And for Mama at the time."

Angela waited for her to explain further.

Willow took a breath and focused on Angela. "Sorry, those were some hard years. It was the time of Jesse's ..." She hesitated.

"Jesse's accident?" Angela tried to help.

Willow visibly closed up. She held her palms in front of her like a stop sign. "That was a long, long, time ago."

Angela instinctively knew it was no time to ask or add anything on the subject. *Geez,* she didn't even know Willow yet, and she would like to know her. Had she crossed a line? She hoped not. "So, how long have you been at this location?" She was trying her best to get back where they were before.

"Oh, ten years or so. I had a small store down the beach, and then when Katelyn joined me, we grew out of it fast." Willow busied herself clearing the greenery remnants from the table.

"Looks like a great location, right across from the pier," Angela said.

"Yes, right in the heart of things." Willow pulled the waste can out from under the table and brushed the pile of leftover greenery into it. "This is prime property. We were lucky to get it. Jesse was friends with Owen, the owner. That helped. Not to mention it holds great memories for me. As teenagers we would hang out here. It used to be *The Tiki Surf Shop.* It's actually where I met my future husband, though at the time I didn't even like him." She looked at Angela and laughed. "It took him two summers to win me over."

The awkward moment had passed. Angela made her way over to the two glass front coolers against the wall. They were filled with arrangements, mostly white with some rose gold accents. "Oh, these are gorgeous!" She walked along the front examining each one.

"Those are for a wedding Katelyn is doing tomorrow. She does a lot of weddings, parties, events, and the like. She has all the work she wants, has to turn down a lot."

"She is good." Angela was scrutinizing a huge centerpiece in the cooler.

"She really is. I'm not saying that just because I'm her mama. She loves flowers like I do. The difference is, she had professional training and learned all the tricks of the trade. When Kate came onboard, she brought us up to a whole new level." Willow furrowed her brow. "Did you see the plaque in the reception area by the front door?"

"Come on." Without waiting for an answer Willow took Angela's hand and led her back to the front of the shop stopping in front of a *Presidential Appreciation* award with Katelyn's name engraved on it.

"Wow, I'm impressed!" Angela said.

"There's an article from the newspaper." Willow pointed to the framed piece next to it.

Angela read the headline.

Local florist invited to the White House to decorate for Christmas.

Beneath the headline was a picture of Katelyn in front of the flower shop. Angela read the article quickly. "It says that thousands of florists apply each year to decorate the White House and only a handful are chosen. But Katelyn hadn't sent an application."

"No. She hadn't. To this day we don't know who nominated her. She almost missed her chance because the invitation came as an email, and at first she thought it was spam. I guess it's not too difficult to see that I'm a proud mama." Willow beamed.

"Was it great... was it fun... did she enjoy it?" Angela's eyes were still feasting on the award.

"She loved it. She was going through a divorce and having a pretty rough time. I was glad when she decided to go. I think it was the best thing that could have happened to her. She came back stronger, almost like her old self." Willow sighed. "Sometimes you just have to get out of town, you know, change the atmosphere."

"I do know," Angela said with a weak smile. "I guess this is my *out of town*." She made air quotes with her fingers.

"Are you getting stronger?"

"I think so." Angela nodded, then tilted her head from side to side. "Most of the time." She could have added, *except when I'm scared, or lonely, or tired.*

"For Katelyn it was really more than getting out of town. If she hadn't gone to D.C., she would never have met Donna, who is also a recovering victim of narcissism."

A victim of narcissism? Angela frowned. "Did you say Katelyn?"

Willow nodded. "That surprises you?"

"Very much. Katelyn seems so rock solid. So together."

"She is now. But her ex had really done a number on her —that's what narcissists do. In the end, the victims need help as much or more than the abusers. Donna spent time talking with Katelyn, helping her understand. She gave her hope."

Angela threaded her fingers together. "Hope is good."

"Hope *is* good, but sometimes hope gets in the way of wisdom. That's what happened with Katelyn. She *hoped* Cory would change. She had two small children and a marriage to which she was committed. She *hoped* she could save it. It took her three times of going back into crazy land before she quit *hoping* he would change." Willow shook her head. "With a narcissist, hope is all you're going to get."

There was that word again. Unconsciously Angela rubbed her forehead. *Narcissist.* It was apparently more common than she had imagined. She'd been told more than once that Brice was one. She hadn't examined that idea. Maybe she should. "Is that what we used to call egotism?"

"It's like that," Willow pondered. "I'd call it egotism on steroids. With the main difference being lack of empathy.

Something in them is missing. They are typically charming, but also controlling, selfish, and dishonest when it suits their needs. There are also different degrees. At the low end of the spectrum—as long as you understand what's going on and guard yourself—you can live with them and just accept that they're obnoxious and unlikely to change. At the other end of the spectrum—well, they can be sociopaths."

Angela shuddered. "That's scary."

"Extremely." Willow's face clouded over. "Cory had made Katelyn so insecure, so unsure of herself that she couldn't even buy the girls clothes without his approval. Fortunately for her, there were plenty of family members around that saw her losing herself. Cory tried to keep her isolated from us. That's what they do oftentimes, but with her working here it wasn't possible. Thank God."

"Yes," Angela muttered. Brice had been controlling, dishonest, and had certainly made her feel insecure. She knew she'd lost herself. Bit by tiny precious bit. He had also alienated her from her family. Wow. She hadn't even realized it. He kept her so busy with *his* plans, *his* needs and wants that whenever she mentioned visiting her folks, he'd throw a fit. Was Brice a narcissist? And if so, did she need help like Katelyn received?

Willow must have noticed the change in Angela's demeanor. Her voice was soothing and helpful when she said, "Donna put Kate in touch with WWA."

"I've never heard of that."

"*Women Warriors Anonymous*—which deals with living with and living without a narcissist. It turns out there is a chapter of WWA just across the bridge. Katelyn goes there a couple of times a month to educate and reinforce herself, but also to help others with what she's learned. It's a supportive group that welcomed her instantly. They're always working to spread the word about abuse and always looking for speakers."

"Wow, poor Katelyn," was all Angela could say.

"Yes, she *was*." Willow smiled. "You've heard the old adage: What doesn't kill you makes you stronger? It's true. Katelyn is a force to be reckoned with now."

After a few more minutes of discussion, Angela bid Willow goodbye and left *Island Floral*. The sun was shining even brighter than when she'd gone in, another glorious Florida day. She drove the short distance to the cove with the top down on her sports car. The wind tousled her hair and cooled her skin. She felt free. Knowledge was power. The accusations that continually bounced around in her head were now subject to this new information.

Angela couldn't wait to tell Jesse about the wonderful morning she'd spent with his sister and meeting his niece, Katelyn. She turned into her driveway, the sign above the gate immediately capturing her attention, *BAKER HOUSE*. She made a mental note to remove it. Glancing over to the gatehouse, she saw that Jesse's car was not there. Disappointed, she drove up to her parking space under the carport of the expansive *Baker House*. She sat for a moment pondering. This was no longer the Baker's house, and she was no longer a Baker. The name would be removed from above the gate, and it would be removed from her. Angela exhaled relief, more chains coming off. She'd be Angela Reed again. Yes. Definitely.

Inside the sprawling mansion, Angela was overtaken by the vastness and the bareness of it all. The walls had a new coat of paint, the new furniture was in place, but it was hollow. No life here. No laughter reverberating off the walls. Only silence. No matter what Brice had done or not done, she had made a happy, fun filled home for their boys. Empty nesting meant a whole new thing to her. She'd lost not only her kids, but her spouse. Still, she knew she'd done the right thing. But should she have to remind herself so often that it *was* the right thing?

Angela walked into the kitchen and checked the answering machine. No messages. She sat her purse and keys down on the granite counter, the sound echoing back at her. She exhaled long and slow and listened as the sound bounced around and disappeared. This was supposed to be her refuge. Shaking off the loneliness that threatened, she went upstairs.

A short time later, Angela bounded down the back stairs into the kitchen in shorts and a faded T-shirt. She pushed her feet into the pair of flip-flops that sat by the door and headed for the beach in a hurry to escape the silence.

The beach was quiet except for the ocean waves gently lapping at the shore and an occasional call of a seagull. But it was a different kind of quiet, it boasted life. Angela meandered over to the banyan tree that stood guard over Wishing Beach. She trailed her hand along its trunk. "What can you tell me? Can you tell me of all the hopes and dreams wished for on this stretch of beach? Were they realized or shattered? Or merely unanswered? Are they even real?" Her eyes moistened at the thought. She wrapped her arms around the tree and gave it a hug.

Angela wasn't sure how long she'd stood there, arms wrapped tightly around the banyan tree, but it was long enough that when she pulled away, the smooth, cracked bark had left its imprint on the tender flesh of her inner arms. Slowly, she walked out to the water's edge where a million flickering lights from the sun's rays twinkled across the water. She stopped abruptly, training her eyes on the bright sparkles. Orbs, she thought. She shaded her eyes against the brightness of the sun, its intensity causing her vision to blur with unshed tears. When she blinked, the water appeared as though each diamond floating on the sea's surface was actually encased in a transparent globe. But before she could focus fully, they disappeared.

These really were wishes, she decided. She laughed out loud, hugging herself as her childhood memory flooded her. *She knew beyond a doubt that these were wishes trapped in sparkling globes.* "I remember. I—captured one."

She'd held it in her hands oh, so many years ago, so many she'd all but forgotten.

And so ... Angela dared to wish. "I wish for my home to be filled with joy and laughter." She spread her arms wide reaching for the heavens. "I wish my home to be filled with family."

CHAPTER ELEVEN

Angela's eyes filled with tears as Ryan told her the story of how Jesse almost died. Ryan's internet research had worked. He'd found a photo of an old newspaper clipping from 1981.

Angela's hands covered her mouth. "Dear God. No wonder Jesse won't talk about it."

In the past few weeks since she'd stood on Wishing Beach hugging the great Banyan tree, she and Ryan had shared several walks on the beach. But one had nothing to do with the other, she'd told herself repeatedly. Ryan was a lovely friend. They enjoyed each other's company. And sure, he was handsome. But Angela had decided that it was all way, way, way too soon after Brice for her to be involved in anything more serious than friendship. Friends, she and Ryan had mutually decided, and it suited them both fine. So what if there were sparks? Physical attraction was only one tiny part of a real relationship. Sparks could be managed. Tamped down. Sure. Of course they could.

She and Ryan had coffee together several mornings each week, and if she were honest, she found him fascinating. Part of that fascination was certainly due to his ability to rise above his circumstances. But also because he was as intrigued as she about what happened over that summer, the summer that began and ended Jesse and Olivia's love story. The summer Jesse almost died at the hands of two unidentified attackers.

Ryan had printed out the article about the attack. He placed it beside her where she sat on his patio. "This account of what happened was hard to find because it didn't give last names. In fact, Olivia's name was completely omitted as was Jesse's last name. Weird. But, you know, I've never studied that much 1980's journalism so maybe that was commonplace back then."

"But you're certain Olivia was with him?"

"Oh yes. The article references a seventeen-year-old female." His eyes narrowed in thought.

Angela had learned his tells. "What's on your mind, Ryan?"

He shook his head and tapped a pencil against his knee. She'd never seen him write with the pencil, but he used it to point things out, as a tapping instrument, and sometimes he parked it behind his ear. "I don't know. Something doesn't add up."

"I'd hate to ask Jesse about it. I know Willow didn't want to talk about it, but I suppose I could try again."

"No, there's something more to this," Ryan said, tucking the pencil behind his ear. "A cover-up."

"What? You've been reading too many murder mysteries."

"And writing them … but that's beside the point. I'm telling you, Angela. This—" He snagged the pencil from his ear and used the end to make small circles over the article he'd printed off for her. "This is only part of the story."

"Well, Ryan, what are we waiting for?" There was a distinct challenge in her tone. A playful, sexy challenge that he quickly responded to.

He sat straighter. "What do you suggest, Miss Baker?"

"Oh, I forgot to mention, I'm going by my maiden name these days. Call me Miss Reed."

"Gladly." He grinned.

"I know you're the internet whiz, but I'm going to introduce you to an old school, fail proof way of doing research."

"What's that?"

"It's called a public library."

Ryan stood. "Sounds kinky. I'm in. You drive."

She laughed. "Of course, I'll drive. Last time you drove, you got us lost."

It was just so easy with Ryan. She never had to straighten her spine or cross her legs at the ankles. She never had to check her makeup or straighten her hair. And it had nothing to do with the fact that he was legally blind because, up close, he could see her. If not clearly, he could see her in the haze.

What she loved about spending time with him was that there was no need for pretense with Ryan. He simply *was*. And when she was with him, she was encouraged to simply *be*. What a life affirming, life altering thing. It was liberty. And liberty felt right. Her new world was a judge-free zone. Oh, sometimes Jesse shook his head at her late-night bowls of ice cream when she'd talked him into watching a movie with her. But there was no real judgment.

Angela and Ryan drove across the island to the small rectangle building that sat between two palm trees. Wishing Beach Library was plastered on a metal sign. Beneath the name, the words, *Dare to Dream. Then, Dare to Do*. Her pace slowed, and Ryan noticed. "What are we looking at?"

"You're so perceptive, Ryan."

He'd threaded his arm through hers in their customary stance as they meandered the beach or walked through town. She liked it. He wasn't dependent on her, yet she felt important to the situation ... something she'd never felt with Brice.

She kept comparing Ryan to Brice. They were worlds apart. Ryan had a quiet confidence that Brice had ever only labored to attain. "The sign. We're looking at the sign."

"It must be quite impressive. Or does it say CLOSED and you're trying to figure out how to break in?"

She squeezed his arm. "Dare to dream. Then, dare to do."

Ryan rubbed his palms together. "All right. Break in, it is."

Angela laughed in spite of herself. "That's what the sign says, silly."

Ryan shifted his weight. "Ah. It's the motto of Wishing Beach Island. In the late 1920s, when the island was newly inhabited and wealthy vacationers began building ridiculous summer places here, Daryl Kane, a rich New Yorker brought his family and arranged to have his prized Aston Martin delivered by an auto delivery service based in New York. Then, as he was leaving town for a business trip, he instructed his wife to hire another service to have the car moved from the driveway into the garage as the delivery people wouldn't do it. She said that was silly. She'd do it herself. Well, Mr. Kane allegedly hit the roof and told her that the last place a woman needed to be was behind the wheel of a fine automobile."

Angela sank into his arm. "Hm. I'm guessing that didn't go over too well. If it had, I very much doubt we'd be talking about it now."

"It did not go over well," Ryan said.

"Let me guess, she not only parked the car, but she took it for a joyride first?"

"Oh, she did so much more than that. Mrs. Kane invited a group of people to the airport. She placed hand painted signs around town advertising the RAISING KANE car race. Ambrosia Kane not only raced, she won."

"Wow. Gutsy."

And for the next ten years, the race was dominated by

Kane's Aston Martin driven by Ambrosia Kane. I mean, seriously, who could compete with that?"

"Did any other women race?" Angela asked.

"Not a one. Not that I've ever heard about, anyway.

"I suppose the men didn't much like losing to her?"

"Well, they stood in line to sign up."

"And her husband?"

"What could he do? She was a racecar driver whether he liked it or not. She had the chops for it, the nerves for it. I suppose it was a Frankenstein he couldn't control, so he embraced it. They made a mint on the race merchandise. One Christmas, he gifted her the car."

"How do I not know this story? Why isn't there a monument to this fantastic forward-thinking woman?"

"There is. Downtown. The copper fountain."

"Of course, the one with a woman and an old-fashioned car. I never stopped to read the inscription. I never really gave it much thought."

"You will now that you know," Ryan said. As he did, he tilted closer to her. An intimate gesture that sent her nerve endings sparking.

She looked up into his eyes and could almost swear he was looking right into her soul. "I certainly will."

The moment stretched. It wasn't awkward, it was comfortable, divine in its simplicity. He was looking at her. In his way and seeing so much deeper than physical eyes could see. After a long pause, he added, "It's why I write, you know."

"Because of Ambrosia Kane?"

"Because our history is filled with inspiring stories."

She cocked a hip. "Wait a minute. You write thrillers and the like."

"Stories, Angela. The world is filled with wonderful stories. There may be murders in my books, but there are also nuggets like this gem. When your imagination can be free to roam wherever it may, *you're* free. And you can even set others free. Don't you feel freer knowing Ambrosia's story?"

"I guess I do."

"Dare to dream. Then, dare to do."

She pulled the sea air into her lungs. Salt, a tang of must and fish. A bit of magnolia mingled and sweetened the aroma. Freedom. This was the taste of freedom. And she never, ever wanted to be a bird in a cage again. Together, they entered the library.

"Ryan, you need a library card." She shoved him forward toward the woman sitting behind the counter. Angela wasn't trying to be sneaky. But with her library card, she was only allowed one piece of historical memorabilia at a time. What if they found two, or several?

Ryan frowned.

Angela smiled at the sixty-something lady across the counter from them. The library smelled of books and love and aging walls. It looked expertly decorated with mid-century styled furnishings. Straight back chairs and a retro color scheme completed the look. Comfortable. Like your favorite hippie aunt's apartment. Oh, who was she kidding? She didn't have a hippie aunt. All of her aunts were business moguls.

When she nudged Ryan's arm, he dug for his wallet and produced a driver's license that he handed to Angela. She found herself staring at it. She knew Ryan's blindness had come after a motorcycle accident years ago but seeing him in the photo with the word DRIVER'S LICENSE stamped in bold black letters gave her pause. What a world-shattering experience he'd been through. People, when motivated enough, could survive anything.

The woman at the counter took his ID. "I'm Sally Tate. I

run the library, and we are always looking for volunteers."
She cast a wide smile at Angela. The motion caused the
corners of Sally's mouth to disappear in the edges of her full
cheeks.

"Do you have a sign-up for volunteering?" Angela asked.

As if by wizardry, the woman produced a paper from
seemingly nowhere and quickly deposited it into Angela's
hand.

"Now, let's get your friend's card started." Sally began to
write, humming as she went. It was the theme to the classic
TV show, *I Dream of Jeannie*.

"Oh, I see you're a local, Mr. North. Locals get all the
perks here at the library."

"Yes," Angela said. "We were hoping to take a stroll
through the history room."

"We're proud to have the largest collection of island
historical documents and photos. I could spend days in that
room alone," Sally gushed.

Angela wondered if Sally had this much energy daily or if
it was a full moon. The last two times she'd come to the
library, there were teens from the local school manning the
counter. Somehow, she'd missed meeting Sally.

Sally tapped the card. "Mr. North, did you know you
share a name with a well-known auth—" When she looked
up into his eyes—now minus the sunglasses—she stopped
talking all together. Sally scrambled behind the counter and
changed out her reading glasses for round tortoise shell ones.
"My … my goodness. Are you Ryan North? I mean, of course,
you are. I'm holding your driver's license. But are you …"

Aw. Fangirling. The older woman's cheeks reddened to a
vibrant shade of enthusiasm. Angela cast a glance to the rock
star writer beside her. His posture was relaxed, smile
genuine, friendly demeanor. Oh. He was used to this kind of
attention.

He stuck out his hand and Sally grabbed it with both of hers. Instead of a pumping motion, Sally cradled his hand and exclaimed. "Oh, I've read all of your books. You've seen me through some dark times, Mr. North."

He clapped his free hand over hers and gave her a congenial squeeze. "Please, call me Ryan."

She continued to hold. "I'd heard that you were staying here. But moved? Permanently? Oh dear, we must get you on the schedule for a reading." She leaned over the counter and lowered her voice when she said, "It wouldn't be too demeaning, our little library?"

"I'd be delighted," Ryan offered, graciously.

Angela could only smile at this exchange.

"And something else." Sally's eyes darted back and forth then finally settled on Ryan who'd placed his sunglasses back over his eyes. Sally's face fell. "I remember hearing about … about your accident." She wriggled one of her chubby hands free and placed it on her chest. "I was so sorry to hear. But so glad you decided to keep writing. I'm sure it isn't easy. I mean. I—well, thank you for writing."

Sally had gone from super fan to super uncomfortable.

Ryan was a pillar of sweetness when he leaned toward her and said, "Thank you for reading. After the accident, I got so many letters encouraging me to keep going, how could I not?"

She shook her head. "Such an inspiration. The article said you weren't completely blind. Honestly, I didn't really understand."

"Well, I can see what's directly in front of me, but it's hazy. A lot of the detail is missing."

"Good heavens. Is that common, what happened to you?"

"Actually, it's extremely rare. I feel very fortunate to have what sight I have. It could have been worse. And as I said, my fans were so encouraging. I started researching and discovered the resources available to visually challenged people are incredible. From all over the world I received encouragement, much of it handwritten notes from fans who are visually impaired. They were a constant source of motivation on my road to recovery and learning how to live with my new normal."

If Angela could reach over and hug him right now, she would. But that would be stupid. And probably obnoxious, so instead, she listened on as Sally fawned and Ryan took it politely.

Angela and Ryan were finally given access to the history room. They went to work straight away with Angela reading aloud the things she'd found and Ryan stopping her when he knew it was a dead end. Sally entered often to check on them. She brought them bottles of water, a plate of homemade chocolate chip cookies and a notebook and pencil. Ryan heard the instrument roll across the table and grabbed it. His motion made Angela smile. She proceeded to watch him move it between his fingers as they pondered their lack of new information. After an hour of digging, they hadn't come up with a thing.

"It doesn't make any sense," Angela huffed. "A young man from this island is nearly beaten to death, and there's barely any mention of it?"

Ryan tapped the pencil on the oak table in the center of the history room. His chair squeaked as he moved. He leaned his weight on the table, the muscles in his upper arms bunching as he did. "I told you. A cover-up."

She just hadn't been able to wrap her head around that. "You're suggesting some kind of scandal?"

"I think the lack of evidence proves it. Someone cleaned up a mess, here."

From the doorway, Sally spoke up. "A mess? Let me help."

Angela cleared her throat. "Not a real mess, Sally." But then a thought struck her.

Before she could speak, Ryan was diving in. "Have you lived here your whole life, Sally?"

"I was five when my parents came. So, I guess that makes me a native."

"Do you know about an incident in the early eighties where a young man from the island was beaten by two attackers?"

Sally pulled out one of the empty chairs and sat down. "Jesse Malone. Of course. It was terrifying. I was twenty-five at the time. That night changed all of our perspectives. You just never think it will happen in your neighborhood."

Angela reached over and patted Sally's hand, encouraging her to continue.

"And poor Jesse. He didn't die, but we all mourned the loss of him."

"What do you mean?" Angela said.

"Jesse was never the same after that night. It was years before he could walk and even talk. He'd always been so open and helpful. He internalized his pain I suppose. He'd never been a quiet sort before the accident. Respectful and so full of life and exuberance, handsome as Michelangelo's David, and always smiling."

Angela's heart broke for Jesse. Sally was describing a man so different from the quiet, reserved Jesse she knew.

"He had months of rehabilitation. Maybe years, I'm not sure. I heard his mama almost lost her house. But someone, some kind soul took care of it."

Ryan leaned forward, catching Angela's attention. His sharp blue eyes settled in Sally's direction. He looked like a freshly released bloodhound when he asked, "What do you mean someone took care of it?"

"Well, paid off her house, of course."

And there it was. Ryan leaned back and a smug smile toyed at his mouth. "Really?"

Angela couldn't explain the surge of emotion that shot into her belly as she watched Ryan.

"All of Jesse's hospital bills too, I understand." Sally took a cookie and ate it.

Angela shook her head. "But if he had months of rehab, the bills had to be astronomical. Who could afford to do that?"

Sally lifted and dropped her ample shoulders. "There were rumors that several businessmen banded together and did it. But no one knows for sure."

Ryan ran the eraser tip of the pencil over his bottom lip. Angela tore her gaze from him and the instrument working over his plump, pink mouth.

"In my experience," Ryan said. "Businessmen typically want some form of credit for the like."

The word *cynical* flashed through Angela's mind, erasing the fun of watching him in his element. *And in my experience, men who are cynical will eventually show their true colors.* She needed to be careful with Ryan. He might be dangerous. If not to her head, at least to her heart because even though they'd decided on friendship, her mind kept toying with more—she could admit that—needed to admit that—to keep herself protected.

ANGELA AND RYAN sat at *1954* for lunch. The sun was high, sparking across the water beyond the terrace where they dined. Around them, a few tourists and locals sat over light seafood dishes and popular salads. "Sally Tate was really impressed with you," Angela said, and took a sip of her berry infused iced tea.

"Sweet lady. You gotta love someone who devotes so much time to preserving and sharing the written word."

Angela agreed. She'd met few librarians who weren't equally enthusiastic. "When did you write your first novel, Ryan?"

"I was sixteen. But my first novel that caught a publisher's attention I'd written in a walk-in refrigerator at an upscale restaurant in Miami."

Angela dropped her fork onto the linen covered table. "What?"

"I was a struggling author, making ends meet by waiting tables at a fine French restaurant called Provence. Before my shift, I'd write in the walk-in refrigerator. My coworkers thought I was crazy. But there, with my fingers going numb and my flesh failing at combating the cold, I wrote the first book that sold. It's titled Silent Ice. Critics called it a haunting tale and an ambitious first book. It's about a young affluent woman whose murder was staged to look like a skiing accident."

"It sounds like a page-turner. Why the refrigerator, Ryan?"

"It was quiet. And it was cold. I'd never been so cold in my life. But I'd had this idea about writing an icy, frozen, unforgiving setting. Growing up in Miami, what did I know about being cold? We don't get snow. Or ice. Or cold of any kind."

"So, the refrigerator put you in the story?"

He nodded.

"I like the title." When Ryan reached slowly for his iced tea, Angela took his hand and guided him to the glass. "The server moved your drink when she placed our salads."

"Glass and other things that are transparent are difficult for me to see—even if I'm looking right at them."

"I noticed once. So, I hope you don't mind my help."

"You're quite perceptive, Miss Reed. And exceedingly kind. You can guide my hand any day." He gave her an appreciative smile that lingered as he lifted his glass and caused Angela to question if there was some hidden meaning behind his words. "Let's drink to new beginnings."

She swallowed the rock in her throat. "To new beginnings."

"What about you, Angela? I could feel your interest when Sally mentioned volunteering. Do I detect a new beginning on the horizon of your life?"

Angela pulled in a long breath. It was time to make some real decisions. "I mean, I wouldn't hate volunteering there."

He chuckled. "Don't get too excited."

"I don't know what's wrong with me. A few weeks back I was at Island Floral and I started imagining what kind of island business I might want to own."

"Are you thinking of buying a business?"

She shrugged. "No. Not really. I just—you know, seeing Willow and her daughter Katelyn—they're Jesse's sister and niece—so in their element. It got me to thinking. What do I do?"

Ryan leaned toward her. They were tucked, side by side in a booth that overlooked the water. He was close. She didn't mind.

"Ryan do you ever feel like the world is spinning around you and you're just stuck in place?"

"Everyone feels like that sometimes."

"I'm not sure what my purpose is. When I was married, I had a purpose. All of my siblings, they have their jobs and believe me they are supremely committed to them. Like you, they're passionate about them."

"Are you suggesting you're not a passionate person, Angela? Because I find that difficult to believe."

"Believe it," she huffed.

Ryan reached over and captured her cheek with his hand. His thumb made long strokes down the side of her face. His fingertips rested along her jaw and the curve of her throat. "You'll find your passion, Angela. Maybe this is the first time in your adult life when you've given yourself the opportunity to learn who Angela really is."

She bit down on her bottom lip. "It's scary," she whispered. "Not knowing."

"You're up to the challenge. I guarantee it." For a few moments, there was only his voice, his words, the scent of pepper and fresh soap that always seemed to linger around him. He was one of the most interesting men she'd ever met. And it felt wonderful to have someone view her as anything other than a wife and a step-mother. "Why did you decide to live here?"

She wished she knew. "It ... *feels* ... like home."

"Forgive me for saying it, but you don't really sound convinced. You've told me you have a history here."

"Brice, my ex-husband owned the house I live in now. It had been a family getaway for his folks when Brice was growing up. My family's winter home is a couple doors down on the cove. We spent Christmases there every year and a few weeks in the summer. Of course, Brice and I weren't friends, not really until I hit high school and my awkward sharp angles became more womanly curves. Then I became more interesting to him. That was when his attention drifted my way." Angie brushed the hair away from her face. "He's a few years older than me."

"Does your family still come to the island?"

"My parents don't travel to the beach anymore. They're just getting a little older and set in their ways. My siblings are too busy. So the house sits empty most of the time."

"You told me you have four brothers and sisters."

"Yes, my parents were the Brad and Angelina of their time

adopting child after child. Two boys, three girls, all of which are adopted except my oldest brother."

"Cool. Now that your life is your own, will you spend time with each of them? Are you close to your sisters?"

Was she close? Not as close as she'd like to be. "Both my sisters are—" *Too busy for me?* No, they'd make time if she'd talk to them. "Tess is a marketing genius. She's developing a new app for iPhone, and Violet is the CEO of a Fortune 500 company."

"Wow. Successful. Good for them."

It wasn't just the two sisters. Angie's entire family was successful. "My siblings had this innate desire to succeed. Each one was so driven while we were growing up."

He tilted so he could look her in the eye. "You seem a bit mystified by that."

Her eyes widened. "I was. I am. I mean, they were each really impassioned about their futures, about their goals. My sister once worked mowing lawns to pay a tutor to help her with chemistry because she didn't want Mom and Dad to know she was struggling. Straight As all the way. All of them."

"That's a lot to live up to. And it doesn't sound very healthy."

She shook her head. "But that's just it. They're all so happy. I mean, they worked hard and had a vision, and they're each at the top of their fields."

"And how did you fit into this lifestyle?"

She shook her head. "I didn't. My parents were continually exposing me to new adventures so I could find my niche. But nothing ever clicked for me. I was happier sneaking into the kitchen and helping prepare food."

"You love to cook?"

She thought for a long moment. "I *like* to cook. I can't say I love it. I like a lot of things. I like interior decorating.

Making a beautiful space for people. I like readying a house for the holidays. I like travel. Okay, maybe I *love* travel. But so what? A person can't have a profession where all they do is travel. And I would assume that if you traveled for your profession, it would eventually get old." She didn't mention her unnatural fear of flying over water which also made a travel profession unlikely for her.

"There *are* professions where you travel."

"But I wouldn't be happy because I like making a home and reading by the fireplace at night and—" Angie was surprised by the sudden rush of tears in her eyes. "Ryan, I don't know who I am. I'm almost forty, and I don't know who I want to be when I grow up."

"It's okay to have wings if you also have roots, Angela. In fact, I think it's beautiful."

She swallowed and tried to absorb his words.

"Just because you didn't appear on the planet with a plan and a lifelong goal—that doesn't make you any less of a person."

Then why had she always felt second rate? Like when God was handing out gifts, He said, "None for you." Why had she always felt like an outcast in her own home? First, the one she grew up in, then Brice's home.

"If you feel like you don't fit in, create a space where you do."

He was close to her. So close she could lean right into that strong and protective nook beneath his arm. The temptation was great, to be sure. But she was done leaning. She was determined to stand on her own. A runaway tear trickled over her cheek. "That might be easier said than done." Her voice cracked.

He reached up and swiped her cheek with his thumb. Had he seen it? Or did he simply know it would be there by the broken tone of her voice? "Just make me a promise," Ryan whispered. "Don't let anyone put you in a box. Stay free, Angela. Freedom looks good on you." Ryan leaned toward her causing the space between them to disappear.

She could smell his cologne and the berries from his tea on his breath, and the two combined in an intoxicating blend. He was going to drop a kiss on her cheek. She knew he was. A tender, sweet peck that would say more than words. Angie's eyes drifted shut. This was a moment she'd treasure. Sweet Ryan kissing the cheek of his basket case friend.

She felt him hesitate for a moment. Maybe she'd read this wrong. Maybe …

But then, there he was. Fingertips and thumb on her cheek and his lips against her own. Warm, soft, full lips pressing into the space of her mouth with a gentleness that was sure to leave her dizzy. Her mind screamed to back away. Get out. Stop. But she didn't. Her body instinctively moved to give him more access to her. A rumble of pleasure slipped from her mouth— most unexpectedly, and before her brain could catch up, she was tilting her head and lacing her fingers into his hair.

The kiss deepened.

Then, Ryan pulled away. He was breathless, forcing out shallow puffs of air. He looked confused. "I'm—I'm sorry. I shouldn't have done that."

Humiliation zinged through her system. Oh God. He looked like he'd just kissed his own sister. Or worse, his mother. "I'm sorry too." The feel of his lips still remained on her mouth and she reached up to try to swipe the sensation away but instead, her tongue slipped out and ran over the now fiery opening, capturing his kiss. Oh dear. She'd kissed another man. Not her husband. Not Brice, but someone else. She'd *kissed* someone.

The breeze blew past. It was cool. It hinted at new beginnings and dreams and wishes. Angela Reed was a free woman. And free women could do whatever they wanted. Even kiss other men. She turned to watch the seagulls diving over the water and soaring to unimaginable heights. A Cheshire smile spread across her face. *I kissed a hot guy. Go me.*

It wasn't until dessert that the conversation picked up again.

The awkwardness had gone, replaced by a comfortable silence until for reasons unknown, she launched into a dissertation about her stepsons and how much she missed them. Still, she was doing the right thing, giving them space. In her heart, she knew it to be true. But her mind poked daggers at her psyche claiming her unfit as a step-mom. All of this she blurted to Ryan over key lime pie. "I need to be stronger. That's all. If I wasn't so weak—"

He chuckled. "*You* and *weak* are not words I'd put in the same sentence. Besides Angela, you don't have to be strong today. Give yourself a free pass."

Tears rushed to her eyes. One overshot the rim and trickled down her cheek, landing on his hand.

"Hey," Ryan whispered and scooted closer.

It had been a nice lunch, sitting on the open patio of the bistro overlooking the water and the boats. Ryan had been a sympathetic ear. But she was done talking. It was getting too deep, too personal, and all the old feelings were rushing to the surface. Why did they come out of nowhere like this?

But she knew why. She was beginning to work on figuring out the rest of her life, and she'd found herself to be a completely boring woman with no real passions and no real interests. She liked things. But she didn't love anything enough to stick with it for the rest of forever.

"Ryan," she sniffed and gathered her moxie. "I'm sorry

you have to see me in this ridiculously emotional state. I don't know what's wrong with me today."

"What's bothering you the most? Is it the divorce? Your stepsons? If we can determine the root, maybe we can work through it together."

"It's … everything." How could she explain it? She didn't even understand it. "I've made my peace with being divorced. But here I am. Thirty-nine. No job. I'm free for the first time in my life. Free to travel, eat dinner at midnight if I want. But all I can think about is how much I want to share it. I just thought that my husband and I would grow old together. I don't have anyone to grow old with, Ryan. And that makes me sad because the thing I love in life the most is sharing my life with others."

"Angela, some people are meant to be alone. Some aren't. Just because your husband was a jerk, that doesn't mean you're done. There are other men out there. Good men."

She blinked. "And what does that say about me? That I can't be happy without a man? Kind of pathetic, isn't it?"

"No. It's not that you can't be happy. It's that you'd rather have someone to share life with. That's beautiful, Angela. Not pathetic."

"How do you do it, Ryan? After all you've been through. How do you maintain such a good attitude?"

He dropped his hand to the table. "What's the alternative? This is the hand I've been dealt. At first, I was so angry. Like God hated me or something. My sight was mostly gone. I'm a writer. But after time and rehabilitation … and therapy, I realized I could go on with my life, with my career. I mean, what if I'd have been a truck driver?"

Angela let a tiny joyless laugh escape her lips.

"The vision loss wasn't going to ruin my life. It just redirected it a bit. I had a lot of anger at first. I wanted to give up.

I wanted to crawl in a hole and never come out. But then, I got some perspective. I like who I am now. I like blind Ryan."

Angela looked down and realized their fingers had interlocked. "I like him too." *She only wished she could say the same for divorced Angela.*

"Well, you might not have liked the old me as much." He bumped his shoulder against hers. "I was kind of full of myself."

"Full of yourself? A superhot, highly successful author?"

Ryan's tongue darted out and licked his lips. "You think I'm hot?"

"No."

"Yes, you do."

"Gah, you *are* full of yourself." The last bits of tension melted. He started to move away, to give her some much needed space. This kind of public intimacy would keep the server from ever returning. He began to move, and instead of letting him, she stopped him by tugging on his hand. "Ryan, I really am so sorry for all you've been through," she whispered.

"Same here. But hey, we survived, right?"

"Mmm. I want to do more than survive. But right now, I should probably get back home." She anchored a hand gently against his chest and pushed off him.

He stopped her. "You haven't told me the whole story, yet."

"Bleah. What's left? My stepsons are college age, but I miss them. My ex will probably never darken my door again, nor will his obnoxious mother. No loss there. I'll miss my ex father-in-law. His name is Cog and he was the only redeeming part of the Baker clan."

A smile stretched across his face. "You're on the mend, Angela. Give it time. And you're not in your old life anymore.

You're here. New place, new life, new opportunities to find—"

She held up a finger. "If you say love, I'll smack you."

The dimples in his cheeks appeared. "Then I won't say it. At least not yet. But I'll be keeping a check on you."

Her heart did a little flop. "What?"

"In the love department."

Heat rose to her cheeks, and she was thankful he couldn't see it.

"Don't be embarrassed."

Ugh. Was there anything he *didn't* see? "There is no love department, Ryan. Not for a good long time." *There's you,* she added, silently. But what were her feelings for Ryan? Friendship. He was her hot writer friend. That was all.

He started to slide out of the seat. "Come on. I'll drive home," he teased.

Just as they left the restaurant, a seagull flew overhead and deposited a chalky-white gift on Ryan's shoulder. He pinched his shirt between his fingers and tugged it away from his skin. "Seriously?"

Angela retrieved a tissue from her small purse. "Hazard of living on an island." She cleaned up the mess as best she could. Once a mother, always a mother.

"Isn't that a sign of good fortune or something?"

She laughed and tossed the tissue in a nearby trash bin. "You really are an optimist."

They fell into step beside one another and rather than slip his arm through hers, Ryan grasped her waiting hand. They threaded their fingers together. And Angela felt like all was right with the world for the first time in months. Sure, they were friends. But maybe … just maybe they were becoming more.

CHAPTER TWELVE

The early morning breeze wafted through the open kitchen windows occasionally ruffling the edges of the to do list Angela was working on. Since proclaiming her wishes at *Wishing Beach* she felt like a new person. Now when she looked at all there was to be done to make the house her home, the task went from ho-hum to love, just like that. *Magical!*

1. *Paintings - call Marco -* ✔*- (Set up an appt for the end of the week)*
2. *Plants - call Katelyn next week – have lunch & order house plants*
3. *~~House name change~~ -* ✔ *- (Jesse has it handled - # 7 Cove Dr .)*
4. *Call the boys - ?*
5. *Confer with Jesse on having the house exterior painted*
6. *~~Send Brax's birthday card~~ -* ✔ *- (sent)*
7. *Buy new guest towels for downstairs powder room -* No Monogram!
8. Ryan????

Angela tapped her pencil on the last line of her list. They'd had this lovely—dare she say magical—lunch at *1954*, and snap! Just like that, he left the island leaving only a brief note behind. Why did he leave so abruptly? Just one short email.

Publisher summoned! On my way to NY and then across the pond. Don't know when I'll be back.

Take care,

Ryan

That was like breaking up with a sticky note on the windshield. Angela threw down the pencil. *Take care. Take care? That's what he has to say after ...* After what, exactly? A little kiss? That's all they'd shared at *1954*. A kiss and a dissertation on her gloomy life. Elbows on the table, she cradled her head in her hands. Ryan leaving was the one bleak spot on what she'd hoped to be a gorgeous sunshiny day.

"Phew," Angela huffed. Enough of that. She stood and cleared the half empty cup and the small plate that earlier held her breakfast, a toasted bagel with cream cheese. The day was still fresh and beautiful, and she wasn't going to let it be spoiled by something she couldn't quantify. As she rinsed the two dishes and deposited them in the dishwasher, she heard whistling through the open window. Jesse was coming up from the beach, a fairly regular occurrence with him. She knew he walked in the surf up to his knees most days, therapy for his legs, she assumed. Angela smiled, it was nice to see Jesse happy ... whistling, even if she didn't recognize the tune.

Her cell phone rang as he stepped into the kitchen. Jesse gave her a wave. She crossed the room and picked up her phone from the table and waved back.

Angela's smile turned to a frown. It was Brice. She was immediately tense. "Hello," she answered.

"Hello, Angel."

That was *nice* Brice's name for her. And she loved it ... *then*, until *nice* became less and less. Brice was handsome, charismatic, and utterly charming when he wanted to be. So much so he made you question if it were even possibly that he had another side—a narcissistic side.

Her throat went dry. "What do you want, Brice?"

"Wanted to see how you're doing." He ignored her cool tone. "It's Braxton's birthday on Sunday."

"I know, I sent a card." Trembling fingers smoothed her hair.

"We want to invite you to come home for a birthday party." He paused. "The boys wanted me to ask."

"I thought they were in Europe for the summer," she said.

"They're here for a week. You know, to wash their clothes." He laughed.

"No one leaves Europe to wash their clothes." Was he baiting her? What was happening, here?

"To tell the truth, I think they were homesick. With everything that happened with us—"

"So, it's my fault that they left Europe? You're saying I ruined their summer."

"Hey, Angel Baby. I didn't say anything like that."

Her heart was pounding. She rubbed a hand over her chest trying to lessen the tightness there. "What are you saying, Brice?"

"They miss us. And I think they'd like to see both of us and know we're okay. You know, with the divorce."

He sounded sincere. But she'd learned not to trust Brice. He always knew how to get what he wanted and used any means necessary. Still, she'd love to see the boys.

"There's actually another reason they came home. They wanted to see their grandfather. Cog had a heart attack. I thought it best they come home ... just in case."

"What?" Angela's throat constricted, making it impossible

to get more words out. Cogburn Baker, Brice's father, was about the only person she liked from that family, him and of course, the boys.

"He's home. He'll be all right. It was a minor heart attack." Brice assured her. "But, since the boys are home and it's Brax's birthday, we thought we should have a party."

Angela pressed a clammy hand to her forehead.

There was a long pause on the other end of the line. "It's good to hear you voice," he whispered.

No, no, no.

"Angel, I've had time to do a lot of thinking. In fact, I've been talking to someone."

Don't ask, don't ask. "Talking to who?"

"You're going to make me say it, aren't you? I've been getting some counselling. I needed to deal with my responsibility in the destruction of our marriage."

What? *What?* She didn't know if she should be angry or happy. She'd begged him to see a counselor and deal with his anger management issues. After talking to Willow a few weeks back, she'd done some research on narcissism. Brice was textbook. And not at the lower end of the spectrum. But people with narcissism rarely reached out for help. Was he doing that? Finally reaching out for help?

"I just, Angel, I want to say I'm sorry."

Her breath caught. He'd never in their married lives apologized to her. Never.

"Listen, I'm not trying to lay all this on your shoulders. Honestly, I wanted to say that in person. As far as coming to the party, I understand if—if you aren't comfortable coming. But I know it would make Dad happy to see you. Mild or not, the heart attack took a lot out of him. And the boys, well, they miss their mom."

Angela squeezed her eyes shut. Brice always knew what strings to pull, this was no exception. The boys, Cog ... he knew her soft spots. And he'd apologized to her. And actually taken some responsibility for the break-up.

Still, she needed to remember all the grief he'd given her about the boys, *forbidding* her to have contact with them. Now dangling them like a carrot in front of a horse's nose. Angela gritted her teeth. "Where are you having the party?"

"Our house." Brice said. "Nothing big, just family. Just a nice family weekend."

Our house ... just family ... Angela heard the caress in his voice. She could almost feel his arms circling her. She sucked in a sharp breath. Her instant reaction surprised her.

"What do you say, Angel?"

Just when she was doing well, he pushes back into her life. She'd almost rather have him railing at her. He was being all the things she'd loved about him. And God help her, that was hard to resist.

Remember. Remember. Memory was her safety net. He never stayed Nice Brice. He turned. He turned quickly and violently into something far different.

"So, can I tell the boys you'll be here?"

"I can't talk right now." She hung up. Angela stared at the phone in her hand. She was shaking. She dropped the phone onto the table and covered her face. "Oh God."

ANGELA STEPPED ONTO THE AIRPLANE. It was a brief flight from Florida to Connecticut, but that fact didn't ease her queasy stomach. Settling into her window seat she experienced a myriad of emotions. First and foremost was dealing with her fear of flying. Road trip? Too many hours, she had decided. Besides, she could do this. On her own. By herself. She could fly. Sure. People flew all the time. Her biggest fear was going over the water. This flight to Connecticut wouldn't be over the water, so all was good. If all was good, why were her hands sweaty?

The way Angela dealt with her fear of flying was to keep her thoughts on something else. So they turned to her next biggest problem. Brice. When Brice called her back the following day, she had expected his usual tirade for practically hanging up on him. Instead, he was still *nice* Brice. And she wasn't equipped to not respond to that. Which was apparent since here she was *on a plane*, going ... *where, exactly?* To what? A future? Maybe at least congenial co-parenting, or just back to the familiar belittling humiliation.

The biggest question of all, could Brice be changing? Could he once again become the man she knew years ago, the man she fell in love with? Did he have to lose her to understand and appreciate what he'd had? Angela's resolve to find out once and for all was becoming necessary. What if life was getting ready to take another sharp turn?

AFTER A WHITE-KNUCKLED LANDING, her boys met her at the airport. They held up a homemade sign. MOM, in big red letters. It melted her heart.

"I missed you two!" she said, hugging both of them for longer than she should. They looked older. Braxton sported a scruffy beard and his little brother Bryan was in much need of a haircut. They hugged again, and she knew they'd missed her as much as she missed them. That made her cry... and hang on a little tighter. Finally, Braxton broke the hug and self-consciously took a swipe at his eyes, Bryan following suit.

"What do you say we get outta here?" Braxton said, a catch in his voice.

Bryan already had a grip on Angela's carry-on. "Good idea."

The three headed arm-in-arm toward the exit. Angela couldn't quit smiling. She had her boys back. And that healed a big hole in her heart.

The boys talked nonstop as they walked across the expansive parking lot. Braxton had offered to get the car while she waited at the building entrance. Angela wanted none of that, now that she had them again, she wasn't ready to let them go even for a few minutes.

When they approached Braxton's car, he jumped ahead and opened the passenger door for her. "At your service." He made an exaggerated bow.

Angela laughed. "I see you still have the ..."

"The bomb!" Bryan finished.

"Oh, yeah. She's still running." Braxton shrugged. "Most of the time."

Bryan tossed her bag into the backseat and climbed in. He started the loud car and they were off.

Angela remembered when they bought Braxton the *bomb.* It was his first car. He was sixteen. They didn't buy him a brand-new car due to Angela's coaxing and rationale. No new cars until they had a four-year degree. Then a reasonably priced new car as they headed out into their chosen fields. She came from a family of financiers, smart, frugal, and rich. Brice respected that and supported her plan wholeheartedly. He usually made all the decisions, except with the boys. He let her raise them for the most part. She was happy he allowed her that since they were *his* sons. In hindsight, she also saw that it had relieved him of the time and responsibility he would have had to invest in raising them. He worked out of town a lot, so it was good for all concerned. Braxton also had to earn the money for his car insurance, part of the plan. She put her foot down when Lorene started giving Braxton the money behind Angela's back. Brice backed her up which was monumental.

There was a similar scenario for Bryan one year later. It wasn't always easy for them, but looking at them now, she knew it had helped mold them into the fine young men they'd become. She felt proud to have been a part of their growing up.

"Mom," Braxton broke into her reverie. "Do you want to drive through *Starbucks?*"

Mom, she would never get tired of hearing it. "Okay." It was what they often did. Oh my gosh, it was all so normal.

As they proceeded toward *home,* they passed *her* mall, then *her* grocery store, *her* hair salon. It was like she had never left. The house and the life that she was building at *Wishing Beach* were what seemed surreal now. Angela sensed she was being drawn back into the other world, Brice's world, but why? She honestly wasn't sure, at that moment, if she was guarding against it… or welcoming it.

Geez, Willow was right. You get so conditioned you fall right back into it, like a drug. This had been a mistake! She rubbed her bare arms. If she was feeling like this already, what would happen when she saw Brice?

In another five minutes she was going to find out.

They arrived at the massive two-story brick house that she'd called home for fifteen years, but Brice wasn't there. Relieved, she took the first few minutes to acclimate. Her crystal vase of hand tied silk gerbera daisies sat in the foyer. The ornate umbrella stand she'd rescued from certain death at a flea market stood sentry by the front door. She'd sanded and refinished the stand herself. Angela ran a hand over the refinished work of art.

Braxton wrapped an arm around her. "He hasn't changed anything in the house since you left. I think he really misses you."

Now that her heart was effectively broken, the boys disappeared. Angela took herself up to the guest room. The familiar walk felt weird. She'd prepared the room countless times for others, and now she'd be staying in it. Each step toward the end of the hall—and the master bedroom—created a panic. Without the boys to shore her up, this was starting to feel like a really bad idea. She tucked into the guestroom and closed the door harder than necessary. Fighting tears, Angela sank onto the bed in the quiet room with the sunny window trimmings she'd chosen and the Egyptian cotton duvet filled with premium goose down. She'd made this a perfect room for guests. But guests weren't hosts, and they had no claim to the surrounding home. Like her, guests came and went, and then were easily forgotten.

It was 5 o'clock when Angela went back downstairs. She heard voices in the direction of the family room. She smiled to herself, the party was supposed to start around six, early enough that Cog and Lorene could attend comfortably. Pizza and German chocolate cake—Braxton's favorite—would be the offerings. Usually, Angela made the cakes for all the family parties. Brice had purchased the one they'd consume later.

Angela made her way to the family room. The large space with a massive fireplace was an extension of the kitchen dining area spreading out to the glass doors that gave a view of the sparkling pool and manicured backyard. The room held so many fond memories, homework, board games, birthday parties, friends over for pizza parties and video game nights. Just she and the boys most of the time, with Brice gone so often.

Many of her fondest memories were of the boys growing up. Brice was in some, but fewer than one would expect, so life here would never be like that again because the boys were grown. There would be no more homework marathons. Whether she was in Wishing Beach or Connecticut, certain things were no more.

187

The realization puzzled her. When she'd heard Brice on the phone, her insides had turned to mush. That much was true. And what that meant, she couldn't yet say. But her memories, the real memories that she treasured—well, those all had to do with the boys. Brice was barely a footnote. She didn't even have time to process these new thoughts or those feelings before she turned into the family room and nearly ran headlong into Brice. He caught her by the arms, and they both laughed awkwardly.

"Sorry," they said at the same time, and laughed again.

His hands warmed her upper arms as he looked deep into her eyes, like he was swallowing her up. "Hello, Angel." His voice was soft and smooth as silk.

She waited for those words to turn her into putty. But … nothing.

"Hello, Brice." Angela questioned her lack of feeling—what it meant or didn't mean. She'd imagined she'd be a blubbering basket case, all the old *good* feelings surfacing after their time apart. That's what had happened during their phone call when all her *smart parts* took a backseat to her unreliable *heart parts*.

And there they stood, his hands caressing her forearms, his gaze intent on hers. Oh, he was reading her—her lack of motion to get away, her stuttering breaths. But Brice was reading it all wrong. She'd expected—after his phone call and her reaction—that she'd fall back under his spell. Brice clearly thought she was under his spell now. He believed he had that power whenever he chose to enforce it, and, for most of their life together it had been true.

"Thank you for coming." He still held her arms and her gaze.

Angela cleared her throat and tried to look away. "Thank you for inviting me. It's been fun catching up with the boys."

He smiled. "Yes, we've got a great family. I think we've both learned a lot from this ..."

The doorbell rang.

"We'll talk later." Brice gently touched her cheek and went to answer the door.

Angela shook off the unsettled feeling and proceeded into the family room where a decorated cake with candles waited on the kitchen counter. Bryan, Braxton, and several friends were already laughing and partying with soft drinks and snacks. The party wasn't just family as Brice had said, but she knew a lot of the boys' friends, so it was a nice time of re-connecting. Besides, the more people and the more activity, the less she'd have to interact with Brice and his mother.

Brice returned with Lorene and Cogburn in tow. He escorted them to their usual spot at gatherings, the loveseat next to the fireplace, it gave them an unencumbered view of the entire room so Lorene could hold court, lording over everything.

As much as she dreaded it, Angela broke away from the kids and walked over to greet Brice's parents. She first said hello to Cog, taking his thin hand in both of hers. He was paler and thinner than she remembered. With a pleased smile, he shook her hand as they spoke. He was a poor thing, far worse condition than Brice had led her to believe.

And then Lorene. "Hello, Lorene." Angela braced herself for the coolness that was sure to come, and she didn't blame her. After all, she'd called the police to have her thrown out of the beach house. But the expected coolness didn't appear.

"Hello, Angela." Lorene had a convincing forced smile on her face as she spoke.

Like Cog, Lorene looked worn down and a little frayed on her perfectly manicured edges. It would seem that the heart attack had taken a toll on both of them. Angela's heart went out. How she could feel bad for Lorene, she wasn't sure

—the woman was pure poison. But she did feel bad. Angela glanced at Brice who was watching it all. He was beaming, apparently pleased with the way things were going. Her mind raced. Was this an intervention of sorts? She knew one thing, if Brice's motives were to win her back, he would have the support of his parents no matter what. He had been running that family since the day he was born. That's why he had the beach house to lose to her. He had it because he had asked for it, and that's all it took. His parents gingerly signed over the house to him. *Angela could feel the cold links of the chains rubbing against her.*

The young people had started a game she wasn't familiar with, but it produced a lot of noise, laughter and running around, so Angela welcomed it. The last thing she wanted to do was visit with Brice's mother, or Brice, she realized. And this time not because he was being cruel or obnoxious as in times past, but because he was being *nice.* She'd always thought that if Brice could maintain *nice* all the time, she'd willingly stay in the marriage. She knew for the first time that was no longer true.

None too soon, it was time for cake and presents which meant the party would be ending. Angela served the cake, like she always had. She wasn't enjoying this anymore. The boys were involved with their friends as they should be, and Angela felt the all too familiar sensation of being out of place. At least now, that made sense. This was no longer her home.

"Brax, you ready for your present?" Brice said with a wide grin.

"I'm ready!" Braxton ran over to his father who was holding up a small black box with a big red bow. He grabbed the box and hurriedly opened it. "What?" he said, holding up a set of keys.

"They're for your new BMW."

"Are you flippin' kidding me?" He danced around laughing. Braxton was clearly overwhelmed. "I can't believe it!" He hugged his dad.

"Believe it, son. You've done well in school, it's your birthday, and you're a Baker."

It felt like a slap in the face. She had been the enforcer of the boys taking responsibility for their cars, everyone knew that. She looked at the smug smile on Lorene's face as she met her gaze. Angela was careful not to show any emotion. Cogburn was stoic. She guessed he wasn't pleased, but he had no say. She realized he never did. Perhaps that was why she liked him so much because he was like her. She saw a weak shell of a man with an overbearing woman at his side. Like she was a shell of a woman with Brice.

Angela searched Brice. He was beseeching her with a big smile, proud as a peacock, waiting for her response of praise. *He didn't have a clue.* This wasn't a slam at her, he hadn't thought about *her* at all. He had tunnel vision, whatever he thought or decided took precedence over anything and everyone. *Narcissist!* Angela finally understood. She understood that he was incapable of feeling or understanding another's pain. All the pain and wrongdoing from him that she had endured and stashed in the deepest basement of her heart was rising. Rising, rising and welling as it moved from the depths of her soul to the tip of her tongue. Angela opened her mouth to speak, but no words came out, instead, something new and fresh swept in.

Another wind of freedom washed over her. It entered her mouth and swept down her throat. None of this was about her. It had never been about her. She finally understood. Knowledge really was power. Angela no longer feared, nor desired Brice. She felt only sadness and pity for him. She smiled sadly back at him.

"Where is it?" Brax asked, so excited. As much as she felt betrayed by Brice, she was happy for the joy Braxton was experiencing. Maybe she would have even agreed with Brice if she had only been asked.

"Before you go, Braxton," Lorene hollered above the excitement.

They all quieted while she spoke.

"Your present from me and your grandfather is that we're going to pay your insurance on the car until you're out of school." Lorene cast a smile Angela's way.

Angela smiled back. Lorene *did* have a clue. She knew exactly what she was doing and took great pleasure in it. This family was not going to get under her skin ever again.

Spending time with the boys went out the window with the new car. Of course they wanted to go with friends and enjoy it. So when Brice asked her to go to dinner at her favorite restaurant, The Waterfront, Angela jumped at the chance. Because she'd only nibbled on the pizza earlier, she was starving. Plus, anything to make the time go faster was a blessing. She couldn't imagine sitting around the house with her ex all evening. She just needed to get through the time until her flight out in the morning.

It was a beautiful restaurant and a beautiful night. The glass doors that created an invisible wall between the diners and the deck overlooking the sound were pulled back, inviting the fresh air and smell of the sea inside. There were candles on the tables and the lights were low, a lovely setting in which to relax. And that is exactly what Angela did. She breathed deep of the salty air and settled back into the comfortable chair. Her composure surprised her.

The dinner conversation was superficial and sparse which pleased Angela. She just wanted to be done in Connecticut and on her way home. *Home*, it sounded so good. Brice poured more wine for both of them. He had become fidgety. It seemed to Angela that he was wanting to say something and was trying to decide how to start. She hoped not. Finally, he asked her to dance. She didn't want to, but she accepted because she knew how to manage Brice. Give him what he wants.

The music was lovely, slow and romantic, and Brice was, like with everything else, an accomplished dancer. She yielded to the moment and enjoyed the dance. When it ended, Brice kept his arm around her and moved right into the second song.

He drew her closer nuzzling her hair. "You are beautiful, Angel."

There was a time she yearned for moments like this—but those moments had been far too rare.

"I want you to come home, Angel." He enveloped her in his strong embrace as they glided across the floor.

No... no ... but the words stuck in her throat.

Her hesitation spurred him on. "Look, it'll be easier on you this time, the boys are out of the house, you'll have a lot of time for yourself."

What he didn't know was that she'd just realized the boys were the reason she stayed as long as she had.

"You can get involved in some women's groups, charity things. And we'll have many more engagements to attend." He drew back and smiled at her. "We do make a handsome couple, don't you think?"

They walked back to their table but instead of sitting down, Angela collected her purse and wrap. "I'd like to go now," she said calmly. She could see the struggle in Brice's eyes and knew he'd never give up that easily.

In the car, as they pulled out of the parking lot, he dove right into the topic he had been pursuing after their dance. "I think, if you would just admit it, what we've both learned from all this, is that we belong together. And we have a family."

Angela took a careful breath. All it took for Brice to explode was to disagree with him. "Brice, we've had a nice day with the boys, a nice dinner, let's just let it go at that for now, okay?" She hoped against hope that he would let it go.

His hands gripped the steering wheel, and he visibly puffed up. "I don't get you. I gave you everything. Everything!" His face turned red under his perfect tan.

Angela shrunk into the corner by her door. *Everything except respect,* she thought.

"All I ever asked from you was to be a supportive wife." His voice rose with each word. "Is that too much to ask?" He tossed hateful glances to her across the car.

She knew Brice's definition—supportive meant never disagreeing. Do what you're told and always, always stroke his ego. That was how she'd kept the peace. Right now, she hoped remaining silent would keep the peace. Sometimes it did, other times it made things worse. His rant continued, listing all the wonderful things he had done for her. She remained silent.

As he raged on, she was reminded why she had come to relish his frequent business trips even though she suspected he was cheating on her. Once, she confronted him about his cheating only to have him turned it back on her. He'd asked, "Are you lacking anything? You knew who I was when you married me. And I knew who you were. I haven't changed ... don't you." And then he added insult to injury. "There are plenty of women who would love to take your place if you don't appreciate what you have." And that had been the end of it.

As soon as they were back at the house, Angela headed straight to the guest room. In the upstairs hall, Brice caught her by the shoulder and turned her to face him. "This is the last time I'm going to say this. Come to your senses and come home."

Angela tensed and tried to turn away. He pulled her to him and kissed her hard. She pushed back at him until he let her go. In times past, his kiss was all it took to melt her. She took a deep cleansing breath, gently tugged away from him. She shook her head slowly, entered the guestroom, and locked the door behind her. She was finally out of love with Brice Baker.

CHAPTER THIRTEEN

The Uber pulled into the drive of #7 Cove Rd. Angela smiled, she liked the way the new signage looked above *her* gate. They continued up *her* driveway, to *her* house ... and *her* new life. A shiver of excitement ran through her as to all the possibilities that lay in wait.

They passed Jesse walking toward the house, rake in hand. When he spotted her in the car, a wide smile lit up his face. Much better than the frown he'd sported she left. He had understood she was in a vulnerable place and had real concern for her. After all, he had seen what Katelyn, his own niece, had endured. But in the end, he came through and wished her well. Angela had always been able to rely on Jesse, and now that she was virtually alone—*alone?* Yes, utterly, truly alone. Unease crept down her spine, but she pushed it away. She had people here—or at least she was well on her way. She had Jesse, his sister Willow, who Angela adored. She could envision becoming friends with Katelyn who was closer to her own age. And then, there was Ryan. But then again, maybe not. Everything with Ryan felt on shaky ground since his little text. And during season, she'd have her old friends. Missy, Donna, Jenny, Gayla, Mimi, Ginger, Kari, and Kara would all be close by for pool parties and movie nights.

On the island, Jesse's friendship and support felt like her anchor. And not just his but his whole family. The way they opened their arms and their lives was beyond anything she could have hoped for.

Angela paid the Uber driver then waited for Jesse to catch up. "I'm back." She waved to him.

"So you are," Jesse answered. "And all in one piece."

"Yes. You want to come in and have a glass of tea?" Angela started for the front door.

"You mean that gawd awful hibiscus tea?"

She laughed. "No, I have to make that fresh. Besides, you know you love it!"

He gave her a wink. Leaning the rake against one of the porch columns, he trailed her into the house, their steps echoing all the way to the kitchen.

"I've got to get some rugs and accessories in here," Angela murmured.

"Yes, you do. It sounds like a tomb."

"Ew." Angela wrinkled her nose. "Now I'll think of a tomb."

"Well, it might help you get it done," he noted.

"Touché!" Angela motioned for Jesse to sit at the table while she got the tea out of the refrigerator. "Everything okay on the home front?" she asked.

"All good." He shrugged. "A quiet weekend. How about you? The boys doing all right?"

"The boys are wonderful. They missed me as much as I missed them." Angela's eyes sparkled. "Oh, and they said to tell you hello."

Jesse nodded his satisfaction. "I told you, you didn't have

anything to worry about. You're their mom. Nothing trumps that."

"I know. Brice had me convinced that they were angry at me, and I believed him. I just thought—"

"That's what you get for thinking." A crooked grin played at the corners of his mouth.

Jesse always had his little jokes and sayings waiting. His humor kept a good balance in any conversation. It wouldn't let it go unnecessarily serious or dismal. Angela chuckled. "You're probably right there." The ice clinked against the sides of the glass as she set them on the table in front of them. "And, yes, I had nothing to worry about."

"Good kids," said Jesse.

"They are."

They danced around with small talk a few more minutes when Jesse finally asked. "So, how did it go between you and Brice?"

She frowned in thought for a few moments. "You know… it went well. Yeah, it did." She raised her eyebrows. "I can't say that Brice would give the same answer. But, for me it was good … and necessary."

"I was afraid you might start second guessing your move here." Jesse took a long sip of his iced tea.

Angela spread her hands on the table. "I can assure you I won't be going back there. As far as Brice and his parents are concerned, I feel totally disconnected from them. It's almost as if I was never a part of the Baker family. More like, I was hired help for all those years."

"That's gotta hurt. Are you okay with how you're feeling?" Jesse raised his eyebrows in question.

"You know, I am. Yes …" She waved her hands in the air in a cheer. "I'm so okay with it!"

Angela spent the rest of the day soaking up the healing

warmth of the sun, waves gently washing up on her feet and legs as she laid motionless on the warm sand of *Wishing Beach.*

She was *home.* For good.

~

AFTER AN AFTERNOON on the beach and a night of deep restful sleep, Angela was ready to tackle life again. She tied the laces on her running shoes, slipped the bluetooth over her ear, her cell phone in her pocket, and headed out the door for her usual morning run. It felt good to get going. She had neglected it for too many days.

The cooling breeze and the salt air invigorated Angela, and she picked up her pace, her body responding to the welcomed exercise. She ran full out for a few minutes, settled back into a jog, and repeated the sequence. When she came to Ryan's house, she slowed to a walk, breathing hard and welcoming the break. She eyed the lanai and the surrounding area looking for signs of life. There was nothing to indicate that Ryan had returned. Deciding to see for herself, she turned into his place and walked up the back stairs. It felt barren, not like he'd just left, but more like he'd never been there. Dread dropped into the pit of her stomach. *Had he moved? And without a word?* It had been nine days.

Meandering around the house, she searched for a window that wasn't covered. She found one. It was high, probably a kitchen sink window. She climbed up on the air conditioner to get a look inside. What she saw confused her.

There were plenty of his personal items around that she recognized. His Panama Jack hat was tossed on the bar, his computer open on the kitchen table, a pencil and a pair of sunglasses next to it.

HEATHER BURCH

What did that mean? Had he not left at all? His curtains were drawn. Was he avoiding her? Had he done all this to avoid her? Now that she had found out what she wanted to know, she realized what a sight she must be peeking into a man's window. Feeling on the pathetic side, she glanced around as she hopped down from the AC unit. What if someone saw her. Worse, what if Ryan caught her.

"Why are you avoiding me, Ryan?" she whispered to the ocean air. She'd thought they were getting close, at the very least they had become good friends, hadn't they? But perhaps she'd read him wrong. A twinge of disappointment settled in her chest. Embarrassment at assuming it was more than it was trickled over her sweat-glistening skin.

Angela's cell phone rang, causing her to jump. She fished it from her pocket. It was Ryan. She nearly dropped the phone, trying to hit the talk button with her butterfingers. Had he seen her? "Hello," she said, looking all around.

"Angie! Are you walking by my place?" Ryan asked.

"Wha-what?" Angela stammered. "Are you home?" The fire of her fresh embarrassment crept up her neck and face.

"No, I wish I were." Ryan laughed. "I know this is the time for your morning run. My mind trails to you at this time every single day."

Well then.

"Anyway, I didn't mean to interrupt your run, but I miss giving you a hard time."

Angela could breathe again.

"I'm back in New York." He sounded excited and alive. "I have so much to tell you."

After his short, curt, email, Angela had planned to be cool toward him when and if she did see him again. But she couldn't dampen whatever it was that made him so excited. "Tell me," she said, wanting to match his enthusiasm.

"Unless you want me to wait until I get home. I should be home in a couple more days."

"Don't you dare make me wait a couple more days." She was happy for him whatever it was, and she wanted to share it with him. And ... she was happy he wanted to share it with her.

"Okay, I'm sorry I couldn't tell you more when I left. But I had to find out for myself first ... so, I ..." He stammered around.

"Just tell me." She wasn't going to make this difficult for him.

"Okay, okay." He cleared his throat. "Where do I start?"

"You said you are back in New York. Where are you back from?" Angela started walking in the direction of her house.

"Israel."

"What?" She stopped just before reaching the banyan tree.

"Yes, this is where it started. I got a call in the middle of the night from my publisher. It's hard to explain. I'll need to give you all the details when I get home. But all of this happened because of Stuart, my publisher ... and friend. Anyway, I had been waiting on something to happen. And he called and told me it had happened, and I needed to be on the first plane to Israel."

"What was it you were waiting for, Ryan?"

"I had word that a research doctor in Israel was doing a breakthrough procedure on the unusual type of blindness I have. It's risky, but it could help me possibly recover more of my sight. Through Stuart's connections, I got my name on the list for consideration."

"Oh, Ryan." Angela's eyes welled with tears of joy.

"Which meant I had to be there, in Israel, for testing to see if I would be a good candidate for the procedure." He took a breath. "So that's why I couldn't stay in touch with you properly. I didn't want to say anything until I knew for sure, and then there was the week of evaluation in Israel, and—"

"Ryan, Ryan. Don't give it another thought." And she meant it. Now her insecurities seemed so petty in the light of what Ryan had been living. If she hadn't been so used to being ghosted by Brice, she would never have reacted as she did. "But did you get accepted? Do you know?" She realized she had crossed her fingers.

"I did get accepted." Excitement and hope echoed from his words.

"That is glorious, Ryan. When will the treatment happen?"

"Well, that's the hard part, waiting. It could be as much as a year before they move forward. And, then there are no guarantees, maybe only partial vision, and maybe I'll lose the shadow vision I have now." That brought him back down to earth.

"The main thing is, you're in the program." Angela consoled him.

"Yes, I am thankful. But, enough about me. What's been going on in your life?"

Angela was pleased he was interested. "Well, it *has* been a busy week. As you know, I've been trying to get the redecorating done in my house. I have a good start. Oh, and I went to Brice's for the weekend." She had an impish grin on her face.

"Wait ...wait ...what?"

"What, what?" She chuckled to herself. He gave her the response she was after. He had a great sense of humor, and so did she. They had become used to baiting each other.

"You spent the weekend with Brice?"

"Just one night. I was back early Sunday morning." Angela sensed the slightest tinge of jealousy, or maybe just surprise. But she liked it.

Ryan was silent on the other end of the line. It was common knowledge the boys were in Europe. Angela could see his mind trying to unscramble what was happening. She finally burst out laughing. "I went to Braxton's birthday party on Saturday. They're home for a couple of weeks. I took the early flight out Sunday."

"Oh, that's nice." Ryan recovered his composure and changed the subject. "Was I right? Are you out on your morning run?"

"Actually, I am. But I'm heading back, I have an appointment with Marco, who is an artist."

"I know who Marco is." Ryan's tone was low and controlled. "Everyone on the island knows who Marco is."

"Oh, well, I'm hoping to commission him to paint some pieces for my living area. I've seen some of his work, and I think he's fantastic."

"Yeah, I've heard he is." His words were overly cheery. "Stuart has me booked for a couple of TV interviews, but I expect to be out of here Friday. No, I *will* be on the early flight Friday."

Angela could tell Ryan was making his plan as he spoke.

"So, if you're free, could you come by my place Friday afternoon? I have so much to tell you." Then he added in a mumble. "And, you might have a little to tell me."

"What?" she asked, though she knew what he'd said.

"Uh, I hope to see you Friday."

Angela held the phone a little tighter. "I'll see you then."

As she loped her way back up to her house, she wondered why *she'd* never heard of Marco. It seemed like everyone else had. She wasn't a newcomer to the island. She'd been here almost every summer for the past fifteen years.

Finally, it dawned on her. She had rarely left the Baker compound when the family summered on the island. Brice was gone most of the time with golfing, boating, and *guy stuff.* She was always at the house with the kids, sometimes Lorene and Cogburn. Brice had a serious jealous streak and sometimes it was just easier to stay home. If Brice were here now, she knew he'd feel threatened by Marco. Brice certainly wouldn't have welcomed the hot artist into their lives. But Angela could, This was her life. She got to make the rules.

NINE O'CLOCK sharp the doorbell rang. She'd showered, changed into real clothes, and after cleaning the bathroom sink, Angela shook her long hair loose from the scrunchie. Tucking one side back behind her ear, she headed for the front door. Punctual. Angela liked that mark of integrity, especially in a person she was possibly doing business with. When she opened the door, she all but reacted the same way she did when she first saw his image on the back of his marketing brochure. Tall and lean and fresh looking, he was dressed in off-white linen slacks and a white gauzy shirt with brown buttons unbuttoned just the right amount down his chest. He wore a ring on each hand and one earring but no other jewelry. His black hair was loosely pulled back in a band at the back of his neck. On his feet he wore Jesus sandals.

"Hi, you must be Marco." Angela extended her hand. His face was clean shaven, his dark eyes bright and inquisitive, but also non-threatening. Trust was her word for Marco. Women had a sixth sense about these things.

"My pleasure." Marco took her hand with a slight bow and placed on it a light kiss. It surprised her. It was probably the custom in the islands where he came from or could be just his own personal branding.

"Please, come in." Angela stepped back to allow him to enter. His cologne was ... crisp, sea spray with a cedarwood base. She drew it into her nostrils and enjoyed the way the scent filled her being. Angela gave herself a mental shake and proceeded to show Marco around the space she wanted to dress with art. "I saw your *Magia* at the flower shop. I found it very interesting."

His dark eyes were intent on her when he asked, "What did you love about it?"

It was a simple question but felt profound and somehow intimate. "I—"

Marco took two steps closer to her—right into her space —but she didn't mind. He simply wanted to capture her thoughts as they left her mouth. How she knew that, she couldn't say. "I—I don't know what I loved about it."

He made a wide gesture with his well-defined arms. "Of course you know. Your heart just hasn't shared it with your mind, yet."

Angela stared into black sparkling eyes. He wasn't smiling, simply inspecting her with this black globes. And he seemed more than happy to wait until she came up with her answer—or until her heart told her mind.

"I loved the motion of the painting. The subjects were together, yet they were apart. And there was emotion and passion in every stroke of the brush. Leaves were more than leaves, branches, more than branches, and when I stepped away from the painting, I felt like it had given me something. Like I'd shared something with it." Where had all that come from? Angela was breathless.

Marco's smile was slow and mesmerizing. "Angela." Her name rolled off his tongue as if he were savoring it. "You understand all that art is." He had a faint accent that suggested island living. It was not unpleasant to her ears. "Are you familiar with my other paintings?"

"I looked through your brochure. I am quite interested in commissioning some work." Angela turned away from him lest she forget the purpose of his visit. She stopped in the center of the spacious living room.

Marco raised his brows. "You enjoyed my brochure?" A smile played at the corners of his mouth. The twinkle in his eyes told her what he hadn't said, *You like the back cover?*

Ignoring the innuendo, Angela continued. "The Wishing Beach painting was a favorite. You know that spot is right out here." She stopped at her massive window and gestured toward the water.

"You have a keen eye."

"I've always loved art, especially oil paintings."

"Angela." Her name again, rolling off his tongue as if this time he'd test it to see if it was a good fit for her. Finally, he said, "Ah, yes, a beautiful name for a beautiful woman." It was said as a matter of fact in his mind now, not as flattery.

And that, she was fast learning, was Marco. He said what he thought, honestly and sincerely. She guessed that was what Willow meant when she said, he doesn't play you.

Different ... but interesting, Angela thought. Although it had been so long since Angela had been in the singles world, everything was interesting and different to her.

The next hour went by quickly. A good share of it in conversation about art in general, the styles, the techniques, the old masters, the new kids on the block. Marco was the first one she'd crossed paths with in years, who loved art as much as she. By ten thirty, Angela decided on the work she wanted created, with Marco's professional input. "I love the Wishing Beach scene. I would like something similar for my main piece in the room. But I'd like it done in an impression-istic, even surreal style, with a limited, subdued color palette. You know, all color and movement." She was swishing her hands and her body, gently swaying back and forth. "Nothing defined."

Marco studied her. He frowned in deep thought, his head

in vague motion following her as she swayed. Finally, he spoke. "I believe I know who you are. I've caught your spirit." He met her gaze with his serious, glinting dark eyes.

Angela was impressed.

"But first, I'll make a small test canvas for your approval."

"Okay." She nodded. "That sounds good."

"When I come back with it, we will then do some measuring for the exact sizes. I'll be photographing the beach in all kinds of weather and at all times of the day. So, don't be alarmed if you see me down there."

When Angela closed the door behind Marco, she was extremely happy about the way the meeting had gone. He was confident and professional. Marco was everything his brochure had promised.

FRIDAY COULDN'T COME SOON ENOUGH for Angela. She and Ryan had decided on two o'clock. Angela was ringing his doorbell right on time. When Ryan answered and she stepped inside there was no hesitation on either part to fall into each other's arms. It just seemed natural. The kiss that followed ... well, it just seemed right.

"I missed you so much." She could hear the smile in Ryan's voice as he rocked her back and forth in his tight hug.

Angela sighed. "I missed you too."

"Good! That's what I like to hear." He let her go, taking her hand. "Come on in and make yourself comfortable. I'll get us something to drink." Letting go of her hand he started in the direction of the kitchen. "You want iced tea or fruit spritzer?"

"Tea is fine, thank you." She followed him into the kitchen. "I can help."

"Well, it's not hard." Ryan reached in the cupboard for

two glasses. "I'll let you in on my secret, either choice comes in a can." He proceeded to fill the glasses with ice.

Angela knew that if she could see into his beautiful eyes behind the sunglasses, there would be a twinkle, a sparkle. That sparkle was in his voice, his smile, and every part of him. Ryan was a joyful person. Period. She felt bad about doubting his motives and their friendship. But she wasn't used to someone being an open book. She was used to having to read between the lines.

At Ryan's suggestion they took the drinks to the comfortable chairs that sat side by side in the living room overlooking the beach and ocean. She wondered why he had chairs placed like that since he couldn't see beyond the reach of his hand. She decided it was for the pleasure of his guests. Ryan was like that she was finding out.

"So, tell me all about your trip ... and Israel. I'm so excited." And she was. "But I can't believe you've never told me about the possibility."

"The possibility that I could see again?"

"Yes."

"Truth is, I didn't want to give you false hope. I may never see." He looked toward the window. And then he turned back toward her. "What you see when you look at me is all there is, and more than likely, all there will ever be. You need to know that." His tone held a serious note. "But," he was back to his joyful self. "Even so, I am vastly excited about this chance, however remote. I wanted to share it with you. I want to be able to tell you when I get news, and when I dream of possibilities, and even disappointments." He sighed, then smiled her way. "Selfish, I know."

"Are you kidding? I was disappointed you had never even hinted to me of something so huge, so fantastic. I mean, I hoped we were better friends than that."

"We are. We are, Angela." Ryan reached for her hand.

"And, my beautiful friend, prepare yourself to hear every exciting detail of my life over the past two weeks."

He began reiterating everything he had told her on the phone a few days earlier while filling in with every tiny detail. Angela hung on each word, delighted he would want her to be a part of his miracle.

After a huge chunk of the afternoon was taken in conversation about his Israel adventure, Ryan took a deep breath and asked. "Now, what do you have to tell me?"

"Hmm, like what?" She grinned, coyly.

"You said Brice invited you to Connecticut."

"He did." She nodded.

"What did he want?"

"He wanted me to come to Braxton's birthday party."

"I'd bet the farm, that he didn't *just* want to offer you a piece of birthday cake."

She rolled her eyes. "You're right."

"What *did* he offer you, other than cake?" Ryan was savvy, he knew how people ticked. He had to ... he was a writer.

"You really want to know?"

"If you want to tell me." He was genuinely interested but not pushy.

"He offered to let me be his *Trophy Wife*."

Ryan's mouth flew open. "Is that what he said?"

"No, not in so many words. But as he asked me to come back—and told me how it was going to be better—the description could only be perceived one way, 'Trophy Wife'."

"Wow!" Ryan combed his fingers through his hair. "Wow." He stood up and paced back and forth. Stopping in front of her chair, he reached a hand to her. She took it and stood up in front of him. "I just want to say ... in Brice's defense ..." Angela raised her brows as Ryan continued. "I think you would make a magnificent 'Trophy Wife'."

She laughed. "Thank you. I think. But that's never going to happen."

Ryan pulled her into his arms for a brief hug. Angela felt good there.

"Well, my friend, after listening so patiently to my ramblings, what do you say I take you out for dinner tonight?"

"That sounds wonderful." Angela said hesitantly. "But, I'm afraid I can't. I have a—"

"Oh, right." Ryan was quick to intervene. "What was I thinking? It's Friday night and a gorgeous summer evening. Of course you have a date." He smiled to cover his disappointment.

"No, no, it's not like that." Angela shook her head. "I am going to a WWA meeting with Jesse's niece."

"Oh." Ryan looked relieved. "I thought maybe you were going out with Marco." He smiled sheepishly.

Angela laughed. "He's doing some paintings for me, that's all."

Ryan looked happy with that. Angela liked that he cared.

"WWA." Ryan frowned. "What is that?"

"It's Women Warriors Anonymous, a support group for abused women. Actually, this particular chapter is specifically geared to dealing with victims of narcissistic abuse—which typically falls under psychological abuse, but not exclusively," Angela explained.

Ryan nodded. "Yeah. They devalue you and make you think it's your shortcomings, not theirs."

"That's true." She nodded.

"You become convinced that if you can just do better, that will fix them. But it won't. Because they're the only ones who can fix themselves. And sadly, that rarely happens."

"Yes!" Angela was surprised at his knowledge on the

subject. "How do you know that? Why am I the only one for which narcissism wasn't a common word with a definition?"

"Well, I didn't come by it naturally," Ryan said as they moved out onto the front porch where she'd first seen him. They sat down. "I was writing a book which had a socio-pathic character. I studied characteristics of sociopaths and came across narcissism. So, I know a little on the subject." He twisted his face as if in thought. "Actually, I could write a book. Oh that's right, I did."

Angela laughed, he was so witty, just one of the things she liked about Ryan. "You would be a great guest speaker for the group. I know they're always looking for speakers, If they're interested, would you be willing to come?"

"A women's group." Ryan chuckled. "Would I be safe?"

Angela knew she'd overstepped her bounds. She didn't know if they welcomed male speakers. And she hadn't even been to a meeting, tonight would be her first. Katelyn had asked her to come and see what she thought and perhaps consider being a speaker, telling her story. But, she did know they would be lucky to have someone of Ryan's caliber to come and speak. She wanted to secure that option in case they could use him. "I'll protect you." She patted his arm. "But seriously, I think it's wonderful they have these groups out there. I would like to find a way to let more people know about the problem and how widespread it is. Women in narcissistic relationships need to know they're not alone."

"I think that's wonderful, too. And, generous of you," Ryan said.

"Take me for instance." Angela went on. "I had no idea what was going on with me and Brice. I just knew I had to get away. I had lost *me*. I know that sounds crazy."

Ryan reached over and took her hand in his, squeezing it in reassuring support. "That's not crazy, that's brave."

"Did you know ... about me?" Angela turned a quick look at him. She suddenly felt vulnerable and exposed.

"No, I didn't know." He shook his head. "You had told me you were recently divorced. All I knew was that you had wounds, you were hurt." He spoke softly. "Everyone that loses someone hurts, whether it be a divorce, death, separation. Even if you wanted them gone, it's all the same. It hurts."

Angela's eyes misted. "Yes, it does."

CHAPTER FOURTEEN

"The three-piece painting of Wishing Beach will be divided and spread along the wall facing the window's panoramic view of Wishing Beach." Angela spread her arms in a sweeping motion. "That way no matter where you look you will be immersed in my favorite spot, Wishing Beach."

Katelyn listened and nodded her approval of Angela's tour, but her attention was captured when her gaze turned to the massive windows. "I must say, I do like your view."

Angela looked beyond Katelyn down to the beach. Marco, in knee length white shorts and nothing else, had a sturdy easel planted in the sand supporting the initial rendering of the final of the paintings. From that and the photos he'd taken, he would finish the painting in his studio.

For a few moments, both women stood at the window watching him. The breeze played in his hair, and he swatted it off his face like a pesky gnat.

"I can't complain," Angela said, voice going husky. "We can go visit him if you like. I go down there regularly. He's a very interesting guy. Unusual maybe."

"Or weird! Mom likes to talk to him. She finds him deep."

Katelyn rolled her eyes. "I find him weird. I do like *looking* at him though."

They laughed.

It was the second time Katelyn had been to Angela's. Today she delivered the plants they had selected for her order. The beautiful house plants were exactly what she needed to finish off the rooms. She had found the perfect area rugs and mats and when Marco finished the final painting, she would call it done. Angela couldn't help but smile. She loved how her space was being transformed. It felt cozy, yet spacious and uncluttered at the same time. She belonged to it, and it belonged to her.

"By the way, thanks again for speaking at WWA. You were a hit with everyone," Katelyn commented, her gaze still fixated on Marco.

"Good to know. I felt like I was blundering along. Uh, uh ... duh." Angela groaned.

"Actually, you sounded like you knew what you were doing. A real professional."

"I guess I fooled them." Angela wiggled her brows.

When she noticed how Katelyn couldn't keep her eyes off Marco, it seemed she must be interested in him in spite of her protests. "Hey, let's take a cold drink down to Marco. Poor guy, he must be hot."

"Oh, he's definitely hot," Katelyn growled.

They laughed and headed to the kitchen. Angela and Katelyn were fast becoming good friends.

～

"You're going to think I'm crazy, but I have an idea." Ryan's excitement was easy to see in the spark in his eyes and the kind of nervous excitement that caused the very atmosphere to crackle.

Angela was intrigued. "Go on or should I run home and shower? I could come back." She'd jogged up the beach and back again, stopping to say hello on her way home.

Ryan reached for her hand and led her into his house. They sat on the couch, her being swallowed by the plush cushions, him on the edge of the seat, as if his uncontainable energy might cause him to burst up from the spot, Yosemite Sam style. "Well, before I dive into my idea, I need to tell you something."

"O-kay."

"I found Olivia."

Shock drove her off the couch. She stood like a statue, staring down at him. "What?"

The nodding of his head did nothing to hide the giant smile on his face. "I found her, Angela."

The excitement of uncovering the truth coupled with the fear of actually *knowing* the truth. And Jesse. What about Jesse? The room darkened around Angela, and she knew she should have eaten something this morning. Her stomach rolled. "I think I better sit back down."

Ryan reached out and found her hand. He pulled her to the spot beside him. "Olivia Lamere lives in Paris, France."

"Olivia Murray was her maiden name. She must be married?"

"Actually, she was married. Divorced. But Lamere is her aunt's name. She took it as a young woman. When she married, she hyphenated. Now, she is back to just Lamere."

Angela's heartbeat soundly against her ribs. At first, she thought they'd find Olivia and learn easily what had happened all those years ago. But when simple searches lead to what Ryan swore were dark cover-ups, Angela began to doubt if they'd ever find her. And without finding her, they'd never know what really happened that night.

"I was beginning to think she was a ghost," Angela whispered. "Now that she's real, I'm not sure what it means." Trepidation worked its bony fingers over her, beginning at her throat.

"We've got to talk to her, Angela."

No. No they didn't. They could just go on with life pretending that there is no Olivia Lamere who lives in Paris, France. "I wouldn't want to cause anyone any pain."

Ryan moved to the very edge of the couch, a racehorse, ready to go. "You mean Jesse? You wouldn't have to tell him until you talk to Olivia."

Her hand pressed against her chest. "Me?"

He gave her a nod. "This is your adventure, Angela. I'm just along for the ride."

Angela bit down on her bottom lip. Her fingers threaded together, palms sweaty. Why had she begun this silly quest? "I'd never do anything to hurt Jesse. But there's also Olivia to consider."

"Will you call her?" Ryan pressed.

Angela tried to envision herself doing just that. But what would she say? How does someone approach a subject that has stayed dormant for four decades? "I don't know."

Ryan waited, patience may not be his strongest attribute, but it ranked in the top ten. He was giving Angela time to process. For that, she was grateful.

After several apprehension drenched thoughts assaulted her, she said, "This is her past. A painful past, it sounds like. I can't just call someone out of the blue and dredge up so much sorrow. It feels mean."

"Good." Ryan gave a nod with his head.

"What? I thought you wanted me to—"

"Why call? When you could talk to her in person."

Her heart jumped. "Is she flying to the states?" Could they be so lucky that she was coming here, or anywhere within a reasonable distance?

"Planes fly both directions, Angela."

It took her mind a nanosecond to catch up. "You're certainly not suggesting I fly to France to talk to this woman face-to-face."

"Oh, I'm not just suggesting it, I'm daring you to do it."

A plane over the water. Her big fear. Traveling alone. Bleah. Oh, but to see the lights of Paris. To walk the streets and watch the sun fall over the city of lights. To sip espresso at a bistro and take pictures of the flower carts. Her eyes were misting. "I've never been to Paris," she whispered. But the vision was shattered. She'd be alone. No one to talk to, no one to hold her hand on the plane while she concentrated on deep breathing to keep herself from completely freaking out and clawing her way out through the plane window. Her hand was hot. She glanced down at it. Ryan's fingers were interlaced with hers. Somehow during her frozen moments of fear and questions, he'd unwound her right hand from her left and deposited his hand there.

"I'd be there with you," Ryan said, the words soft, little more than a whisper.

"You would?" Hope's fire shot into her belly.

"You know, if you want me to go."

"Yes! Oh my gosh, yes. I mean, the idea of going alone is terrifying. But if you go with me…"

He laughed. "You're gonna love France. And, I'm a good traveler, Angela. I swear you won't have to babysit me."

Babysit him? Oh, it would be much the opposite. It was rare that he talked about himself in any negative way. Ryan was nothing if not upbeat. But as he sat there beside her, she saw the insecurity. "Ryan, I'm afraid I can't make the same promise. I'm scared of planes. It's not so much the plane as the loud noise at the takeoff and landing when I know I'll be flying over water. I know it's ridiculous. Plus, you're an expert traveler, right? You've been everywhere. I'm going to seriously cramp your style. Even in New York, I do the whole head-back-gawking-at-the-skyscrapers-thing." She shook her head to clear it. "You—You've been to Paris?"

"Many times. I can show you around. In fact, I already called a friend who owns a hotel. He can give us a two-room suite. You'll have your own bedroom. If you're comfortable sharing a place."

"Yes." Of course. They were friends. "I'm going to Paris." The reality of it needed time to set in. She'd say it again and again to assure herself.

"You're going to Paris."

But one thing first. She had to tell Jesse where and why she was going. Anything else would seem deceitful. Jesse had a right to know that Olivia was alive, divorced, and living in France. Maybe she'd moved there as a young girl. Maybe that was why she never returned to the island or tried to reconnect. Maybe Angela and Ryan could get answers as to why she never even came to the hospital to see Jesse after the attack. Angela tried to always think the best of people. But not visiting Jesse—well, that was close to unforgivable. It would be her first inquiry to Olivia.

Answers awaited her. In Paris. The very thought of traveling to France—on a whim—left her eager, energized, and more than a bit apprehensive. Tiny particles of hope unfurled in her stomach as she considered strolling the streets that lived only in her dreams. Paris. Freaking Paris. Why had she not gone before now?

Angela poured a fresh cup of coffee and used a kitchen towel to swipe absently at the already clean counter. Years ago, her lingerie drawer had been littered with brochures touting the beauty of Paris and the French countryside—a place she was equally keen to visit. Had she really allowed Brice to fully dictate every movement that her lifelong fantasy to visit the city of lights had become nothing more than a pipedream? Whenever she'd mentioned Paris to Brice, he'd snort a sardonic laugh and tell her she'd hate it. Food is bad. City smells. People are rude. When she finally left him, she'd thrown away the travel brochures much as she'd thrown away many of the mementos that reminded her of the life she'd left behind. She should have kept them—by not doing so, she'd cemented the reach of his hold over her.

Angela didn't care about any of that now. Paris had been and always would be just one step below heaven in her opinion. The mystery and excitement were as much an intoxicant as the city itself. No, Brice's Paris was not *her* Paris. Brice's Paris was not Ryan's Paris. For Ryan, it was a city of light and life, a city he loved. And she'd go there with him. A thrill raced up the muscles along her spine. With him.

WHAT THEY WERE PLANNING to do weighed heavily on Angela. What if Jesse didn't want to know about Olivia? What if it made him sadder than he already was? What if … what if …

`She decided she couldn't take it upon herself to ruin Jesse's life. Angela picked up the phone. Willow would know what to do. She had lived the tragic past along with Jesse and the rest of their family.

Angela and Willow sat at an outdoor table at the Yacht Club sipping iced drinks and waiting for the lunch they'd ordered. Angela was hoping they could talk candidly about Jesse and Olivia. She remembered the last time she'd asked a question on the subject and how Willow had put a dead stop to further discussion. Willow was noticeably agitated now, hope was waning.

"I don't understand why you're digging up old bones." A frown creased Willow's brow. "Those were terrible times." Willow looked out across the ocean. "We'd all like to forget."

Angela sighed. She might have made a big mistake

coming here. She was about to say never mind when Willow turned and looked her straight in the eye with resolve.

"I'll tell you what happened." She hesitated only for a moment. "The first few months after Jesse was horribly beaten, we didn't know from day to day, sometimes minute to minute, if he would live or die. Then for a long time, we didn't know if he would ever walk or talk again, or if he would be bedridden. My mom spent every moment of the next seven years nursing him back to health. She had to teach him how to eat, how to walk, how to learn, as if he were a baby all over again. That was our life."

"Oh, Willow, I'm so sorry. I knew it was bad … but, I had no idea."

"One of the worst parts of the whole thing is that the two college boys that beat him nearly to death, got off with not much more than a slap on the wrist." Anger and pain flashed in Willow's eyes. "They came from wealthy families. You know what they say … money is power. Well, it's true."

Angela bristled. Ryan had been right, it was a coverup. The more she knew, the more she felt their pain. "I see why no one wants to talk about the past. I'm sorry. I just wanted to make Jesse happy. He spends time every day on Wishing Beach just staring across the ocean. And he carries that faded picture of Olivia in his billfold."

Willow looked surprised. "He does?"

"Yes," Angela said. "Everyone talks about closure these days. Maybe Jesse needs closure so he can live his life."

Willow studied her for a long moment. "Has Jesse ever told you what he does with his life? I mean apart from taking care of your place."

"No. He's never offered to tell me, and I don't pry. That's the boundary he set between us. I've tried to respect it."

"Like you're respecting it now?" Willow pressed. "Why are you so obsessed with this, Angela?"

"I—I don't know." She should explain. But she simply couldn't. It didn't make sense. "My marriage ended because my husband was abusive. I see that now. My marriage was destined to end. But Jesse and Olivia, they had their whole lives ahead of them. And it seems like their love story ended not because of them, but due to outside circumstances. Unforeseen hands meddled in their love story, and it seems they should have a chance to set the record straight."

Willow leaned forward. "Angela, it was forty years ago."

She nodded. "I know. I know." Silence surrounded them for several long seconds. "You were going to tell me what Jesse does besides take care of my place."

"Jesse is *supposed* to be retired, but he can't seem to keep his nose out of his work. He's a victim's rights advocate. Hands on, here on the island." Willow waited for Angela's surprise. "In the beginning his focus was on victims like himself, where money or politics got in the way of justice. In time, it evolved into much more. Folks who live around here know that the first person you call for help if you've been victimized is Jesse Malone. Even in the world of crime and drugs, and other criminal activity, they know to call Jesse. He's worked with a lot of recovering criminals. If they're sincere about wanting to do better, he will fight for them, and he'll get them help. Because the justice system sometimes has a lock-them-up-and-throw-away-the-key mentality."

How could she have not known this? Of course, Jesse probably wanted to keep it on the downlow. Maybe he was afraid she wouldn't want someone working for her who consorted with criminal types.

"And boy do they call, all hours of the day and night." Willow rolled her eyes. "I should know, I'm the screener, if you will."

"What does that mean?"

"Like I said, he's mostly retired now. But once in a while,

calls still come to me through an agency he used to work with. I pass those calls to one of the fulltime advocates here on the island. Leftovers and hard cases go directly to Jesse."

"Were you always involved in this?"

"Not at first. But people kept stopping in at the flower shop looking for Jesse back before the days of cellphones. Over the years, I found I liked being his first line of defense. I could listen to someone for five minutes and determine if they needed Jesse or the cops. Sometimes I refer them directly to the police if I think it's an especially threatening situation or if it feels it's likely to escalate. The job sort of stuck. Cellphones came along and, though we're not official anymore, people still call. If I hadn't filtered, he would have taken too many risks. But it doesn't ring all that often anymore. The fulltime advocates in the area have their hands full, so Jesse does what's needed. He only takes the extra work these days."

"You're like 911." Angela barely noticed when their lunch arrived. Her mind was racing trying to understand the man she thought she knew.

"We called ourselves *Lifeline*. People called when they were at their lowest and most desperate. Sometimes, they would prefer to avoid police intervention until Jesse can help them work things out."

"Oh my gosh. That sounds dangerous." Angela's mind was spinning. This sounded like something from a Grisham novel, not her quiet, caring, groundskeeper.

"It can be. There were a few precarious incidents in the past, which is what led us to do screenings." Willow shook her head. "I could tell you stories."

Now that she'd gotten started, Willow was on a roll. She dug into her fresh greens salad as she continued. "Jesse spent his life with his nose in law books and on the computer researching. Do you know where he goes every month?"

Angela shook her head. "No." She had wondered but wouldn't pry.

"He goes to the capital a few days each month. He works closely with the governor and the powers that be to legislate good laws and change bad ones."

"I had no idea. Wow." Angela was stunned. *You think you know someone ... wow!*

"Because of Jesse's work here, Senator Perry created a state Victim's Task Force years back and appointed Jesse to head it up. It has been hugely successful. Jesse has stepped down now, you know, retirement and all." Willow added. "But he made a difference on the state level, and a big difference on our island, for sure."

"He must have been good if he caught the eye of the senator," Angela said.

"Well, Jesse knows Senator Perry ... Travis. He has for a long time. Roy Perry, his father, was the primary person who helped Jesse and my mother after the ... *incident*. Roy was a senator at that time and carried a lot of weight. Not to mention that the college boys who beat up Jesse were acquaintances of Travis's. Travis had invited them here to a party they were having that night at the Perry house. If not for that, none of those horrible events would have happened. Also, Olivia and her family were good friends and neighbors of the Perry clan back in Boston." Willow stopped to take a bite of her food.

"So, Perry took care of the medical bills?" Angela was perplexed.

"Um, nope." Willow finished chewing and swallowing. "The fathers of the two college boys met behind closed doors with the judge and agreed to pay all hospital bills, generously, and completely, in exchange for light sentences and no records for their sons."

Angela gasped.

HEATHER BURCH

"I know, terrible right? I thought so too for a long time. But as I've been involved with Jesse's work for so long, I have come to find that nothing is black and white." Willow took a drink of her water.

Angela raised her brows in question. "Meaning?"

"Meaning, that with the lawyers they could afford, the outcome may have been worse for Jesse. He had huge medical bills for years, and he was able to get the finest procedures available at that time. He may not have had that if they had gone to court."

"I see what you mean." Angela nodded.

"Even better than that, Senator Perry—at the urging of his son, Travis—threatened the boys with a lawsuit for all the pain and suffering they had caused." Willow smiled as Angela's mouth hung open. "Well, the fathers knew that would mean all the details of that night would come out, including what they had done to protect their sons from punishment."

"What happened?" Angela was transfixed.

Willow answered, a big smile on her face. "Senator Perry sued them, on behalf of Jesse, for five million dollars."

"Oh, my, gosh!" Angela's eyes bulged. "Five million dollars."

"Not quite the end of the story." Willow Held up her index finger while she chewed. "They settled out of court for two point three million."

"Yes." Angela gave Willow a high five. She wished Ryan were here. He was not going to believe this. "Justice shall be done."

"It was well deserved." Willow gazed at the water thinking back. "Jesse wanted to buy Mama a new house or build her one where hers stands now to help make up for all she'd been through. He wanted to make her life *better*. But she wouldn't have it. She told him in no uncertain terms to just do all the repairs, but don't change a thing. 'This is where I keep all my memories, the good and the bad. Life is made up of both, you know. If there were no bad memories, how could we truly appreciate the good? This is our home. It doesn't get any better than that'. Mama Grace always did have a way with words."

After their moment of jubilation, Angela laid her fork down while she tried to digest this new information. Jesse was a successful statesman? Then why live and work at her house? She mentally shook the confusion from her brain. "And Jesse works for me. He has for years. Why?"

"Why does he work as a caretaker?" Willow finished for her.

"Exactly."

"That was my question." Willow took a sip of her water maneuvering around a fresh lemon wedge. "Here's Jesse's answer in a nutshell, #1. It's a quiet place to work, #2. As groundskeeper it requires him to get plenty of fresh air and exercise, instead of sitting at his desk, #3. The ocean water is good therapy for his leg, and #4. He gets paid for being there. It's a win-win!"

"But still, he doesn't have a wife, or anyone," Angela pushed her agenda ahead, "to share his life with."

"He's dated quite a bit, off and on." Willow shrugged. "He says he hasn't found the right one. Back in the day, he was married to his work." Her brow furrowed in thought. "I didn't know he was still pining over Olivia. I just assumed after forty years he'd managed to put that behind him."

"He hasn't." Angela sipped her drink.

"Wow." Willow sighed aloud. "Maybe he does need to face it, bury it once and for all."

"Soooo, should I tell him what I'm doing, or wait until I've talked to Olivia?"

Willow gave her a long, thoughtful, look. "I don't know Angela. But, whatever you decide, you have my blessings."

∾

ANGELA HAD BEEN WATCHING Jesse through the window while he'd rested under the banyan tree at the edge of her property. It stood watch over Wishing Beach, the glorious stretch of coastline that never seemed to gather seaweed—even in the violent storms that raged during hurricane season. Wishing Beach stayed pristine.

Beneath the branches of the massive banyan, Jesse folded his hands. Angela straightened. Almost a prayer posture on the jean clad caretaker who'd become one of her dearest friends. Was Jesse wishing? What would he wish for?

Angela knew what she'd wish for right now. Answers about Olivia. Why had Olivia gone without a word? Had she been forced? The answers were for Angela, but they were also for Jesse whom she knew had never really made peace with the disappearance of the girl he'd loved.

She'd be crazy to believe that traveling around the globe to get answers from a woman he'd known for one summer could somehow change the world for him, but in her heart of hearts, that's what Angela believed she'd be doing.

A secondary voice assured her she was setting them all up for a giant fall. An epic dive down a razor-sharp cliff edge and possibly into a pool of old pain made fresh.

Lost in her thoughts, she hadn't heard Jesse approach until he was inside the kitchen and the back door whooshed shut behind him. Angela blinked her surprise and hoped everything she felt wasn't as easy to read in the concern lines on her face as she imagined.

"I cleared the perennial bed of weeds. Doggone snakes will be trying to nest there if I don't stay on top of it. The hibiscus has overgrown its spot. I'll trim it up tomorrow." He helped himself to a bottle of water from the fridge and drank half of it before Angela mustered her nerve.

"I noticed you from the window," she said, forcing some cheer into her voice. This conversation was bound to get heavy soon enough.

Jesse nodded and dragged a shop towel from his back pocket. He wiped the sweat from his brow.

"I saw you pausing at the banyan tree. It's known as the spot for leaving wishes on Wishing Beach, is it not?"

He stopped in mid-motion for a fraction of a second then slowly returned the towel to its resting place. "Old island proverb says to be wary of women who ask questions they already know the answer to."

Angela toyed with the handle on her coffee mug. "Were you making a wish?"

Jesse's deep green eyes were trained on her for a long moment, not unlike a curious animal sniffing around the opening to a cage. "I don't think the Wishing Beach works for me, Angie. I suppose I've sat under that tree a hundred times wishing for this thing or that. In my estimation, if it works at all, it's choosy about who it bestows its power upon."

His words made her sad. "Jesse, can I talk to you about something?"

"Anything," he said, without hesitation.

For a moment, Angela changed her mind about telling him, about digging around in things that were none of her business, about going to France at all. There were real people with real feelings involved, and it could all blow up in their faces. Jesse had always been open with her. Except of course, about the work with victims he'd done over the years. Why did she feel the need to press about his personal life? "I'm going to Paris, Jesse," she blurted.

His face lit. "Ah, that's wonderful. When do you leave?"

"Two weeks. I'm going with Ryan."

A cloud came over Jesse's face. "You don't really know him well enough to be traveling so far with him, do you?"

"It's not like that."

Jesse tilted his head and rubbed a hand over his chin. "I'm certainly no expert in the love department, but I know what a rebound is."

Angela crossed the kitchen and placed her hands on his upper arms. "Your concern touches my heart, Uncle Jesse."

"Well, isn't that what you wanted to talk to me about, my advice?"

Angela smiled and dropped her hands from him.

"Well, it's not my business to tell you who you can and can't travel with. But ... I don't want to see you get hurt."

"I do appreciate your concern. But Ryan and I are not going together. I mean, we are, but we're not a couple." Exactly. What were they? "We'll have separate rooms."

Under his deep tan, Jesse turned red and dropped his gaze. "That's none of my business, for sure."

"We're friends. We're mostly just really good friends. We're not going away together for a romantic getaway. There's a purpose to this trip." Her last few words were slow, cautious.

Outside, the wind had kicked up. Hurricane season, so that wasn't uncommon. This particular wind pressed hard against the windowsills, shoving its way inside through every crack in the walls and window frames. It was a bossy wind. "Uncle Jesse." Her tone was soft. "We're going to Paris because we found out that Olivia lives there."

The edges of his mouth turned down. The frown looked out of place on him. His voice was gone when he whispered, "Why would you do that?"

Once, when Angela was seven, she'd gotten caught

stealing a five-dollar bill out of her mother's wallet. She'd wanted to use the money to buy food for the stray cat that was skin and bones and slinked through their neighborhood with a limp. She'd left out table scraps, but the cat had always turned her nose up at them. Angela's mother saw her stealing the money. It was the most embarrassed Angela had ever been. Until now. She opened her mouth to explain, but words failed. Why was she doing this? Inside her head, it all made sense. But hearing Jesse, seeing his face—it confirmed this idea was one hair shy of crazy. "I know how it sounds. And I know you probably don't want me to do this, but Jesse, if she's the girl you told me about, I don't think she left town of her own free will."

His eyes pleaded. "We were kids! Whether she left or not of her own will, doesn't really matter in the big scheme of things. Things happen ... probably, the way they need to happen. She didn't come back. Okay? The reason is of no consequence."

"I just want you to have some answers."

Jesse's mouth became a hard line. "I didn't ask you for answers. I don't want this. I can't stop you from going to Paris, but I don't want any part of it. And I don't want any details about Olivia when you return." Jesse left the kitchen.

Angela sank onto a nearby barstool. Would she never learn to mind her own business?

OLIVIA WAS LIVING IN PARIS, France. Jesse had said the words over and over again in his mind. He felt bad for the way he'd handled Angela, but there was a whole lot to consider. He'd always felt like Olivia deserved more out of life than he could give her. She came from another world, rich, beautiful, a Travis Perry world. But they decided they could make their own world. Just the two of them. What they'd shared had been special—star-crossed lovers kind of special—and the one thing he clung to was that it really was special for both of them. In his mind, nearly forty years ago, a boy fell in love with a beautiful girl, and if it weren't for ... parents, society, a couple of college kids with meanest in their hearts, and who knows what else, maybe they would be together today. This was a past he could live with. Whatever Angela may find in Paris might not be.

Reality had a way of shredding the single thing that held your memories together.

CHAPTER FIFTEEN

Angela found her seat while Ryan lifted her carryon into the overhead bin. She'd struggled with it, and he'd taken it gingerly, mumbling about if the spot directly overhead was clear. She'd mumbled a "yes" back to him, and this was how their navigation of things seemed to go. It was becoming second nature for Angela. She was beginning to "see" what Ryan saw. It wasn't until she glanced around that she noticed a few people were watching them. An elderly lady sitting nearby watched Ryan's every move as his white cane dangled from his wrist while he situated the carryon, then slid his backpack off his shoulders and expertly placed it beneath his aisle seat.

Angela grinned as he dropped into the seat and folded his long legs. "You really are an expert traveler, aren't you?" She'd marveled at the small suitcase he'd checked and the backpack he carried. She'd over packed, of course. And now, she was going through the long list of items she may have forgotten. It didn't take her mind off the impending flight. Her fingers drummed the cool metal of the armrest.

"Nervous?" Ryan asked. His voice was smooth as glass and calmed her if only for a moment.

"Nope," she squeaked.

"Liar."

"I'm nervous as a cat. Talk to me, Ryan, tell me something. Anything."

The look on his face changed. It was a small thing, but one that sent a shiver over her chest. Heightened nerves, that was all it was. His warm hand closed around hers. How did he always know exactly where to find her fingers? He always knew when she needed shoring up. "Okay. I'll tell you something if you promise not to freak out on me."

"You may have missed the point of talking. I'm already trying to not freak out."

"How's it working?"

She squeezed his hand. "Not well."

"Then allow me to change the subject." Ryan's voice was low and so close to her ear that each exhale moved the hair against her throat. Still, he leaned closer and when her mass of curls was in the way, he gently reached with his free hand and dragged a finger along her hairline. His lips brushed her ear when he said, "There's no one I'd rather be going to Paris with than you."

Black spots dotted her vision. Her head pounded, and she realized she needed to breathe. A moment of euphoria was replaced with all the reasons why he needed to not say such things.

Another puff of air danced over her ear, and Angela fought the urge to drink it in, drink him in. "Angela," he whispered. "I'm not going to push for anything romantic because I know you don't want that, but I'm also not going to ignore the fact that I'm extremely attracted to you. I'll bide my time, but the truth is …" His lips moist and warm dropped a kiss on her earlobe. "I want you, Angela."

She tried to swallow. Nothing. Even her eyelids were sweating. He needed to stop, just stop talking. They were sitting in a crowded airplane, and yet this was by far the most intimate conversation they'd ever shared. It felt … naughty. And that alone heightened every sensation. The slowly hissing air from the overhead vent, the tightness of her seat belt along her hips, the scent of Ryan and his womanizing cologne. It should be called Doomed. Because a girl was pretty much doomed when she breathed it in. There was a sudden deafening roar that drowned out the last of his words.

Beside her, she felt him moving, gentle shakes of his shoulders. Angela was confused, dazed. She opened her eyes and looked over to find a grinning Cheshire cat excuse of a Ryan beside her. His tongue ran over his teeth, but this wasn't sexy, it was cocky. Way too cocky, like he was in on a secret she hadn't figured out. He was chuckling. "Take offs and landings, huh?"

It was then that Angela noticed the smooth hum of the engine. They were in the air. She'd been effectively baited. "You jerk." She'd be angry if it wasn't so funny.

"And you said I wasn't hot." He brushed his fingernails over his chest. "That makes you a liar."

"Me? You're the one seducing an innocent woman in public. What does that make you?"

He laughed. "Not my fault. You're the one who said to talk to you. Tell you anything."

"Well, I didn't mean *that*."

He tilted his seat back and closed his eyes. "Wait until you see what I have planned for you before we are over the ocean."

She pulled away so they were no longer touching. "I might change seats."

"Good," he grumbled, but smiled after. "Let someone else babysit you."

She punched his shoulder, causing him to jolt. The elderly woman beside them gave her a dirty look.

"Hey, don't abuse the blind guy when there are witnesses," Ryan said. Angela buried her head in her hands and prayed the flight wouldn't be long. There were worse things than takeoffs and landings and flying over the ocean, she decided. There was mock seduction.

THEY ARRIVED TIRED and went straight to the hotel. A small taxi with hazy windows offered little view of the city. Daylight would be in a couple hours, so they decided to get settled in, then freshen up and attack the city. Angela yawned as they stepped off the elevator, then worked their way down a hallway. The ceilings were high, heavy with ornate crown moldings that created a beautiful tapestry as they walked. Beneath their feet, deep burgundy carpet was a welcoming river, leading the way to their room. She'd noticed Ryan— one hand grazing the wall—counting as they passed tall white doors with wrought iron knobs and small numbers.

Their room was on the ninth floor of the hotel. "We're getting close, yes?" he asked.

Even though they'd spent a lot of time together, Angela still marveled at his almost superhuman senses. "Right here," she said, stepping toward their suite door. With key in hand, she opened the door expecting a somewhat casual room on the other side. Angela gasped. The impossibly high ceilings were a perfect backdrop for a fairytale space. Along the far wall, tall narrow French doors led to a balcony. Her gaze jetted past the beautifully appointed room and straight to the Eiffel tower that rested far in the background, perfectly framed by their French doors.

Ryan bumped her shoulder. "Nice, huh?"

"Nice? It's a palace." Inside, she dropped her purse and bags—along the wall so as not to trip Ryan. "I mean, it's huge!"

"I know. Unusual for Paris. This is our America equivalent of a penthouse. The owner, Matthew insisted. I haven't been here for a while, and I guess he thought I could impress you with this fabulous place."

She moved to his side and realized he was still carrying a backpack and holding one of her bags. She slid the overnight case from him. "Consider me impressed. Please give your friend my deepest thank you."

"He's out of the country for a couple of weeks. But he assured me he'd alerted the staff to take good care of us. Do you want to rest for a bit?" He took the backpack off and Angela began walking him around the room, making sure he knew where the furniture and any tripping hazards were.

"Rest? No. No way! I slept on the plane, and I know you did too because I could hear you snoring."

"What? I did not snore." But Ryan grinned.

"Like a freight train," she teased.

"I'm surprised you heard me. What with all the mumbling and moaning you were doing. What were you dreaming about, Angela?"

She was glad he couldn't see the red stain on her face. "Which room is mine?"

He reached out for her. "Come on, I'll show you."

Angela took his hand and found it deliciously scandalous to be following a handsome man into a bedroom in a foreign city known as a place for falling in love. She pushed those devilish thoughts from her mind and concentrated on her surroundings. They left the living room, and she glanced into the kitchen—galley styled, stone countertops, all black and white with cranberry accents. Very elegant and very French.

The rich four poster bed made her heart sigh. This was a place for a queen. Not for her.

Ryan was beside her. Her shoulder grazing his bicep. "What's wrong, Angela?" he whispered.

Gah. Her nose tingled. "Wrong? Nothing. Everything is perfect."

He slipped an arm around her and hugged her shoulders. It wasn't intimate. Just brotherly. And she was suddenly thankful for Ryan, for his kindness, his friendship. "While you unpack, decide what you want to see first."

"Everything!" She'd burst if she didn't get outside and begin exploring.

Ryan laughed. "Okay, okay. We'll see everything. But what do you want to see first?"

Angela gave a half shrug. "Everything."

"We'll start at *Notre Dame*. We can't tour inside right now —it's closed due to the fire, but it's such an amazing structure. For the best view, we'll visit the *Brasserie Le Notre Dame* for an espresso or a café au lait. Their croissants are delicious. They melt in your mouth, and we'll need the fuel. Although, I'm not sure you need the caffeine."

He was correct. She was bouncing like Tigger on the inside. One little push and she'd be springing up and down on the fine Egyptian rug beneath her sensible shoes.

Angela unpacked in record time after showing Ryan to his room and alerting him where the hazards were. Since he'd stayed here before, he appeared to be at ease, so she rushed back to her royal quarters and tossed her things in the armoire. She arranged her toiletries in neat rows on the bathroom counter, and then she stared out her bedroom window at the city beneath, scarcely believing she was there. Less than a dozen hours ago she was on Wishing Beach Island. Now, she was in Paris. When Ryan hollered to ask if she was ready, she bounded from her room.

They walked arm in arm, and Ryan used his cane—something he didn't do often back home. "Is it easier to navigate here with your cane?"

"It's more about feeling confident. It keeps my mind from wondering if there's suddenly something that might trip me up. Even the sidewalks date back hundreds of years. Level they are not. Plus, it frees you up to look around instead of constantly making sure the path is clear."

While staying in step with the other early morning travelers, they walked until she saw the cathedral. As they neared the massive structure, she noticed how much grander it was than any photos or movies could ever portray, even with the various tell-tale signs of renovation, the cathedral was breathtaking. For a few moments, she could only pause and stare. "Stunning."

"I used to come here in the early morning hours with an espresso and a laptop. "The inspiration is pretty intense. In the fall, fog rolls up over the cathedral and it looks like something from another time and another world. Ethereal."

Angela glanced over. He was wearing sunglasses, as he so often did, but she could see his profile and had to wonder if Paris was as inspiring for him now. Now that he was mostly sightless. She squeezed his arm a little tighter. Her gaze trailed across the street. "I'm so aware I'm no longer stateside."

"Well, the French signs will do that."

"Not just that. It feels different. And the architecture. Everything is gloriously old." Excitement was getting the better of her again.

"Come on, we need coffee." They crossed over to the corner café.

"Hey, I've seen this place before. In movies, maybe. Or travel guides." The tight row of outdoor tables spanned the entire corner and were already nearly half full, even though the streets weren't crowded. A thin green and beige awning sheltered the seats. They found a spot in the far corner and ordered.

"You probably have seen it before," Ryan said. He'd chosen to sit beside her, instead of across from her. She liked that. "*Brasserie Notre Dame* is quite famous because of the celebrities that often drop by."

For a time, they sat quietly while Angela watched couples and families pass. She ate a large *pain au chocolat* croissant, and Ryan ordered his favorite, *pain aux raisins*. "I'd love to see Notre Dame from every angle—since we can't go inside."

He shot her a winning smile over his pastry. "We will. I promise. But not today."

She glanced over at him. "Why?"

He leaned closer to her and ran a hand over her exposed arm. "I have something else for you today," he said, his low tone melting a little piece of her heart. "But you have to trust me."

Trust him? Yes, she realized. The resolution of her trust caused a breathlessness she couldn't explain, leaving Angela surprised so could extend such trust in such a short time. But with Ryan, that came easily. There never seemed to be an ulterior motive. There never seemed to be an agenda. Plus, Ryan had a talent for seeing things in the splendid way they were intended to be seen. Had he always been like this? Is that what made him such a good writer? "I trust you, Ryan."

He gave a quick nod of approval. "Angela, when do you want to call Olivia?"

She dropped her head. "I can't believe I came all this way to make a phone call."

"I'm good with knocking on her door."

"Well, that seems even more creepy and stalker-ish than a phone call."

"What are you going to say?" he pressed.

"I'm going to tell her I live on the island, we have a mutual friend, and would it be okay to meet for coffee?"

"You could say you admire her art," Ryan offered.

"That would be a lie. I haven't seen her art."

Ryan produced a piece of paper from his front pocket. "It wouldn't be a lie if we go visit the gallery where her sculptures are sold."

Tigger again. "Really? You didn't tell me you had this!" She plucked the paper from him and stared at the address he'd scribbled on the page. It was legible. But Ryan had a habit of placing the words and numbers very closely together. Probably from not being able to see them as anything but a shadow. Still, the address of the *Beaute de L'Art Gallery* was easy to decipher.

"It's a few blocks down. Shall we?"

They left the café and meandered along the Seine while Ryan gave her a rundown of French art terms he'd learned doing research for a book. From Neoclassicism to Cubism, Ryan talked on, his voice a perfect complement to the scenery. His words were velvety, each one a symphony. She stopped at the edge of the river.

"Are you okay?" Ryan asked.

She had tensed. He noticed. Of course. "It's just a lot to take in," Angela admitted. This was the second time she'd been overwhelmed by the city around her, and in only a short time. But it wasn't just the city. The tiniest of voices far in the deepest corner of her mind whispered. Her reaction to this place also had to do with who she was sharing it with. Ryan saw everything. Or more aptly, he chose to experience everything rather than rush past.

He gave her time. When they'd stood quietly for several minutes, Ryan began talking again in his soft, warm tone. "We'll visit the *Louvre* tomorrow. You can spend an entire day doing the *Louvre* alone, but we'll add *Pompidou*. If you're a fan of the impressionists, we can spend a few hours at the *Musee d'Orsay*. The museum is housed in a former railway station. The building is as spectacular as the artwork with its high arched ceilings and surround window architecture. You're going to love it, Angela."

When she turned to face him, she could easily detect how much joy this adventure was bringing him. There was an expectancy about him. "Like Christmas morning," she whispered.

"What?"

Angela tilted her head back and let the sun dry the fresh tears in her eyes. "You look like it is Christmas morning, and you're getting ready to unwrap an amazing gift."

Ryan reached to her cheek. "I'm watching you unwrap the gift, Angela. Paris is the gift." He leaned toward her and dropped a light kiss on her cheekbone. "Fits perfectly, doesn't it?"

She didn't pull away from him after the kiss, instead she wound her arms around his waist and rested her head against his chest. There, they stood for a long time with the sounds of Paris enveloping them.

Yes, in fact. It did fit perfectly.

As evening fell, the city changed from bright and cheery to warm and sultry. The blanket of night created an almost utopian atmosphere. The day had been amazing, and now they were sitting at a bistro just outside their hotel. Angela couldn't stop thinking about the sculptures they'd seen at the *Beaute de L'Art Gallery*. "Be honest with me, Ryan. I'm not making this up, right?"

"Are you talking about the statues Olivia sculpted?"

Angela sipped her espresso and thought back to the room filled with tall, beautiful contemporary statues that resembled bodies intertwined. Each one had been unique and more than a little on the *avant garde* side. From stone bases, two pillars—the male a sepia tone, the female an off white—were wrapped together. Each statue stood placed on a base of ocean waves crashing up the sides of the subjects and a sandy bottom beneath them. Some of the sculptures were no more than two to three feet tall. Some were as tall as Ryan. But the intention was evident. Two opposing shades—a perfect complement for each other, interlocked in an ethereal dance of strength and beauty.

Angela had described each to Ryan as they worked their way through the gallery. But when the gallery owner came near, he suggested Ryan feel the statue to get a sense of it. He'd done that with several. "Yes … the sculptures."

"No, Angela. You're not making up what they symbolize. Even without sight I could see they are personal to the artist."

"Those sculptures represent Olivia and Jesse, don't they?"

"We may be making a giant leap, but yes." Ryan finished his baguette and dusted the breadcrumbs from his mouth. "I think they do."

"She still loves him too, Ryan. Why else would she still be sculpting likenesses of the two of them?"

Ryan grinned. "The city of love may have gone to your head. I never pegged you for such a romantic, Angela."

She brushed a hand through her hair. The Paris breeze had worked its way through the strands the better part of the day. "I never would have pegged myself as a romantic either. All I know is forty years ago, two people who were in love were ripped apart. And if those statues are any indication, Olivia is still broken about it. We already know Jesse is. Ryan, maybe we can reunite them."

Ryan slid his plate away and rested his forearm on the table. "Angela Reed, did you get me here under false pretenses?" When she didn't answer, he continued. "Did you bring me to Paris under the guise of learning what happened all those years ago when in fact, this is a Cupid mission?"

She pressed a hand to her heart. "Excuse me, but *you're* the one who brought *me* here."

"New plan. The *Louvre* will have to wait. Tomorrow you call Olivia."

A fresh wave of apprehension hit Angela. "Maybe we should wait—"

"No. Tomorrow. Deal?"

Their server left with their tab after Ryan handed him a credit card. "No backing out."

"Okay. Tomorrow I call Olivia and see if she'll meet us to talk."

"Great. Now, let's get you back to the hotel so you can collapse into that heavenly bed."

A thrill raced down Angela's back. There was so much to love about Paris.

$\sim$

"I CAN'T BELIEVE we're standing here." Angela's throat had gone dry.

Ryan reached to knock on the door of the apartment. It was in a beautiful building with high ceilings and windows that viewed the park. They stood on a freshly polished marble floor hallway. Angela grabbed Ryan before his hand made contact with the door.

"Wait," she said. "I'm not ready."

Earlier that morning, she'd dialed Olivia's number from Ryan's cell, but she couldn't bring herself to connect the call. Over and over she'd done this. Each time, changing what she'd say then hanging up before the call was actually connected. She'd finally uttered, "We need to do this in person."

"Knock, Angela. You're stalling. This is why we came, remember?"

She knew it was why they'd jumped on a plane and flew to Paris. Ryan gave her arm a gentle squeeze. When she remained statue stiff, he lifted her hand, kissed her knuckles, and proceeded to place them against the door. "The rest is up to you," he whispered.

Angela drew a steadying breath, then knocked. She jumped when the door flew open as if the woman had been waiting on the other side. "Hello," Angela said, a shake in her voice.

"Oh, hello." The woman looked from one to the other. "I didn't realize someone had knocked. I was heading out."

She was lovely. Silvery blonde hair and bright blue eyes. She didn't look almost sixty years old. The woman wore a black sleeveless turtleneck—very stylish and black capri pants. Angela tried to find her in the photograph of Olivia.

The moment stretched, and the woman blinked. Concern sifted into her features. She had a faint French accent. "I'm sorry, can I help you?" Where her tone had been friendly, it now sounded forced. Angela needed to speak. Where were her words? Was this Olivia?

Ryan stretched out his hand. "Are you Olivia Murray?"

When she didn't answer, he continued. "My name is Ryan North, and this is a close friend of mine, Angela Reed. We are so sorry to bother you, but—"

Angela's brain kicked in and she took over. "But we have a mutual friend and Ryan and I both live on an island you once visited. We're from Wishing Beach."

For several moments there was silence. Outside a delivery truck sailed past, the hum of traffic filled the air. His hand had not been taken in greeting, so Ryan dropped it slowly to his side. The woman at the door swallowed, a myriad of emotions playing across her face. "Wishing Beach," she whispered.

"Yes. Do you know it?"

"Of course. And the two of you are on vacation here?"

Ryan leaned toward Angela. "She'd never seen Paris. We're staying at the *Bleu Lavande* Hotel near the *Louvre*."

"I see." Her chin tilted up a degree. Her eyes were moist. "Perhaps you two should come in for a few minutes."

Ryan took Angela by the elbow so she could guide him into the unknown atmosphere. They stepped inside the well-appointed apartment. Contemporary artwork decorated the walls and the furniture was an eclectic blend of old-world charm and sleek new pieces all pulled together with brightly colored accent pillows and high-end details. A perfect fusion of old and new. It was definitely an artist's house.

When she turned to face them, Olivia said, "Wishing Beach. Such a very long time ago that I was there."

"So, you are Olivia?" Angela couldn't help but take a step toward her.

Olivia smiled, and Angela could finally see the girl in the photograph. She'd been right there all along, just hidden. "Yes, I am. And your name is Angela *Reed*? There were Reeds on the island when we visited. A house just down from the Perrys' on—" she snapped her fingers, "Oh, what did they call that section of beach?"

"Millionaire's Cove," Angela answered her.

"Yes. My mother and Mrs. McGovern often had lunch with Mrs. Reed."

"Claire. Claire Reed is my mom. I live at Baker House—which I no longer call Baker House. Ryan lives just down the beach from me."

Olivia nodded. "I only visited the one summer. You said we have a mutual friend?"

"Yes," Angela said. She hadn't offered them a place to sit,

so they continued to stand in the center of Olivia's living room. "Jesse, Jesse Malone is a friend of ours."

The concern returned to her features, shadowing those inviting blue eyes. Olivia seemed to travel a million miles away, the pressure of her past, a heavy weight, stealing the air from the room. Olivia's fingers covered her mouth drawing Angela's attention to the giant, bewildered globes that were Olivia's eyes. "He's alive?" Her words were barely audible. She sank into a nearby chair.

Angela reached out a steadying hand, concerned Olivia might faint. "Oh, yes. Jesse is fine. He's just fine."

Olivia's shoulders dropped as the color drained from her. She lowered her quivering hand to her lap.

Heart pounding, Angela shot a look to Ryan. He slipped his hand into Angela's. What was happening here? Why would Olivia assume Jesse was dead?

And more importantly, were they getting close to hearing what had happened after that horrible day?

Olivia was chalky white, a stark contrast to the black she wore. Angela knew she needed to ease Olivia into this. The woman was too tightly strung to launch headlong into the answering of questions. "Ryan and I toured the art gallery, Olivia. I might be way off, but I think your work is a monument to the love you and Jesse shared."

"It was so long ago," Olivia said softly, her gaze far off as memories seemed to carry her away from them to another time. She threaded her fingers together.

Angela waited for her to continue. Olivia was getting agitated. They were losing her.

Angela sank onto the nearby loveseat so she could look Olivia in the eye. "Why did you leave, Olivia?"

"Well because I—" The lost look returned. Lost and frightened. Then her features hardened. "What did you say your names were?"

Ryan, still standing, spoke. "Ryan North."

"And I'm Angela Reed. I live on the Cove. Jesse lives on the grounds there. He works for me."

Olivia jetted out of the seat, her composure back as if their conversation hadn't happened. "Um, you know, I think we need more time. I was just headed out when you arrived. I have to spend a couple of days in London. How long are you visiting Paris?"

"We leave Saturday morning," Ryan said.

"I see. Could the two of you meet me Friday evening for coffee? We have a lot to talk about." She moved toward the front door, so Angela and Ryan followed.

Olivia held the door open, and when they stepped outside, Olivia touched Angela's arm. "Angela, it was very good to meet you both. Seven o'clock on Friday evening at the coffee shop across from your hotel?"

"Yes," Angela said with a soft smile.

"Will you be talking to Jesse before Friday?" Olivia's perfectly arched brows tilted into a frown.

"I don't think so."

"If you do, please don't tell him that you found me. When we meet on Friday, things will make sense, I promise."

Before Angela could answer, Olivia locked her door, tossed her keys in her shoulder bag, and hurried down the hall toward the steps.

CHAPTER SIXTEEN

Two more days of sightseeing had taken Angela—along with her ever indulgent guide, Ryan—to Versailles as well as the top of the Eiffel Tower. Touristy, yes. But these landmarks were unlike any in the states. They'd been here for hundreds of years instead of decades. They'd survived world wars and seen their population diminished by famines and disease. And still, they stood. Glorious. Beautiful. Monuments to life.

Angela remained quiet while they'd toured the catacombs. Six million skeletons had been moved, back in the nineteenth century, when a wall collapsed under the weight of too many bodies in the adjoining graveyard. The task began. The movers worked at night and over the next several years. Skeletal remains were relocated to the catacombs creating an eerie place to visit, one that was thick with the presence of the quiet dead.

Angela pulled fresh breath into her lungs as they left the catacombs.

"You didn't like it?" Ryan asked.

"Fascinating. But also kind of heavy. If that makes sense."

He nodded. "Let's get coffee."

"Better idea. Let's get gelato."

She snaked her arm through his and rested her free hand on his forearm. She'd spotted the gelato shop earlier in the week and was hoping they'd try it before she left. "I can't believe we're able to eat anything, the way we've feasted for days."

"Well, we've eaten small meals."

"Small meals a dozen times a day," Angela corrected. They stopped at a streetlight and she watched cars zooming by. "I think I've gained ten pounds since we've been here."

Ryan turned to face her and lifted his hands to her cheeks. Slowly, he moved his fingers and palms over her skin, unsettling her sunglasses. "You haven't gained anything."

Her cheeks were hot. Could he feel the heat in them? "Let's hope I haven't gained all the weight in my face."

One of Ryan's brows shot up and he shrugged, taking her words as an obvious invitation to explore more. He dropped his hands to her shoulders and then tucked them under her arms, slowly grazing over her ribcage on either side as he worked his way to her hips.

Angela's breath caught. She glanced left and right, but the truth was, she didn't care who saw them. She didn't care that they were on a busy street corner waiting to cross the road.

When Ryan's hands landed on her hips, he grinned and murmured, "You're perfect."

Well then. What did one say to that? Nothing. Words could only ruin this faultless moment, so she remained quiet.

They ate gelato tucked into a small table overlooking the park.

"I was thinking about how awful it would be to get lost in the catacombs with the lights out." Angela searched her gelato for more bits of toffee. "But I realized that you would be able to navigate just as well. Lights. No lights. Is it wrong to say that made me feel more at ease?"

"Are you claustrophobic?"

"No. Well, yes. A little. Only when my mind goes wandering. I was standing there thinking what we would do if the lights suddenly flickered and went off."

Ryan grinned around his hazelnut gelato. "Flickered and went off, huh?"

"Mm hm."

"Angela, you have the mind of an author."

She shrugged past those words. "I was thinking how scary it would be to reach out to find your way and feel a skull. But then I remembered that you were with me. You can navigate anything, Ryan. I have so much respect for that."

They were no longer talking about lights in the catacombs. Ryan had navigated the path of being sighted to going blind. He'd kept his joy, his humor in the face of insurmountable odds. "I'm really impressed with you. That's what I'm trying to say."

He grinned. "Impressed *and* you think I'm hot."

She scoffed. "I never said you were hot. *You* said that."

"You agreed."

"I did not," she countered. The sun shone down on them, throwing sparks off Ryan's aviators. His elbow was propped on their small round table, and his spoon was about to drip onto his arm. Before she could stop herself, Angela reached over, grabbed Ryan's hand, and dragged the spoon to her mouth. She licked the melting gelato.

Ryan, who'd been at ease, suddenly seemed as frozen as the statues at the Palace of Versailles. But not frozen in a bad way. Not frozen because of being horrified or even shocked. He simply went perfectly still as if he didn't want to miss what was happening.

Angela blushed. Her hand was still wrapped around

Ryan's and she slowly loosened her grip on him. But he caught her hand before she could move away. There, with their gelato melting in tiny cups between them, Ryan slipped the spoon into his own mouth. Angela's hand was trapped between his two and the moment took on a whole different feel—one that was far too intimate for a busy city sidewalk. Even in Paris.

"Mm," he said, and let the word linger on his tongue. "I've been wanting to taste you."

Ice cold gelato had done nothing to cool her off, Angela realized as she lay on her ornate bed staring up at the detailed ceiling and watching the lights of Paris at midnight flash shadows and highlights across her room.

Ryan. What to do about Ryan. It was too soon after her divorce to be involved with anyone. Then again, was it? She and Brice had been separated for months before the divorce was final.

Whether she liked it or not, her friendship with Ryan had morphed into something more. She felt it. She knew Ryan felt it. But oh my. What to *do* about it?

She punched her pillow and rolled for the hundredth time trying to find a comfortable spot on the heavenly bed.

Ryan. He was everything Brice wasn't, and just the fact that she was comparing the two proved she wasn't ready for a relationship. Then again, maybe it was too late. She and Ryan were in—well, something. Some inexplicable friendship—not exactly a full and hearty meal, but more like a kind of soup. That was it. Soup. Relationships were meat and potatoes. What she had with Ryan was thinner, less filling. Soup. Or maybe stew. Yes. She had Ryan stew. Angela had always loved stew.

Oh Lord. She really needed to get some sleep.

"You're fidgeting again."

Angela exhaled and drew her fidgeting fingers into fists. "She's late."

"Only by a few minutes," Ryan-stew interjected.

They sat at the coffee shop across from their hotel as instructed by Olivia. Angela had chosen three different tables since they'd arrived, moving their drinks and bumping into other customers as she rearranged their seating. She'd finally settled on a table that overlooked the street where she could watch the main doors of the hotel in case Olivia went there instead.

Angela rested her elbow on the table and propped her chin on her upturned palm. "Where on earth is she?"

For the next two hours, she continued to ask that. One at a time, they'd taken turns leaving the table and going over to the hotel to pack. They'd leave the following morning, and right now, it looked as though they'd leave without seeing Olivia. Anger and concern took turns on Angela's psyche. "Should I try to call her again?"

"Sure," Ryan said.

Angela could see the truth hidden behind his aviators. "You think she stood us up."

He rubbed a hand over his chin. "I don't know, Angela. Something changed in her while we were standing in her apartment. After that, it felt like she was just trying to get rid of us, to be honest."

Why hadn't Angela noticed that? She'd been so wrapped up in the fact that they'd found her, the fact that she had certainly loved Jesse. Making this nightmare worse, Angela had told Jesse when he'd called the following day to check on her. She'd said they'd found Olivia and were meeting her for coffee on Friday night. He'd been full of hope, he'd kept his words to a minimum, but she knew him well enough to hear the excitement in his voice.

"And don't forget, she made a point to ask if you'd speak to Jesse before we saw her again. And instead of saying to tell him hello, she said to keep the fact that we'd met her a secret. Why? What's her goal? What's her motivation?"

Angela's heart couldn't sink much lower. She opened her mouth, but nothing came out. "I don't know. You're the writer. You tell me what her motivation is."

"If she was one of my characters—and she cared for Jesse —she'd rather he not find out we'd met her. She doesn't want to hurt him, but she also *clearly* doesn't want to have anything to do with him. She got rid of us. She had no intention of meeting us here today. It was a snap decision to get us out of her apartment."

Angela's heart sank. "Once she was a no-show, we wouldn't bother to tell Jesse we'd ever found her. Is that what you're suggesting, Ryan?"

"Yes. But only because something changed. I don't recall exactly what we were talking about with her, but I remember sensing the change in the atmosphere. She seemed..."

"Angry? Frustrated that we were there? What?"

"Anxious maybe, or frightened."

THEIR PLANE LANDED LATE in the night. The Uber dropped Ryan off at his house and drove the short distance to hers. Angela expected the house to be dark and silent. But lights were on, not off, and though she liked the idea of not coming home to an empty cavern, the last person in the world she wanted to see right now was Jesse. Why had she opened her big mouth and told him they'd found Olivia?

When she stepped inside, the scent of hot cocoa filled her

nose and the unmistakable sound of someone puttering around in the kitchen drew her deeper into the house. Jesse used a ladle to scoop a steaming cup of cocoa, then held it out to her. She hugged him as she took it.

"How was Paris?" Jesse's usually wavy dark hair was ruffled, and he looked like he could use a good night's sleep.

"Uncle Jesse, I need to talk to you about Olivia. I—"

Intensity gathered around his eyes, making the dark irises almost unbearable. "I can't tell you how much it means to know she's alive. To know that she's okay."

Angela placed the cup on the counter with a little too much force. As the hours had passed, she'd become increasingly angrier with Olivia. What a horrible thing to do. "Jesse, she may not be the person you remember."

"Of course," he agreed. "It was forty years ago. She was just a girl then. But I bet she still has that beautiful smile and those gem-like blue eyes."

Angela's heart sank farther and farther in her chest. "Oh Jesse. I don't know how to say this." She'd thought she'd have all night to worry over the words and to get them right. Instead, here she was.

"What's wrong, Angela?"

"Olivia. She—"

He stepped back. "Did something happen to her?" The tension around him thickened to the point Angela thought she could cut it with a kitchen knife.

"No. She's okay. She just—"

"She what?"

"She didn't show up for our meeting."

Understanding worked its way over his features, filling his eyes with questions. "Maybe something happened—"

"No, Jesse." Angela's words were stern. "She used the meeting to get rid of us at her house. When I look back on it, I don't know why I didn't see it."

"I'm sure she had her reasons." He looked away but not soon enough to hide the disappointment in his eyes.

Angela reached out and took his hands in hers. "I believe the Olivia you knew all those years ago loved you, I could see it in her eyes ... in her work. She just—she's changed. She's no longer that person."

"What do you mean in her work?" When Angela didn't answer, he became more forceful. "What do you *mean*?" His tone was sharp, the kind reserved for bad little children who'd disobeyed.

Feeling as though she couldn't sink any lower, Angela recalled the artwork. "Oh Jesse, I know she loved you. Then. She has an entire collection of sculptures that are a man and woman intertwined with waves and beach sand holding them captive. They're ... the most beautiful things I've ever seen." Giant tears slipped from Angela's eyes. She brushed the back of her hand at them and tilted her head back hoping to capture more before they fell. It was then that she realized Jesse too had tears. They spilled over his eyelids and onto his ruddy cheeks. "I didn't tell you about those on the phone, Uncle Jesse because I wanted you to see them. To see the monument she built to your love, but now—"

His lips were quivering when he said, "Now what?"

"Well, as I said. She's not the girl you knew. Not anymore. Of that, I'm certain."

He slowly drew his gaze away from hers. "That's a lot to assume from one missed meeting."

"When I look back, it all makes sense. I so badly wanted this to go differently." She looked down to hide her shame. "I'm sorry, Jesse."

"Hey ..." He put his hands on her upper arms and gave her a gentle shake. "It's okay. It's all okay." He dropped his hands. "Come, let's sit down and enjoy the delicious cocoa I worked so hard to prepare. And you can tell me all about Paris."

Angela looked up at his smiling face but the usual gleam in his eyes was gone. Because of her, it was gone. She gave him a weak smile. They settled themselves at the table. Jesse brought over the hot pan from the stove being careful to set the pan down on a potholder he'd tossed on the table with his bad hand so that he could dip the steamy treat. He topped off the hot chocolate in their cups.

He toyed with his mug, his curved hand holding the handle. "What I said about not wanting to find Olivia, I take that back. I'm happy to know she's all right," Jesse said.

"After all you went through, what she did, and what she continues to do?" Angela's gaze focused on Jesse's unbending fingers. "I don't see how you can be so generous toward her." The frown of anger was still on her face. She couldn't help it. She was furious with Olivia. It was unforgivable.

"I rather expected it. Oh, not to say I wouldn't have liked it to be different, of course." Jesse let out a tired breath. "I've done a lot of soul searching while you were gone. What do I really think … you know, down deep?" He hesitated a moment gathering his thoughts. "First of all, I think, some things don't turn out the way you plan. I think it's not about the coulda, shoulda's, but about savoring those special, *magical* times. I think, if you do other than that, the magic will die." He looked Angela in the eye. "And wouldn't that be a shame?"

Angela had nothing to say to that. If Jesse could be so forgiving, she should be able to, shouldn't she? Perhaps in time.

～

255

IT TOOK Angela four days to get her suitcase emptied. All of the wonderful memories of Paris and Ryan, and Ryan and Paris, were mixed in with her failure of matching up Jesse and Olivia again. If Olivia would've just shown up like she was supposed to. Or maybe Angela was just deflecting the blame lest she take it on herself. After all, Olivia had told her not to tell Jesse that they had found her. So in reality, it was one hundred percent Angela's fault. Then again ... Well, it hardly mattered now. Olivia was an ocean away, and as far as Angela was concerned, it couldn't be far enough. On the upside, Jesse appeared to be better than ever, happy, peaceful —like he'd come to terms with the past. He seemed content. And he didn't blame her. He thanked her. She was going to take that as a win.

Angela wiggled into her hot pink and black stretch running gear. She inspected it all around in the full-length mirror. She loved the color, so she wore the outfit a lot. It made her wonder if she shouldn't change it up more. Ryan might get tired of the same-o same-o. Angela chuckled. Ryan only saw her in shadow. How often she forgot. That was indeed a testament to him.

She'd barely seen Ryan since coming home, and that was okay because she was still trying to define exactly what her feelings were for him. She had decided it was definitely too soon. Too soon after a difficult divorce to be in a serious relationship—even with Ryan-stew. At the same time, no one had supplied her with a rulebook, so she didn't know the appropriate number of weeks, months, years. Ryan wasn't pushing for anything. He simply was a wonderful calming force in her life. And once again, because of her own stupid choices, she needed a calming force. Maybe they just needed time. Eventually, could she and Ryan ...? That was a question not ready to be answered.

But today, they were going to walk-jog on the beach and

then have lunch together. She had to admit she was eager to see him.

~

JESSE WAVED BACK to Angela from the riding lawn mower as she headed across the lawn toward the beach. He knew she would more than likely be seeing Ryan. He smiled to himself. Ryan made her happy, and he was proving himself to be a man of character. As Jesse contemplated such things, he felt his phone vibrate in his pocket. He cut off the mower's engine and answered.

"Hello." There was no answer. He looked at the number on the screen, didn't recognize it.

"Hello," he said again.

"Jesse?" The voice was soft, a bit hesitant.

Every nerve in Jesse's body stood on end. He knew the voice. It was a sound cemented in his memory. "Olivia?"

"Jesse, I didn't know." A sob caught in her throat. "I'm so sorry."

"Know what? It's okay." He swallowed hard at the knot that was in his own throat. He didn't know what she was talking about, but he couldn't bear to hear Olivia cry.

"I thought you had died." This time the tears were not held back.

Jesse could hear her crying and the anguish in her voice. "Livi, it's all okay... don't cry."

"They told me ... Jesse, I wouldn't have left if I'd known." Olivia was now sobbing.

"It's okay." He didn't know how to console her, so he let her cry. Her sobs tore at his heart, and he cried silently with her.

Finally, Olivia quieted. She struggled to regain her composure. "I need to talk to you, Jesse."

257

"All right." He nodded, trying to retain some form of composure. Her voice, Olivia's voice—the one he heard in his dreams for four decades—now telling him they needed to talk.

"Do you have time now?" She said between sniffs. "It could be lengthy."

"Now is fine." He climbed off the mower and headed toward his house. It was hot out and the gravity of her tone told him there was much to be said—even more than he'd imagined. He swiped the sweat from his brow as he entered the house. Feeling a little off kilter, Jesse steadied himself against the doorframe for a few moments before heading to the kitchen. He wanted a cold drink and a good place to sit for this—a place that could hold him steady because right now, he felt like the entire earth had shifted on its axis, and he was hanging on by a thread.

Olivia was quiet for a long time. Then she said, "I buried my father this week."

Standing in the kitchen doorway Jesse stopped again. Was this why she'd called? He was puzzled. But then, he remembered, Olivia always was a puzzle. "I'm sorry, Livi. Is there anything I can do to help?"

"Thank you, but no. He was ninety-three and had been ill for a long time. Cancer. He'd outlived his four-year prognosis. Still sad, but it didn't come unexpectedly."

Fully in his kitchen, Jesse washed his hands at the sink and splashed cold water on his face, then dried off with paper towels. "So sorry for your loss. And your mom?" Grabbing a bottle of water from the refrigerator, he dropped into his favorite easy chair in the adjacent living room.

"Mother passed away five years ago."

"I am really sorry. I know it must be hard for you."

"Thank you." She paused. "This brings me to what I want to talk to you about. I want to share this with you as I heard it." She sniffed. "I'm going to start at the beginning, if you'll bear with me." She waited. Jesse was silent. "It started with the visit from your friends who came here to Paris. I assume you know about that."

"I do know about that. But I assure you I had nothing to do with it. They did it all on their own." What can of worms had they opened?

"I'm happy they came. They told me you're alive." He heard the catch in her voice. "All these years I believed you were dead. I was happy to hear you were alive, so happy. But I had to find answers, so I left. I cleared my schedule, even cancelled an art show because I couldn't rest until I understood—well, everything."

The gravity of Olivia's words caused Jesse to squeeze the water bottle. When he heard the pressure popping and clicking the plastic, he swallowed hard and loosened his grip. What on earth had Livi been through?

"I want to take you through what happened next, so you'll hear it as I did."

He could hear the desperation in her voice again. "I drove to the *Palmiers en Bord de mer* in Nice, it's a nursing home by the sea where my dad had been for some time. Dad loved the sea. As I told you, I believed you had died after ... after the night we were attacked. That's what my parents had told me." She gulped for another breath. "So, after your friends arrived here in Paris, I went to see my father. My parents had lied, Jesse. They lied about you, and I had to know the truth. All of the truth."

"Take your time, Olivia."

"My dad, he was so frail and weak, it broke my heart to look at him. When I walked into his room, he smiled and held out his hand to me. I didn't want to, but I had to know. I asked, 'Daddy, why did you tell me Jesse died?' His face crumpled and a tear fell onto his wrinkled cheek."

"He said, 'I'm so sorry, sweetheart. I'm so, sorry. Your mother ... and I felt it would be best for you to get on with your life. You were so young. You had your whole life ahead of you.'

"He broke down and just cried for the longest time. His face covered with his thin hands. Finally, he said, 'There is more ... The baby didn't die. She was put up for adoption.' He went into convulsive sobs. I put my arms around him and held him and cried with him because everything I'd believed I now knew had been a lie." Olivia choked back a sob. "Jesse, I was pregnant when I left the island, though I didn't know it at the time. Your baby, Jesse. Our baby."

Jesse didn't speak as he tried to understand. "A baby? But we ... we ..."

"I know. We only made love once." She gave a little laugh through the tears. "I guess that's all it takes."

Stunned, Jesse tried to sit his water bottle on the edge of the table. He missed and the bottle landed at his feet on its side. He watched as if in slow motion as the liquid spilled out. "I'm a father," he whispered.

"Do you hate me for not telling you?" Olivia ventured. "And for not raising the baby myself?"

"No. No, you thought I was dead. How could you tell me? We made a child, Livi. You and me. Are you ... okay?"

"No. But yes. I mean, I'm happy we made a child. I'm happy our child didn't die. I hope she has had a good life." And then, the sobs began again. "We missed everything. We missed her birthdays and her boo-boos. We missed her first love and her prom. Jesse, I don't know how to feel. On the one hand, I feel cheated. On the other, I'm so thankful your friends came. Otherwise, we'd have never known."

"I am so sorry, Livi. This must have been horrendous for you to go through alone." Anger gripped his soul. "God, I wish I had been there for you." He grabbed the empty water bottle from the floor and crushed it in his hand.

"I'm not alone now. You are alive and Jesse, we have a child."

"Maybe Wishing Beach really does grant wishes," Jesse whispered.

"My father said when they finally realized that life for me was not going to just continue as if the summer at Wishing Beach had never happened, it was too late to change what had been done. Oh, it was so sad, he was so broken." She was crying softly again. "He said, 'We thought of this terrible thing we had done every day of our lives. The only bright spot in it all was that the baby lived and was raised by a good family. The Reed family, who summered on the cove, raised your child."

"Olivia, what are you saying?" Jesse's voice was raspy.

"Yes, Jesse. It's Angela. Angela Reed is our daughter."

Caught between disbelief and euphoria, Jesse didn't know whether to laugh or cry. This might explain why he was drawn to work at the Baker House for so many years. And why he had always felt protective of Angela. He thought it had something to do with Brice's uncaring behavior. But no, it was a blood tie. "Are you sure?" Even though his heart knew it to be true, his mind wasn't catching up.

"Well, when we were on the island, my mother was mesmerized by Claire Reed and how she adopted children. Angela has brothers and sisters, am I right?"

"She does. A whole passel of them. All adopted, except her eldest brother."

"My folks had no ties to the island. Heaven knows they never intended to go back there. So, when Mrs. McGovern suggested adoption to my mother, she told her that Mrs. Reed could walk her through it. By the time Angela was born, Claire had decided she wanted Angela."

"And you didn't know any of this?"

"No. It was all kept from me. Although, I wouldn't have done anyone much good. After they said you'd died, I fell into a deep depression. I only ate because I knew the baby needed the nourishment. Half the time, I couldn't keep food down. It was a hellacious nine months. But they never let on that we weren't keeping the child. I'd picked out names, Jesse Paul for a boy and Angel Grace for a girl."

"Oh, Livi."

"I want to hate them for doing this, but at the same time, I was a wreck. And there just wasn't help for depression in those days like there is now. No wonder they did what they did."

"When did you move to Paris?"

"Right after the child was born. I had a C-section and, in those days, they put you under. I was not coherent. But I'd dreamed that I saw Mrs. Reed there at the hospital. When I questioned my mother about it, she said it was just the strong medication I was under."

"But now you know that Claire Reed really was there. Was Angela's adoptive mother part of this scandal? This lie?" Jesse found himself suddenly angry at the Reeds.

"No. My father was very clear about that. Claire Reed only knew that she was adopting Angela. They told her I didn't want to see the baby after the birth. The nurses told me I kept saying the name Angel over and over again. Maybe that's why she's named Angela? Maybe they told Claire Reed?"

"Olivia, we created a fine, beautiful, caring daughter. You would be proud of her."

"I know I would." She sniffled. "I'm glad you've had a chance to know her."

"Someday, you too, will get to know her."

"Are you going to tell her?" Olivia asked, there was a new trepidation in her voice.

"Of course I will …" Jesse stopped mid-sentence. Not telling her was something that hadn't crossed his mind. He'd just assumed … but should he? He frowned. It was a sobering thought. "I guess … I don't know yet."

"There's a lot to consider." She sat silent for a moment. Then she said, "Knowledge changes you. Sometimes forever. That summer changed me. Losing you and our baby changed me in another way, forever. Even finding out the truth has changed me. I'm still trying to figure out what I think. I know when I was with my father this week there came a point when I'd wished I didn't know the truth. He was so soul-broken and sorrowful, I could barely stand it. I told him I was sorry for bringing it up. I thought, to what good? To cause so much pain to this man, this father who only had done what he did out of love. Nothing will change the past. People have moved on, built their lives. There's no going back. So again, to what good?"

"Did he leave this earth on bad terms with you?"

"No. In fact, he thanked me and said he was finally free of the burden and could die in peace. Is that why he held on so long, Jesse? Is that why he was skin and bones but his frail body wouldn't give up?"

She was asking questions Jesse had no answers to. "Oh Livi," he whispered.

"I'll always remember that pain in his eyes. And, I still don't know, not completely, if I did the right thing." Another sob caught in her throat.

Jesse listened, pushing his own feelings aside so he could be there for her.

"He died that day." Olivia's voice was barely a vapor. "So, I don't know if Angela needs to know. I'll leave that for you to decide. But I knew for certain that *you* needed to know. You have a right to know everything. We can't go back, we can't be young again, but we can share the answers ... and the memories. Share the good times." She sighed. "We did have good times ... didn't we Jesse?"

"That summer ..." He said past the lump in his throat. "It was the best time of my life."

"Me too." Olivia's answer was a teary whisper.

For the next two hours, they dared to go back there, to a world, to a summer where no one else existed. They approached it carefully lest it be too painful. But it wasn't. They fell back into it comfortably, reliving it once again. They were able to brush aside the tears for the moment and even laugh. In fact, they laughed a lot at the carefree boy and girl and that magical summer. That was one thing they both agreed on. It was *magical*.

After the two-hour time warp, they settled into bringing each other up to date on their past, nearly forty years of it. Olivia had spent all of that time in France. She never returned to America, not even for a visit. So her life was fully and deeply rooted there. She spoke French as well as she spoke English. She'd excelled in the art world, was half owner in a highly respected gallery, and taught as well. And, she had a non-profit foundation that provided art lessons and materials to underprivileged people of all ages at no cost. They covered all of France and were branching out into neighboring countries. When Olivia spoke about the non-profit project, her excitement was evident in her voice. She was passionate. As was Jesse when he talked about his victim's advocacy endeavors. They both had found purpose in life which they embraced.

As Jesse put down the phone, an unusual peace settled over him. He leaned back in his comfortable chair, closed his eyes, and breathed deeply. The decades old questions were finally answered. He allowed himself a few minutes of what seemed like perfect peace, then he picked up his cell phone and placed a call.

"Mom."

"Yes, Jesse. I've been expecting you to call."

Jesse frowned. "Why?"

"Aren't you calling to tell me you've talked to Olivia?"

"Well, yes, but how did you know?" His mind was running in circles trying to find how that could happen.

"Olivia called me, and I gave her your number."

"Wait …" Jesse gave his head a shake. "How'd Olivia get *your* number?"

"She called the business line at the dock, and they forwarded it to me." She hesitated. "Olivia told me that she never knew you were alive."

"Yeah," Jesse acknowledged. "She said her parents told her that I was dead. Trying to protect her."

"You poor kids. Secrets … hardly ever good. After all you went through, and nothing to show for it."

"Well, Mom, That's not entirely true." He thought he'd better ask. "What else did she tell you?"

"That's all. I gave her your number … I thought you'd want to talk to her," she said, although it sounded more like a hesitant question.

"Yes, yes I did," Jesse assured her. "You did the right thing. Thank you." He could hear her sigh on the other end of the phone. "There's more. And I wanted you to be the first to know." He took a deep breath. "Olivia had a baby … my baby." Saying the words out loud ran chills down his spine. *It was real.* Saying it caused his skin to tighten.

"A baby?" It was a breathy question. "A baby! A boy or a girl?"

"It's Angela, Mama. Angela is our daughter. Your grand-daughter."

"Angela … your Angela?"

265

"Yes, my Angela ... at the cove!"

There was a long moment of silence on the line.

"Mom?"

"I'm here," she finally said. "This is a lot to take in." They talked for several minutes, laughing one moment, crying the next. Finally, Mama Grace said, "Angela is a lovely girl. I think it's wonderful, just wonderful." Her voice was filled with emotion. "I'm so happy for you, son."

After he'd hung up, Jesse pondered what his mother had said. *Secrets ... hardly ever good.* Hurtful and destructive, they were. And in that moment, Jesse knew what he must do. Angela was not a secret to be kept. She deserved to know the truth.

CHAPTER SEVENTEEN

Present Day
Angela

Angela stood at the giant mirror in her master bedroom. Jesse and Olivia were—in fact—her birth parents. It seemed unbelievable. Yet, it was true. She'd called her mother who verified the information, explaining everything and not casting blame. That was her mother, Claire Reed—who'd agreed that the terms of the adoption were to be kept secret. She hadn't known they told Olivia the baby died, but she'd also kept her word. Claire told Angela to call with any questions, and she'd answer every single one—if, of course, she knew the answers.

In light of it all, Angela had to wonder if this was why her parents never came to Wishing Beach anymore. In fact, their visits had stopped about the time Jesse became caretaker of Baker House. They still owned a house a few doors down from her, but they'd stopped coming. She reached for her phone and called her mother. Without bothering to offer a greeting, Angela said, "Did you know Jesse was my father?"

Claire sighed. "Not for certain, no. In fact, we thought it was most likely Travis Perry. Even though Olivia spent a lot of time with Jesse over that summer, she and Travis had always been close."

"Okay, Mom." Angela hung up the phone. She'd already called her mom three times since learning the truth. She only seemed able to get out one or two questions, then she hung up only to call back five minutes later. Her mother was patient and understanding. Claire had always been a wonderful mother.

Angela—although she'd never felt like she belonged in the family of driven overachievers—had always known she was loved and adored by her parents and her siblings. She hadn't fit in with them, and now that made sense. She'd always been more interested in art than numbers and in music rather than business.

And in all of her life, she'd never cared to know about her birth parents. Angela had always envisioned a young woman alone, possibly a teenager who'd gotten pregnant and was in no way equipped to raise a child. In many ways, Angela had been right about the circumstances. But the tragic story that she and Ryan had pursued until it was finally unveiled, now included her. And that was a hard concept to grasp.

She studied her reflection in the mirror for the umpteenth time but still couldn't see a resemblance. She and Jesse both had dark hair—hers curly, his wavy—but his eyes definitely were green. Olivia had blue eyes, but Angela remembered them as being much lighter than her own. No. Nothing. She searched for either of them in her face.

Her cell phone rang. She hoped it was Ryan. She'd left him a message earlier to return her call. She grabbed it off the bed checking it to be sure it was him. Jesse had called several times. He rang her doorbell rather than come on in like he used to do. She'd sequestered herself in her house—not ready to talk to him.

"Hi, Ryan."

"Hey, what's up?"

"Do you have a few minutes to talk." Angela knew he was working with his publicist doing a bevy of virtual interviews for TV. She hoped he was finished.

"You can have me for a whole hour, then I have just one more set to go."

Upbeat Ryan, that's what Angela loved about him. *Yes, I said loved... so?*

"Ryan, I have something to tell you. It's kind of ... big."

"In that case, come over. Be here in five minutes."

Without bothering to freshen up, Angela grabbed her purse and ran downstairs to her car. She noticed Jesse's Jeep was gone from in front of the guesthouse. Good. She couldn't face him yet.

As soon as she entered Ryan's house, he drew her into a hug. There, he held her for a long time, but she didn't cry, she didn't react, she simply drew strength from the man who'd become so much to her.

He eventually led her to the couch and held her hand. "I'm listening. Shoot."

So shoot she did. Every detail. Angela talked non-stop, about when Jesse came to her door the night before until now.

"Wow," Ryan exploded. "You wanted to uncover a mystery and, when you did, you discovered you were part of it. What are the chances? That's cool!"

"Is it?" She honestly didn't know what to think. Ryan's response was not what she expected. But then, what did she expect? *You poor thing ...* Or what? What was she supposed to think, or feel? She was numb.

269

"Remember I said we could write a book about the mystery of Jesse and Olivia?" Ryan said playfully. "Well this could be the final chapter."

"We're not talking about a book, Ryan. We're talking about my life."

"You're right. I'm sorry. I guess I didn't see a problem, just ... a mystery solved." He exhaled aloud. "What is the problem?"

"What is the problem?" Angela bristled. "I'll tell you what *the problem is*. My life has just been turned upside down. And I don't know what to do."

"Hey, hey, maybe you're making this too hard," Ryan soothed. "Think about it. Your life is not really different today than it was yesterday, right?"

Angela considered what he was saying. She had more information than yesterday. Other than that, he was essentially correct. She knew she'd needed to talk to him. He was her stabilizing force, always. "You're right," she conceded.

"Think of it like this, Angela. You've always known that you were adopted. Which meant you had biological parents out there, somewhere. That part is no surprise, right?"

"Right."

"And I have to imagine it is a bit of a shock to have your parents suddenly show up."

Angela nodded. "Yes."

"That part's over. So, it leaves just one question." Ryan softened his tone. "Would you rather it have been some other couple out there in the universe, someone other than Jesse and Olivia?"

"Other than Jesse? No." She didn't even have to think about it. "But I don't know how I feel about Olivia."

"What? Why?"

"I've built up such a dislike for her, imagining how she hurt Jesse. She left us sitting at a coffeeshop for hours. And then to find out she's blood. I don't know. I mean, all those years and she never came back to the island? Hard to believe forty years can go by and you have a child on the planet, and you honestly don't *know*? We're just trusting that she's telling us the truth. Is it a true story or just convenient?"

"You know what they say, truth is stranger than fiction. Which is actually true," Ryan added. "Jesse believes Olivia, right?"

"Yes, he does." Angela sighed. "Jesse is partial, he has never said anything bad about Olivia."

"Maybe because there's nothing bad to say," Ryan offered.

"I don't know. She left us, Ryan. In Paris."

"You're angry with her. It makes sense. You feel like she abandoned you twice. Once at birth and again in Paris."

Well then. She hadn't thought about it that way, but yes, she did. "How do I trust her? I'm not sure I can."

"That's okay." Ryan's voice softened. "*Trust Jesse*, Angela. Trust your father."

CHAPTER EIGHTEEN

Present Day
Jesse

The evening sun was setting into the horizon across the dark, cool ocean waters, a profusion of gold and orange ribbons lacing the sky. Jesse saw Angela there on Wishing Beach. Not moving, her silhouette was caught in the beauty of the encroaching twilight. His heart went out to her. She'd had so much to deal with lately, the divorce, the boys, just having to start over and build a whole new life was a lot. Now this.

The previous evening when he'd told Angela the circumstances of her birth, she hadn't said a word—no flash of excitement or anger, no questions, not even curiosity. She just turned and walked upstairs leaving him to let himself out. He'd never known Angela to be rude, but she was this time. In shock, he guessed. But that was last night. Taking a deep breath, Jesse headed toward the beach.

Hurting Angela was the last thing Jesse wanted to do. Yet this new revelation may have done that, in a way, he didn't understand. He knew she would be surprised but the possibility of rejection never crossed his mind. She didn't want him to be her father? He thought he and Angela were solid. How could he have been so wrong? He kicked at the sand. Probably time to move on and let her live her life. They say you can't pick your relatives. Well, Angela can and will. He'd miss her, but his biggest regret would be that he had caused her pain. Some things are just not meant to be. In this case, everything possible had been against them from the beginning.

Jesse walked over and stood beside Angela. And for a few long minutes they both just gazed across the sea at the ever-unfolding sunset.

"Beautiful," Jesse offered.

"Yes, it is." Angela gave him a tentative look and a weak smile. "Jesse, I'm sorry for the way I acted last night."

Jesse shook his head. "I'm sorry for springing such huge news on you like that. I should have known better."

"I just didn't know what to do with it. I mean ... you're my father?" Angela pushed her hair off her forehead, keeping her hand there, holding her head. "What am I supposed to feel? How am I supposed to act? How do I wrap my head around that?" She looked at Jesse. "How do you?"

"I know this has been a shock to you. To me too, actually." Jesse smiled. "Look, you have great parents. I'm thankful for that." He brought his hand to his chest. "And they will always be your parents. I just believe you have a right to know where you came from. And, you don't have to do anything with that."

She smiled and nodded. "Okay."

"I can't tell you how to feel, Angie. You'll have to figure

273

that out for yourself." Jesse looked at the ground. "It's probably best if I move out, so you can think with a clear head."

"Uncle Jesse! You want to leave? Why?" Angela was visibly shaken. Tears formed in her blue eyes.

"I want to do what's best. Give you time to find out what you think, what you want." He looked at her, a sad, troubled expression on his face.

"No." She grabbed his arm. "I don't want you to ever leave. I do know that. You've been one of the best parts of my life since I met you fifteen years ago." She laid her head against his arm. "I just don't know where or how to start, now."

"Angie, nothing has to change. I'm still Uncle Jesse, and you're still Angie." He laid his arm around her shoulders and pulled her closer. "Except now, maybe we can understand why we were drawn together in the first place. Why you've always had a special place in my heart."

"And you in mine." Angela circled her arms around Jesse's waist and ... *she hugged her father.*

JESSE DIDN'T like midnight calls. That meant some poor soul had so much trouble, it couldn't wait until morning. Which also meant a lot of uncertainty as to the danger and the outcome. But tonight, those thoughts were pushed aside so as not to spoil the euphoria he had been feeling since he'd talked with Olivia and then Angela. No more secrets.

The drive out of Millionaire's Cove in his Jeep, the top down, the wind blowing in his face, and breathing the sea air, was exhilarating. He slowed as he reached the town proper. Typically, he didn't feel threatened by the late meetings, but tonight, apprehension crawled over him. He brushed the thought aside. "You got something to live for now, that's all," he muttered to himself. Still, he intended to stay sharp.

The usually bustling streets and businesses were silent. He met only one car on his way to the pier, his meeting place of choice, out in the open, safer for all concerned. Instead of parking in a designated space next door or across the street, Jesse pulled right up to the pier entrance and looked around. He didn't see anyone, but that was usual for a late-night meet. They apparently wanted to get a good look at the situation ... and had he brought the cops? Jesse turned off the key. He hoped this initial meeting would be a short one. Then, he could take them to a safe house and tackle the rest in the morning—maybe get them in touch with one of the fulltime victim advocates on the island. Glancing at the dashboard clock he breathed a loud sigh and waited. Ten minutes, fifteen, went by. Thirty minutes was as long as he was going to wait until he would call it a no-show. He leaned his head back on the headrest and peered up at the sky blanketed with stars, reminding him of other nights so long ago. He could smile at those memories, finally. Those memories trapped in his pain where he kept them buried, were now free. Jesse suddenly sat up straight and looked down the pier. It was his meeting place, but he never went out on it. He hadn't been *on* the pier more than a handful of times in almost forty years. The few times he'd walked out there, pain hit him hard like a vise crushing his heart. It was probably ten years since he'd last tried. He could go out there now. He was free to remember.

Jesse jumped out of the Jeep and boldly stepped on to the planking. Taking his life back, feeling liberated, he walked out to the end of the long dock and looked across the vast ocean as he and Olivia had done so many times. He couldn't deny that tiny ache buried deep in his heart. It would probably always be there in remembrance of a girl with long blond hair and precocious ways and bright blue eyes that resembled his daughter's.

Jesse looked up to the heavens and found the brightest star and smiled. He was free to remember the first time they'd met. He looked down at the water where she'd jumped in and where he'd saved her. That same girl stole his heart as they met on the pier and talked, and sang, and danced. Oh, how she loved to dance. And, then that last night when they danced as one, yielding to each other, begging the night to never end.

"Jesse Malone?"

Jesse froze. He knew that voice. Slowly he turned around.

"Jesse?" The word was full of hope.

His breath caught in his throat. For a second, he thought his imagination was getting the better of him. Jesse couldn't speak, he just opened his arms and Olivia rushed to him, his embrace engulfing her. They clung to each other and wept. Finally, he looked at her face, still as beautiful as the day they'd met. He brushed away her tears with his thumb. "I always loved you, Olivia."

Olivia's eyes searched his face, finding everything she was hoping for. "And I loved you too, Jesse Malone."

They kissed, a kiss so tender, so perfect. "I can't believe you're real." Jesse tried to breathe but there was no oxygen.

"I know. It's been so long." Olivia gave a little laugh. "But being in your arms again ... it feels the same. It feels perfect. Just like that last night dancing when you sang me a song. Do you remember?"

"How could I forget? I remember everything, Livi. Everything about you and everything we were," Jesse said, and started humming. They began to sway. He looked deep into her crystal blue eyes, so lovely, searching for the answer to the question he had to ask because he had to protect his heart. "How long will you be staying?" The words stuck in his throat. Jesse feared that if he spoke them it would bring an answer he didn't want. Livi was back in his arms. The years had melted away. But was it only for a moment? He'd lost her once. He'd survived. But he wouldn't survive it again.

She searched his face. "That depends … on you."

"Depends on me?" Jesse frowned, perplexed.

"…if we still have a deal?" Olivia's eyes searched his. She reached into the neckline of her blouse and pulled out a chain that hung around her neck. On it was Jesse's high school ring. "I'd like to trade this in for that diamond now. I finished high school and even college—as was our agreement. I don't think I want to wait any longer."

Jesse laughed in spite of himself. "I never renege on a deal." He picked her up and swung her around.

They hugged, they kissed, they danced. Jesse began to hum as they glided around their moonlit ballroom, fitting together perfectly, as if they were one. "I've changed the last verse of your song," Jesse said.

"Keep the chorus, though," Olivia said.

"Always." He kissed her hair.

As if on cue, together they began to sing.

"Forever and ever
Forever together
I love you.
Yes, forever and ever
Forever together
I love you."

"HERE'S THE NEW VERSE," Jesse whispered.

"All of the moments we've shared together
Are forever sealed deep in my heart.
Now that you're back in my arms once again
No one nor nothing will keep us apart.

Forever and ever
Forever together
I love you
I love you."

EPILOGUE

Christmas Day, now

ANGEL STOOD under the banyan tree with Ryan at her side. A beautiful winter sun shone down on them and cast sparks of life upon the water.

"You're glowing," he said.

"Ummm," She laid her head against his arm. "I have so much to be thankful for." She patted his arm. "Wonderful family. Friends. It's been an amazing day. What can I say?"

"I saw you watching your mom and dad today. I love that you're getting to see them so happy."

"Yes, after a lifetime of hurt." Jesse and Olivia were like two smitten young people. "Did they fall in love all over again, or are they simply still in love?" That was a question Angel had pondered since Olivia first came to the island.

Olivia and Jesse had married soon after she'd come back from France. They bought a large home closer to the island's downtown area and were redoing it to include an art studio. Her interests in Paris still flourished. She hoped to do some of the same things there. The two traveled to Paris a couple of times a year ... together. They never wanted to be apart again.

Angel had become close to them as parents, as if they always were. And she had eventually become Angel rather than Angela to those who knew her intimately because that was the name her birth mother had given her, and with all that had been stolen from Olivia, being Angel seemed right.

Jesse was still Angela's caretaker and used the gatehouse as his study. Things remained much the same at her house, only with a lot more hugging and people constantly dropping in. Aunt Willow, her cousin, Katelyn, her nieces ... and Angel loved it all. Fishfrys and shrimp boils had been moved to Angel's house where the kids could swim in the pool while she and Aunt Willow sang Mama Grace's favorite hymns.

She loved Jesse's family, her family now. She and Katelyn had become best friends. Katelyn brought officer Chris North to Christmas Eve dinner last night. Holidays with her new, loud and boisterous family provided everything Angel could ever want. Bryan and Braxton were here this Christmas and visited often. They along with their girl-friends were spending more and more time on the island.

Angel and Ryan had spent almost every day together in the last few months. A trip to his doctor confirmed that he had been, in fact, seeing more and more lights. Though he would likely never regain his full sight, he could see shapes and shadows more vividly, light and darkness, some color and even make out faces from farther away. He'd regained more than he'd ever dreamed and could now look at Angel. He said regaining a measure of his eyesight was enough for him. It was a gift.

· · ·

AT THE EDGE of Angel Reed's property, Wishing Beach beckoned. On its sandy shore, the giant banyan tree draws all who venture near. Angel and Ryan stood arm-in-arm beneath its branches with only the rustling of the majestic leaves and the sound of the waves to keep them company.

Ryan kissed her cheek. "I wished for this, you know?"

"For your sight to return?"

"No," he said. "For you. For someone who could love me even though I couldn't see them."

"But you *always* saw me, Ryan. Always." They kissed and something sparked at the edge of Angel's gaze. She scanned the beach. Tiny iridescent balls floated on the water. "Do you see those?"

She left him and walked to the water where wave after wave lapped at her ankles. Ryan joined her just as she swooped down and lifted one of the sparkling balls into her hands. "It's a wish," she whispered, reverently. "It's for a young woman named Catherine." Angel rubbed her hands together cracking open the treasure. "She's in trouble. But now, her wish is going to come true."

Ryan reached out and touched Angel's hand. "You're beautiful when you're being mysterious and whimsical."

"It's not whimsical. It's Wishing Beach. And it's not my fault I still believe." There, in that moment, she remembered a day not unlike this one. A day long ago when she stood on this same shore as a small child and told her adoptive mother Claire Reed that she'd opened a wish for a woman named Olivia. And because she'd broken it open, Olivia's wish would come true. "Wishes are delicate things, I suppose. Maybe sometimes it takes years for the answer to reach its intended party. Maybe the magic of Wishing Beach only works for people who believe. Either way, I'll take hope over skepticism any day."

Ryan grasped her hand. "And that's why I love you."

"I love you too, Ryan."

"Come on, let's get back to the house. You've got a lot of guests waiting for that famous Christmas pudding."

She'd made Christmas dinner so many times for people who didn't value it, didn't value the work and effort she put into it. But this year was different. She was surrounded by people who loved her, appreciated her, and cherished their time with her. Angel's heart was full. Though she'd done her share of wishing at Wishing Beach, she'd been blessed with more than she dared hope. And this Christmas she'd share with her birth mother and father, her stepsons, her new aunt and cousins, a slew of kids, her grandmother Mama Grace, and Ryan, the love of her life. She'd visit her adoptive parents over the new year's holiday as they'd made their plans according to Angel's siblings needs. But right now, she'd cherish her new family and her new love. Life was good. There, on the distant horizon, the world crackled with the substance of hope. Hope had mended bridges that seemed impossible to cross. Hope was the glorious substance that now comprised her life. And everyone knew a good life was built on nothing less.

THE END

I truly hope you loved the story of Angela, Ryan, Jesse, and Olivia. If you'd love to read more of my novels, follow the link to my Amazon page where you'll find other titles.
Heather Burch's Amazon Page

Book Club Discussion questions are available upon request.
Get Book Club Questions

If you'd like to know more about the author, please drop by her website and take a look at her other award winning books.

Heather is an avid traveler who loves coffee, chocolate, and spending time with her amazingly supportive family. Her books are published around the world, and she'd one day love to do a book tour in every country where her books have been translated. That tour would include Italy, Germany, Turkey, and Norway to name a few.

Does she love to hear from readers? Why yes. Yes, she does.

Does she adore readers who write reviews? Absolutely!

If you'd like to leave a review of this title, here is a direct link to the Amazon Review Page. REVIEW WISHING BEACH